"Your bedroom is at the end of the hall," he reminded her.

He needed her gone. The scent of her was maddening, elusive, bewitching.

She moved into the formal parlor, taking a seat and looking at him out of those warm brown eyes. "I want to know what Beloch meant. What kind of test is he expecting you to perform?"

He knew what Beloch wanted. He was supposed to fuck her and then prove he could walk away from her, turn her over to the shattering destructiveness of the Truth Breakers and then celebrate the destruction of one more demon.

He looked at her and his body stirred, and he despised her—and himself. He could tell himself it was simply her wiles, her powers, that were doing this to him. But he wasn't asleep, he wasn't drugged.

And he wasn't going to do it. Not tonight, when need vibrated through his body and he wanted to shove her up against a wall and take her. By tomorrow he'd be back in control.

"Go to bed," he said gruffly. "Or you'll wish you had."

She simply raised an eyebrow, the foolish creature. It was unwise to underestimate him. He could squeeze the life out of her in a moment, end her as he'd come so close to doing, more times than he could remember.

"I'm not afraid of you."

"You should be," he said. And before she knew what was ha[...] hoved her up against the door and sla[...]

Der[...]

Also by Kristina Douglas

Raziel

Available from Pocket Books

THE FALLEN

DEMON

KRISTINA
DOUGLAS

Pocket Books
New York London Toronto Sydney

Pocket Books
A Division of Simon & Schuster, Inc.
1230 Avenue of the Americas
New York, NY 10020

First Pocket Books paperback edition June 2011

POCKET and colophon are registered trademarks of Simon & Schuster, Inc.

For information about special discounts for bulk purchases, please contact Simon & Schuster Special Sales at 1-866-506-1949 or business@simonandschuster.com.

The Simon & Schuster Speakers Bureau can bring authors to your live event. For more information or to book an event, contact the Simon & Schuster Speakers Bureau at 1-866-248-3049 or visit our website at www.simonspeakers.com.

Designed by Jacquelynne Hudson
Cover design by Lisa Litwack
Cover illustration by Craig White

Manufactured in the United States of America

10 9 8 7 6 5 4 3 2 1

ISBN 978-1-4391-9193-4
ISBN 978-1-4391-9195-8 (ebook)

For Sally,
because she likes world-building

On the Subject of Angels

The world of the Fallen is my own creation, based on Apocryphal works like the Book of Enoch and other obscure texts that didn't make it into the current Old Testament. Being a new age liberal Christian, I've always been fascinated by the inexplicable behavior of the Old Testament God and his tendency to use the smite key on his celestial computer at random. It's easy enough to do a little Internet research to find references to all the less than charitable things that God supposedly did, and I wanted to come up with a world that explained the difference between a just and loving God and the big old meanie from the past. Hence the world of the Fallen and the Archangel Uriel.

I took bits and pieces of mythology and changed them to suit my story—the Nephilim are generally considered to be the offspring of the fallen angels, but I decided to make them the next wave. There are countless references in the Bible that argue against the "eating of blood," so it seemed an obvious curse. And fallen angels are so much more interesting than the ones who are still supposedly perfect.

So you need to take it all in the spirit in which it's intended. Most of the Old Testament is open for debate, anyway. I just shifted things the way it worked best for my fallen angels.

Beginnings: The Real World

Chapter One

He was following me again. I knew it instinctively, even though I hadn't actually seen him. He was just beyond my vision, on the outer edges of my sight, hiding in shadows. Skulking.

Not stalking. There might be huge gaps in my memory, but I had a mirror and absolutely no delusions about my totally resistible charms. I was determinedly average—average height, average weight, give or take ten pounds. I had short hair, the muddy brown you get when you dye it too often, and my eyes were a plain brown. My skin was olive-tinged, my bone structure unremarkable, and there was no clue to who or what I was.

Here's what I knew: My name was Rachel. My current last name was Fitzpatrick, but before that it was Brown, and the next time it might be

Montgomery. Average names with Anglo-Saxon antecedents. I didn't know why, I just went with it.

I'd been Rachel Fitzpatrick for almost two years now, and it felt as if it had been longer than usual, this comfortable life I'd built up. I was living in a big industrial city in the Midwest, working for a newspaper that, like most of its kind, was on its last legs. I had a great apartment on the top floor of an old Victorian house; I had an unexciting car I could rely on; I had good friends I could turn to in an emergency and have fun with when times were good. I was even godmother to my coworker Julie's newborn baby girl. I kept waiting for the other shoe to drop.

It was November, and I thought that probably I had never liked November. The trees were bare, the wind was biting, and darkness closed around the city like a shroud. And someone was watching me.

I didn't know how long he'd been there—it had taken me a while to realize he was back again. I'd never gotten much of a look at him; he kept to the shadows, a tall, narrow figure of undeniable menace. I had no wish to see him any better.

I was very careful. I didn't go out alone after dark, I kept away from secluded places, and I was always on my guard. I had never mentioned him to my friends, even Julie. I told myself I didn't want them to worry. But I didn't go to the police either, and it was their job to worry.

I spun any number of possibilities out of the big gray blank that was my memory. Maybe he was my abusive husband, watching me, and I'd run away from him, the trauma of his brutality wiping my mind clean.

Maybe I had been in the witness protection program and I'd gone through some kind of horror, and the mob was after me.

But it didn't explain why he hadn't come any closer. No matter how careful I was, if someone wanted to hurt me, to kill me, there was probably no way to stop him short of . . . well, there probably *was* no way to stop him. So my watcher presumably didn't want me dead.

I was working late on a cold, rainy Thursday, trying to get a bunch of obituaries formatted. Yup, doing obituaries late at night was not my favorite thing; but with the *Courier* on its last legs, we all put in overtime whenever asked and worked on anything that was needed, though I drew the line at sports. I was ostensibly home and health editor, *editor* being a glorified term for the only reporter on the beat, but I generally enjoyed my work. With obituaries, not so much. It was the babies that got to me. Stillbirths, crib deaths, miscarriages. They made me feel like crying, though oddly enough

I never cried. If I could, I would weep for those babies, weep for days and weeks and years.

I didn't wonder whether I'd lost a child myself. Instinct told me I hadn't, and besides, grieving for lost babies was a logical, human reaction. Who wouldn't feel sorrow at the loss of a brand-new life?

The wind had picked up, howling through the city and shaking the sealed windows of the new building the *Courier* had unwisely built less than three years ago, and I logged off my computer, finished for the night. I glanced at the clock; it was after ten, and the office was deserted. My car was in the parking garage—there had to be someone there. I would have my keys out, make a dash for my reliable old Subaru, and lock myself in if anything loomed out of the darkness.

I could always call Julie and see if her husband could come and escort me home. While I hadn't told them about my watcher, I had explained that I was extremely skittish about personal safety, and Bob had come to the rescue on a number of occasions. But they had a brand-new baby, and I didn't want to bother them. I'd be fine.

I grabbed my coat and was heading for the elevator when the phone at my desk rang. I hesitated, then ignored it. Whoever it was, whatever they wanted, I was too tired to provide it. All I wanted was to get home through this blasted wind and curl up in my nice warm bed.

The elevator was taking its own sweet time, considering the entire building was practically deserted. My desk phone stopped ringing and my cell phone started. I cursed, reaching into my pocket and flipping it open just as the elevator arrived.

It was Julie, sounding panicked. "Rachel, I need you," she said in a tear-filled voice.

Something bad had happened. My stomach knotted. "What's wrong?" And like a fool, I stepped into the elevator.

"It's the baby. She's—"

As the door closed and the elevator began to descend, I lost the signal.

"Shit," I said, very loudly. My office was on the twenty-second floor, and I'd pushed the button for the second level of parking, but I quickly hit a lower-level floor to stop the descent. The doors slid open on the dark and empty eighth floor and I jumped out. I pushed my phone's call-back button as the doors slid closed, abandoning me in the darkness, and a shiver ran over me, one I tried to ignore. I had nerves of steel, but I was never foolhardy, and there was no reason to feel uneasy. I'd been in this building alone on numerous occasions.

But I'd never felt so odd before.

Julie answered on the first ring. "Where did you go?" she said, her voice frantic and accusing.

"Lost the signal," I said briefly. "What's wrong with the baby?"

"I'm at the hospital. She couldn't breathe, and I called an ambulance. They've got her in the emergency room and they kicked me out, and I need you here for moral support. I'm terrified, Rachel!" Her voice was thick with tears.

"Where's Bob?" I said, trying to be practical.

"With me. You know how helpless men are. He just paces and looks grim, and I need someone to give me encouragement. I need my best friend. I need *you*. How soon can you make it?"

Strange how we could become such good friends in so short a time. It had felt like an enduring bond, not an office friendship, almost as if I'd known her in another life. But she had no more clue about my past than I did. "Which hospital?"

"St. Uriel's. We're in the emergency waiting room. Come now, Rachel! *Please!*"

St. Uriel's, I thought. *That's wrong, isn't it? Was Uriel a saint?* But I made soothing noises anyway. "I'll be right there," I said. And knew I lied.

I flipped the phone shut, mentally reviewing the contents of my desk. Nothing much—a copy of *House Beautiful,* the latest Laurell K. Hamilton, and the Bible, which was admittedly weird. I didn't understand why I had it—maybe I'd been part of some fundamentalist cult before I'd run away. God knew. I only knew I needed to have a Bible with me.

I would find another, as soon as I checked into a hotel. There was no need to go back. I traveled light, and left as little impression behind as I could. They'd find no clues about me if they searched my desk. Particularly since I had no clues about myself.

My apartment was only slightly less secure. There were no letters, no signs of a personal life at all. I had a number of cheap Pre-Raphaelite prints on the wall, plus a large framed poster of a fog-shrouded section of the Northwest coast that spoke to me. I hated to leave it behind, but I needed to move fast. I'd have to ditch the car in the next day or two, buy another. It would take Julie that long to realize I'd gone missing. She'd be too busy hovering over baby Amanda, watching each struggling breath with anxious eyes.

But Amanda wouldn't die. She'd start to get better, as would all of the other newborns that I knew were filling the hospitals as I lingered. All I had to do was get far enough away and they'd recover. I knew it instinctively, though I didn't know why.

I pushed the elevator button, then paced the darkened hallway restlessly. Nothing happened, and I pushed it again, then pressed my ear to the door, listening for some sign that the cars were moving. Nothing but silence.

"Shit," I said again. There was no help for it—I'd have to take the stairs.

I didn't stop to think about it. The time had come to leave, as it always did, and thinking did no good. I had no idea how I knew these things, why I had to run. I only knew that I did.

It wasn't until the door to the stairs closed behind me that I remembered my watcher, and for a moment I freaked, grabbing the door handle. It was already locked, of course. I had no choice. If I was going to get out of town in time, I had to keep moving, so I started down the stairs.

In time for what? I had no clear idea. But baby Amanda wouldn't survive for long if I didn't move it.

I tripped on the next landing and went sprawling, slamming my shin against the railing. I struggled to my feet, and froze. Someone was in the stairwell with me. I sensed him, closer than he'd ever been before, and there was nothing, no one, between him and me. No buffer, no safety. Time was running out.

I had no weapon. I was an idiot—you could

carry concealed weapons in this state, and a really small gun could blow a really big hole in whoever was following me. Or a knife, something sharp. Hell, hadn't I heard you could jab your keys into an attacker's eyes?

I didn't know whether he was above me or below me, but the only doors that opened from the stairwell were the ones on the parking level. If I went up, I'd be trapped.

I started down the next flight, moving as quietly as I could, listening for any matching footsteps. There were none. Whoever he was, he made no sound.

Maybe he was a figment of my paranoid imagination. I had no concrete reasons to do the things I did, acting on instinct alone. I could be crazy as a bedbug, imagining all this power. Why in the world should small, insignificant Rachel Fitzpatrick have anything to do with the well-being of a baby? Of a number of babies? Why did I have to keep changing my name, changing who I was? If someone was following me, why hadn't he caught up yet?

What would happen if I simply drove home and stayed there? Joined Julie at the hospital?

Amanda would die. I had no choice. I had to run.

AZAZEL MOVED DOWN THE STAIRS after the demon, silent, scarcely breathing. He could sense its panic, and he knew it was going to run again. He had taken longer to find it this time—it must be getting better at coming up with new identities. If the demon vanished once more, he had no idea how long it would take him to find it again. The longer it roamed the earth, the more destruction it could wreak.

It was time to make his move. He didn't know why he'd hesitated, why he'd watched it without doing anything. His hatred for the creature was so powerful it would have frightened him, if he were capable of feeling fear. He was incapable of feeling anything but his hatred for the monster. That must be what had stayed his hand. Once he killed it, he would feel nothing at all.

How difficult would the demon be to kill? It looked like a normal female, but he felt its seductive power even from a distance. It didn't need any of the obvious feminine wiles to lure him. It didn't wear makeup, didn't flaunt itself in revealing clothes. It tended to dress in dark colors, in loose-fitting T-shirts and baggy pants. There was nothing to make a man think of sex; yet every time he looked at her—at it—he thought about lust. He must never underestimate her.

It. Part of the demon's power was to make him

forget that it was merely a thing, not the vulnerable female it appeared to be. So easy to slip, to think of it as a woman. A woman he would have to kill. Maybe it had been female once, but not anymore. Now it was simply a repository of all the seductive female force in creation, channeled into a demon that looked like a soft, vulnerable woman.

He could catch her in the parking garage, break her neck, and then fly up high and fling her body into the sun. He could bury her deep beneath the earth in the belly of a volcano. He sensed he would need fire to eradicate her completely, her and her evil powers. Only when she was dead would the threat dissolve.

The threat to newborn babies. The threat to vulnerable men who dreamed of sex and woke to find only a demon possessing them.

And the threat to him. Most of all he hated her for the connection that was foretold, with him of all people. And the only way to make certain that never happened was to destroy her.

He was standing in the corner of the stairwell on the bottom floor, watching her. He'd pulled his wings around him, disappearing; though she searched her surroundings, she saw nothing, and moved on.

More proof of her power, the power she was

trying so hard to disguise. No one else sensed him when he cloaked himself. But she did. Her awareness was as acute as his. And he hated that.

Tonight, he told himself. Tonight he would kill her. Whether he'd present proof to Uriel was undecided. He might simply leave him unknowing. He could finally return to Sheol, take the reins back from Raziel if he must. And see Raziel's bonded mate in Sarah's place.

No, he wasn't ready. Surely there must be something else he had to do before he returned.

She'd escaped into the garage, and he followed her, the door closing silently behind him. The place was brightly lit, but there were only a handful of cars still there. She was already halfway to the dark red one he knew was hers.

He knew where he would take her—as far away as humanly possible from this place. To the other side of the world, one of the few places where the scourge known as the Nephilim still thrived.

What better place for a demon?

He waved a hand and the parking garage plunged into darkness, every light extinguished. He could feel her sudden panic, which surprised him. He wouldn't have thought demons feared the darkness. She started running, but her car was parked midway down, and he spread his wings and took her.

15 Demon

I SCREAMED, BUT MY VOICE was lost in the folds that covered me. I couldn't see, couldn't hear, could barely move, so disoriented and dizzy that I felt sick. I felt the ground give way beneath my feet, and I was falling, falling. . . .

Something tight bound me, but I couldn't sense what. It felt like irons bands around my arms, holding me still, and my face was crushed against something hard, something that felt like cloth. I breathed in, and oddly enough I could smell skin, warm, vibrant, indefinably male skin. Impossible. I smelled the ocean as well, but we were at least a thousand miles away from any salt water.

I squirmed, and the bands tightened, and I couldn't breathe. My chest was crushed against whatever thing had done this, and I was helpless, weightless, cocooned by the monster that had grabbed me. I tried to move once more, and the pain was blinding. As if my heart were being crushed, I thought, as consciousness faded and I fell into a merciful dark hole.

I COULD HEAR SOMEONE SINGING, which was absurd. Either I was dead or I'd been captured by some science-fictiony creature who'd sealed me in a cocoon or a hive, probably to be eaten later. I'd seen those movies, could remember them even though I couldn't remember my own parents.

I hurt everywhere, but most particularly my chest. It felt as if someone had reached inside me and crushed my heart in his hand. Another movie, I thought, feeling dizzy.

But one thing I did remember was that life was never like the movies. I didn't believe in ghosts and ghouls and things that went bump in the night. Whoever had done this to me had to be human, and therefore I could fight back.

Cautiously I opened my eyes.

I was lying in the middle of a lumpy bed in what looked like a seedy motel room. A radio played in the background, something soft and depressing. Another bed was beside me, empty, but with a depressed area on the pillow where someone had been, so presumably I wasn't alone.

I tried to move, just a little, and while my body screamed in protest, I was no longer restrained. I was lying facedown on the mattress, as if someone had dumped me there, and I was relatively sure I hadn't been raped or otherwise interfered with. Someone had simply managed to scoop me up and run off with me.

The watcher. I rolled over on my back, very gingerly, half-afraid he was waiting to pounce again. I kept picturing him like a bat, swooping down on me, dark wings beating at my head. Either I had hit my head and had a concussion, or someone had drugged me.

The room was even worse than I'd thought, more a flophouse than a motel. Not that I'd ever been in a flophouse before—at least, I didn't think I had—but the small table and two chairs, the hot plate, and the dismal china sink all looked like my idea of one.

I turned back and almost shrieked. The other bed was no longer empty. A man lay there, watching me out of hooded eyes.

I opened my mouth to speak, but my voice was strangled in my throat. He must have seen the fright and fury in my eyes, but he didn't move.

There was one small, grubby window, and I could tell from the color of the sky that it must be a little past dawn. And then I remembered Amanda and the others, and real panic set in.

"Have to . . . get out of here," I managed to wheeze.

He didn't move, didn't react, and I wondered if he'd heard or understood me. Maybe he didn't speak English.

I couldn't afford to waste time. I began to pull myself to a sitting position, ignoring the pain that shot through my body. "You have to listen to me," I managed to say, my voice still thick with pain. "I can't be here. I have to get far away. People will die."

He still didn't move. The room was murky in the predawn light, and I couldn't see him clearly. All I could tell was that he was long and lean, and he was most definitely not from around here. They didn't grow them like that in the Midwest.

I sat up, my feet on the soiled carpeting. "I'm getting out of here," I said, starting to push myself up from the bed. I hurt like hell, but I could make it. I *had* to make it.

"No." Though I hadn't seen him move his lips, the word was, sharp, definite.

"I told you—"

"You told me people will die," he said in a bored voice. "The only one who is going to die is you."

His cool words should have chilled me, but I'd already figured out I was a lost cause. "Look," I said patiently, "you can do anything you want. Stab me, strangle me, shoot me—I don't care. Just do it miles away from the city."

I suppose I should have looked him over more carefully to see if I could find a weak spot, but I was too wound up thinking about Amanda. *No more,* I thought. *For God's sake, no more babies.*

"We are in Australia," he said.

I stopped trying to get up, finally looking at him. "How long have I been unconscious?"

"Not long."

Okay, now I knew he was a certifiable fruitcake. Not that I should have had any doubt—a sane person doesn't swoop down on you like a bat and abduct you. I tried once more to get off the bed, and this time I made it, as if whatever had held me back finally let go.

"Go to the window if you do not believe me."

I went. I didn't see koalas or kangaroos bouncing by the window—it looked like any dingy waterfront. Even so, it would take more than a couple of hours to reach the ocean from the last place I remembered being. So clearly I'd been out for longer than he'd said, but that didn't matter. All that mattered was that Amanda and all the other newborns would now be safe.

"Okay," I said, turning back to face him. I was tired of running, tired of the fear and panic that had threatened to strangle me. "Go ahead. Make my day."

And I spread my arms wide, waiting for him to kill me.

CHAPTER TWO

THE MAN GAZED AT ME, HIS FACE expressionless. "You have seen too many movies."

I sighed. "Look, I don't know who or what you are and I don't care. I'm tired of running, tired of questions with no answers. If you want to shoot me, then go ahead and do it; otherwise, give me some answers or leave me alone."

"I don't possess a gun." I was still deciding whether or not I was relieved when he continued, "You know as well as I do that I do not need a gun to kill you."

I sat back down on the lumpy bed. "I don't know shit," I said flatly. "I don't even know who I am, much less who you are. I'm sure you could overpower me if you wanted to, but I'm also going to presume that if you were planning to kill me you would have already done it."

"You should not presume anything. I can come up with half a dozen reasons why I have yet to kill you. Perhaps I need a better place to dispose of your body."

"Like Australia?"

His face was impassive. "Perhaps I want to draw it out, let you suffer. Or maybe I have decided to give you a chance to talk me out of it. Or even give you a head start."

Okay, none of that sounded even the slightest bit reassuring. I took a good look at him. By some standards he might even be considered attractive. Hell, freaking gorgeous—if it weren't for the incredible coldness in his blue eyes. He had long, straight, very black hair, pale skin, a narrow face with finely chiseled high cheekbones, a thin mouth, and a strong nose. He looked as cold as Antarctica, and his faintly formal diction made him seem even more impenetrable.

"You know, for some reason none of those possibilities seems very likely. You don't strike me as someone filled with the milk of human kindness."

"I am not human."

This barely struck me as odd. Impossible as it was, I had begun to guess as much, considering that we had apparently managed to travel thousands of miles in a matter of hours. "Then what the fuck are you?"

"You know."

I was facing death with what I considered a fair amount of noble equanimity, but he was getting beyond frustrating, ruining the whole Joan of Arc bit. "I *don't* know. I told you, I don't even know who I am, and even though you came swooping down on me like a bat out of hell, I'm having a hard time processing the idea that you're anything but a crazy stalker who's probably going to dismember my body and gnaw on my bones."

"We do not eat flesh. That would be the Nephilim."

That word, that name, struck an odd chord inside me, a surge of nausea that it took all my willpower to control. Yet the word meant nothing. "Who are the Nephilim?"

He didn't answer. He rose, and I watched him, looking for any sign of weakness. Presumably he wasn't lying about the gun—he was wearing a black T-shirt and jeans and I could see no sign of one on him. For a moment I was afraid he was going to approach me, and I steeled myself to fight, but instead he walked over to the window, pushing open the curtain to let in the early morning light. The soft singing on the radio finished, and the announcer came on—most definitely Australian. I felt a shiver wash over me, and tried to control it. At least Amanda was safe.

And then he switched off the radio, turning to look at me. "It is time to go."

"Go where? Are you going to explain anything at all or leave me to die of curiosity?"

He didn't make the obvious answer. He just stood there waiting, and slowly, painfully I rose to my feet again. I felt as if someone had used me as a punching bag—presumably this man. I wondered if I looked as bruised as I felt. As I started after him I glanced at my reflection in the mirror. And screamed.

Even before the sound erupted he was on me, one hand clamped over my mouth, the other around my waist, imprisoning me as I struggled against the rising hysteria. I didn't know that woman in the mirror—a stranger looking back at me out of warm brown eyes. In fact, in that first horrifying glimpse, it was only the eyes that seemed familiar.

I might have been fighting a machine. His body was impervious to my struggles, my frantic kicks. And as quickly as the panic had come on, it drained away, leaving me staring at myself in the mirror, with him behind me, holding me.

My hair was red. With all the bottles of dye I'd used over the years, the one color I'd never used was red. I'd been blond, brunette, and everything in between, but the very thought of red hair had made me ill. My skin was pale, almost transparent, and the hair was thick and curling, hanging below my shoulders when I'd favored something short and manageable. His hand covered half my face, but I'd seen my mouth—wide and curving, different from the small mouth I'd occasionally augmented with lipstick. My own eyes stared out from the face of a stranger, and I wanted to throw up.

He must have felt the fight leave my body, because he slowly released me. I had no doubt those iron hands could clamp over my arms again at any moment, and I did my best to make my body soft and pliant.

"You do not fool me," he said in my ear. "I am not going to turn my back on you for a minute."

"Probably a good idea," I said out of the stranger's mouth in the mirror. "I'd run."

"You would be more likely to disembowel me."

Startled, I looked up at him. Again, he was totally without affect—I'd picked up that word during one of my lifetimes, but I couldn't remember where. His eyes were cold, his face blank. He'd said he wasn't human. Impossible as that was to comprehend, looking into his soulless eyes made it marginally more believable.

"Not likely, unless you're going to hand me a knife." I was pleased with the caustic tone I achieved, until his next words hit.

"You wouldn't need a knife."

"I think I'll just stop talking," I said, feeling ill at the picture his words conjured. That was twice he'd sent me to the edge of nausea. Probably a combination of jet lag and hunger. My brain was still trying to make sense of it all. So he said I hadn't been out long, yet somehow we'd gotten to Australia. Clearly he was lying, and I must have been unconscious for days. It was no wonder my stomach was in an uproar—I was starving. "Just feed me," I added, "and I promise I won't bother you."

He stared at me, and I thought I could feel his eyes on my throat. He still clasped one of my wrists, but the pain of that manacle-like grasp was nothing compared to the rest of my body, so I'd barely noticed.

Then he nodded. "After you." And with a none-too-gentle shove, he pushed me out the door.

Yes, it was Australia, or he was going to great lengths for a practical joke. The license plates were different, and the ordinary-looking sedan he pushed me into had the steering wheel on the wrong side. He closed the door and moved around to the driver's side, not even bothering to see whether I was going to try to run for it. He must have known I was past fighting.

We drove in silence, into the dawning of what was presumably going to be the last day of my life. I leaned back in the seat, watching the landscape whiz by with incurious eyes. We'd been in some kind of port city, but by full daylight we were already past the suburbs and into the countryside. Oddly enough, he'd turned on the radio once we got in the car, and quiet music filled in the blank spaces in my mind. It seemed an anomaly—he was much too cold and empty a person to care about music. I figured that was the least of my worries. I listened to plaintive voices, some familiar, some not, and waited to die.

I must have slept. When I awoke, the sun was blazing brightly overhead and we'd stopped outside a restaurant that seemed to have erupted in the middle of nowhere. I glanced at my nameless companion, wondering if this was one of his creations, but it seemed real enough, and as I followed him out of the car I noticed a sign announcing that they had Foster's. At that point I was grateful for small favors.

"Nice of you to feed me," I muttered gracelessly after we'd slid into a booth and my captor rattled off an order to a sullen waitress. "But you might have let me order for myself. The condemned woman should get to choose her last meal." Though a hot lamb sandwich with gravy and chips wasn't a bad choice, come to think of it.

"Deal with it." He'd ordered a veggie burger for himself. So he could kill people but not animals. Great. I sat back in the booth, taking a surreptitious glance around me. He hadn't used the bathroom since I'd been with him, but sooner or later he'd have to, wouldn't he? Unless he truly wasn't human, which I took leave to doubt.

I wondered if I could hot-wire a car. Newer ones might be tricky, but there were enough older cars parked outside the restaurant that I might have some luck, if I could just manage to distract my kidnapper for a short while.

I didn't know his name. I didn't want to. For some reason, thinking of him as an abstraction made the situation easier to deal with. If he had a name, like Joe or Tom or Harry, that would make it more real, and as long as it stayed a little otherworldly I could handle it.

When he went to the bathroom I could make a run for it, I thought. I could beg for help from some of the rough-looking customers—surely they'd help a lady in distress. There were two burly ones at the counter, another one toward the back—

"No one will help you."

It didn't take a rocket scientist to know what I was thinking. "Why not?"

"Because you cannot get up from that seat. You cannot speak."

What the hell do you mean? I began, and then realized my mouth hadn't moved. No words had come out, not even a mute squeak of protest. I tried to move, but my butt might as well have been superglued to the booth. I put all my fury and panic into my eyes, but he simply looked away, bored, as the waitress brought a foaming mug of beer. One. For him.

I reached out, planning to either grab it or dump it in his lap, but my hands couldn't move past the centerline of the table. It was as if there were a Plexiglas sheet between us, thick and hard and invisible. A diet soda had been left at my place, and I found I could reach it. Couldn't swipe his beer, but in fact I was happier with the Diet Coke.

I waited for him to lift his voodoo spell, but he simply drank his beer, looking out at the dusty landscape, ignoring me. I went from fury to pleading to tears and back again, and it was a waste of time. When my food came I could reach it, but my appetite was gone and I just stared at it.

"I do not care whether you eat or not," he said, not looking at me. "You have another ten minutes and then we leave."

I glared at him, a wasted effort. And then I ate, because if there was a chance I could make a run for it, I'd need my strength.

He must have drugged me. That, or hypnotized me. Some way he'd managed to fuck with my mind, convincing me I couldn't move or speak.

For a last meal, it wasn't bad. He'd ordered dessert as well, and when the waitress cleared the dishes and brought me a huge slice of coconut cake, my stomach did another leap. I loved coconut cake. How did he know?

I couldn't very well ask him. I smiled my thanks at the waitress, then ate every single crumb of that damned cake.

The stranger rose. "Time to go."

My feet were no longer stuck to the ground, but my enforced silence was still in effect. He took my arm in a fairly brutal grip and led me back to the car, and it wasn't until he shoved me inside that I could speak.

"I have to pee," I said in a flat voice. It was a lie, but I figured it was my only chance at getting away.

He shot me a glance. "Then I expect you'll be uncomfortable for the next few hours."

I subsided, not bothering to try the door. Even normal people could lock car doors from a distance. He pulled out onto the empty road, his expression the same. Empty. Grim. Purposeful. He really was going to kill me.

"What's your name?" I hadn't wanted to know, but the silence was driving me crazy.

"Does it matter?"

"Hell, yes, it matters. I want to know why you've been following me all these years."

"I thought you failed to remember beyond the last year or so."

"I don't even remember my own name. But I remember you."

He looked at me then, the deep black emptiness of his eyes chilling me. "Azazel."

AZAZEL CONCENTRATED ON THE NARROW, sun-baked road ahead. Her cluelessness was beginning to annoy him, but if that was her main line of defense it was easy enough to deal with. As long as she didn't shift into her real form, his job would be relatively easy. What he couldn't understand was why she wasn't putting up a better fight.

She had weapons she hadn't begun to use, not the least of which was her ability to shift into Lilitu, the storm demon, the birdlike monster who could claw the entrails from a man, given a moment of inattention. It would be useless against him, but she wouldn't know that. She never remembered.

It wasn't the first time he'd battled the Lilith.

With the curse of eternity on his head, he'd come face-to-face with her in many demonic forms, and each time he'd vanquished her. But never completely.

He'd destroyed other demons and abominations in the thousands upon thousands of years he'd been on earth. Most obviously the Nephilim, as well as others that Uriel had allowed to run free in an attempt to vanquish the Fallen. But the she-demon Lilith was beyond even his control. And he'd waited long enough.

He hated to think of her as female, but now that he was around her he couldn't continue putting her in the nongendered group to which most demons belonged. Her destructive power was like that of no other female, and he'd always tried to think of her as *it*. Particularly given the unacceptably prophecy he was determined to avoid. She was dangerously female, and even now he could feel her seductive power.

She hadn't reacted to his name, but she should know exactly who he was. It was always possible she was telling the truth, that she didn't remember anything. He'd been watching her for the last five years, and her behavior had been odd, supporting what she said. By the time he'd finally taken her, she'd already lived under four different names in four different cities. He'd assumed it was an effort to avoid him, but there was the slight chance she really didn't remember. He could sense very real distress coming from her, and he needed to fight it.

Demons were expert at clouding expectations. And most creatures felt distress when they saw death staring down at them. He had no room for pity or second thoughts.

The landscape had gotten scrubbier as the day wore on. They'd reach their destination well before nightfall—he'd have more than enough time to take care of things. He wondered vaguely if he'd return afterward, to see if there was anything left. The idea should have filled him with grim satisfaction. For some reason it was no longer as soothing.

She—it—was doing too good a job.

"Azazel?" she said, obviously trying to sound normal. "That's an odd name. Is it Middle Eastern?"

"Biblical," he said briefly.

"My name is Rachel Fitzpatrick." At his uncontrolled snort, she changed tacks. "All right, so Fitzpatrick isn't my real last name. Since you seem to know more about me than I do, why don't you tell me what my real last name is?"

He said nothing. Richard Thompson was on the radio, and he leaned forward to turn it up, wanting his mournful voice and stinging guitar. The moment he pulled his hand away, she reached out and turned it off.

He glared at her. "If you want to be able to move and talk," he growled, turning it back on, "you will keep your hands off the radio."

She sat back, folding her hands in her lap. They were normal hands—pretty, even. Odd—she wore no rings, no polish, none of the adornments women had used since the beginning of time. Yet he could almost imagine those hands on his body.

He shuddered, fighting it. It was so easy to forget, to see her as a desirable female, when he'd done his best to submerge his sexual nature. He glanced at her face. Her curling red hair was the same as always, a snake's tangle to ensnare men, to make them want to bury their faces in the silken strands. He was immune—the moment he felt even the slightest pull, he was able to slam a lid on it. She wouldn't reach him as she had so many men. He couldn't let her.

RT was singing "Can't Win," which seemed absurdly prescient. When it was over he turned the radio down again, glancing over at her. "That isn't your name."

"Then what is it?" she said, her voice breaking with frustration. "For God's sake, if I'm going to die, don't I deserve some answers first? At least to know why I've been targeted by a killer? I've done my best to be a good person. If I did something bad in the past, something that deserves punishment, then at least I should know what it was."

"Your crimes are too numerous and horrific to detail."

Her forehead creased, and he wanted to smooth it. She was working her wiles, and he forced down his reaction. "That's wrong," she said. "Now I know you've got the wrong person. If I committed horrible crimes, I'd know it. I couldn't commit . . . atrocities and then live a normal life. You've got the wrong person. You've got me confused with someone else."

"I'm not confused."

"Then who am I? What did I do?" she cried.

And tired of her whining, he finally answered.

"You are evil, a succubus and a murderer of infants. You are a nightmare, a horror, a monster." He looked into her dazed face. "You are the Lilith."

Chapter Three

"You're out of your mind," I said. My voice shook, even as I tried to be firm. I felt as if the universe were suddenly made of sand and everything were shifting beneath me. "Not that that's news—I already figured you had to be demented to want to kill me. So who told you I was Lilith? Your neighbor's dog?"

He stared at me. "What are you talking about?"

"Son of Sam," I said briefly. "You know, the serial killer? I imagine you've studied his work."

He shook his head. "I am not a serial killer. Think of me as an executioner."

"Oh, that's extremely comforting." I was clenching my hands tightly together, so tightly they were cramping. I was getting nowhere with my whines—I needed to work on this logically.

"Look, assuming by some wild chance I actually were this Lilith, why would you want to kill me? She was Adam's first wife, wasn't she? Trust me, I don't feel anywhere near that old. For that matter, I don't think I believe in Adam and Eve. It's a nice story, but that's about it. And even if I were Lilith, is that any reason to kill me?"

"Do I need to tell you all this?" he said, ignoring my protests. "You were Adam's first wife and you refused to lie beneath him. You ran away, and when he begged you to return you refused. You chose to consort with devils and take the souls of babies, as bloody and terrible as Kali the Destroyer or any of the bloodthirsty demons that have roamed the universe. You fornicate with beasts, you seduce men in their dreams, and you slaughter newborns."

I stared at him, stunned, and managed to pull one last ounce of attitude from my weary soul, not quite ready to give up. "Honey," I drawled, "I don't seduce anyone, in dreams or out. Nor do I fuck animals or murder children."

"I said beasts. Other demons, neither animal nor human. And you can argue all you want—I know who and what you are, and you have admitted you do not."

"In that case, don't you think you should think twice about killing me?"

'"No."

There was something implacable in that short, cool word, and I gave up, staring out into the scrubby, deserted brush. None of this made any sense—he might as well be talking about a stranger.

Except for the part about newborns. Why had I felt the desperate need to get as far away as I could from my newborn goddaughter? It had been nothing but instinct, strong enough to make me throw everything away and vanish.

And what exactly had I thrown away? No memory, no history, no family. Could he possibly be right? I leaned my head back and closed my eyes, closing out everything, doubts and stray thoughts and fear. I closed my eyes and waited for what would come to pass.

It must have been hours later when the car came to a stop. I sat up, looking around me with dazed acceptance. The sun was close to the horizon, and we had pulled up to a deserted building that might once have been some kind of farmhouse. The windows, doors, and most of the roof were long gone, and it looked as if no one had been anywhere near it in decades.

Azazel looked over at me. He must have sensed that I was past fighting him. I unfastened the seat belt I'd been wearing, the seat belt I'd been silly enough to wear, considering I was going to die anyway, and slid out of the front seat to stand in the scorching heat of the late afternoon, waiting for him to come around the car.

"Inside," he said. I went. I was past romanticized visions like Marie Antoinette on the scaffold. Impossible as it seemed, what he'd said made an eerie amount of sense. I knew there had to be some reasonable explanation, but I couldn't find it, and I was tired of running. If there was any truth to his crazy allegations, and I was beginning to believe there might be, then . . . then I wasn't going to fight it. If I had somehow been involved in the deaths of babies, of innocent newborns, I would rather die than risk doing it again.

The inside of the house was empty, nothing but a single chair bolted to the floor in the center of the main room. There were chains and ropes in a neat pile beside it, and belated panic swept through me. "No," I said. "You're not going to burn me alive."

"No, I am not. Sit."

It wasn't as if I had any choice. He could move faster than I could, he was stronger, and if I was the demon he said I was, all my abilities had vanished along with my memories. "Is there anything I can say to make you change your mind?" At least I didn't sound as pathetic as I felt. Though why dying with dignity should matter was debatable. If I screamed and cried and begged, no one would know but this son of a bitch. No one would pass judgment.

I sat. He knelt at my feet and began to tie my ankles together, and I looked down at him, at the broad shoulders, the silky black hair that had fallen forward, obscuring his cold face as he prepared my execution, and I had no idea why I moved my hand.

I put my fingers under his hair and stroked his hard face like a lover, my fingers caressing his skin and dancing across his mouth. He froze and looked up at me, his deep-blue eyes burning into mine with such heat that my entire body was swept with arousal, and I swayed toward him, wanting his mouth.

He stumbled back away from me, cursing, and cold reality hit me once more. I dropped my hand and turned my face away, refusing to look at him.

"If you do that again," he said in a harsh voice, "I'll strangle you myself. Though you would probably prefer that, would you not?"

He moved back in, grabbed my wrists, and tied them with quick, jerky moves. I ignored the pain—it no longer mattered. I was sickened by what I had done, by the rush of emotion and longing I'd felt for my soon-to-be murderer.

I managed one last salvo. "Prefer strangling to what? You said you weren't going to burn me. Are you just going to leave me here to starve to death?"

He shook his head, threading the heavy chain around my tied wrists and ankles and clamping it to the floor. He really wasn't taking any chances. He moved away, and that shaken expression was gone, leaving him stark and cold and beautiful in the waning light.

"I'm leaving you for the Nephilim."

"And they are . . . ?"

His disbelieving snort would have been annoying under any other circumstances. "They are an abomination. As are you. You cannot be killed by human means, and I prefer not to touch you. The Nephilim are a fitting end for you."

"And just who are the Nephilim?" I demanded again, not certain I wanted to hear the answer.

"They prey on the unearthly. You. And my kind," he said. "We have killed most of those that roam the world, but there are still some here in Australia. I am leaving you for them." He brushed the dirt off his dark clothes, almost as if he were brushing off the guilt of killing me. "It will hurt," he said. "But it will be over quickly. And you shouldn't have too long to wait."

There was almost kindness in his voice. An executioner's mercy. I watched as he moved toward the door, his figure outlined by the setting sun, and my voice stopped him, for just a moment.

"Don't." My voice broke this time. "Please."

But he left without looking back, and a moment later I heard the car start up, heard the tires on the rough terrain. I listened until I could hear nothing, and the darkness began to close in around me.

And I waited to die.

HE DROVE FAST. HE OPENED all the windows, ignoring the dust that was swirling into the POS Ford, his foot down hard on the accelerator. A car accident wouldn't kill him. What was true for the Lilith went for him as well. It would take an otherworldly creature to finish him, and as appealing as that sounded, there would be no one around to do the job.

He could have waited. Bound himself to that chair beside her and let the Nephilim come. When he'd felt her cool hand slide over his hot skin, he'd wanted to. Nothing could make him want to release her, nothing at all, but dying with her might have had a certain desperate symmetry.

He could have waited to make certain they'd finished her, but he knew what he could and couldn't do. And there was no way he could watch as they tore her into pieces, feeding on her flesh while her heart still pumped blood. He would come back in the light of the new day and find traces, blood and bone and skin. The Nephilim left destruction in their wake, and there would be enough left to bring proof to Uriel, if he chose to do so.

He was driving east, and in the rearview mirror he could see the sun on the horizon, sinking low, bright splintery shards of light spearing outward toward him. They would come for her as soon as the sun disappeared. They would come, and they would feast, and it would be over. There would be no way for any of the insane prophecies to come true. The Lilith would take no more innocent newborns; she would steal into no man's dreams and take his very breath.

And she would never marry the king of the fallen angels and rule over a hell on earth.

That particular prophecy had been scorched into his brain since the beginning of time. He had no idea who had existed longer, the Lilith or the Fallen, but they were both from before time was measured. The harsh judge who'd cast out Azazel's kind and cursed them was the same who'd cursed the first human female much more cruelly. The Fallen were left alone, simply to serve as couriers for souls between death and the hereafter, cursed to subsist on blood. The Lilith was taken up by demons and forced to lie with them, and she'd disappeared.

He would hear of her—stealing into men's dreams and leaving them drained and near death during the Middle Ages, leaving infants lifeless in their cribs—but then she would vanish again into obscurity. This time she would be gone for good, and the Fallen would continue with their endless quest to find the First. Lucifer, the Bringer of Light, entombed in a living darkness, waiting for them.

After the death of Azazel's beloved Sarah, the Fallen's stronghold had become not a haven but a prison, and he'd left Sheol in search of the demon destined by a sadistic Ultimate Power to be his bride. To destroy her would be to destroy one more source of evil in this misbegotten world—and ensure that that particular curse never came to pass.

The speedometer was climbing, but the road was empty, and if he lost control he would walk away. Nothing could kill him but fire or another otherworldly source—the Lilith, the Nephilim, Uriel's host of angels, who were more like Gestapo storm troopers than seraphim. But no one would put him out of this pain that had slid from unbearable to merely numbing.

He heard the unearthly howl, ululating as the

last spike of sunlight shrank below the horizon. He was too far away—there was no way he could actually hear the Nephilim as they caught the scent of her and moved in—but the sound shrieked into his mind, and he could see her, the tangled red curls, the pale skin and soft mouth, the frightened eyes. The eyes that called to him. The soft mouth that moved him more than he wanted to admit.

He slammed his foot on the brakes.

The car went into a spin in the swirling dust, coming to a stop sideways at the edge of the road. He soared upward, smashing through the metal roof as if it were aluminum foil, straight into the rapidly cooling air.

The Nephilim were already advancing on the deserted house. He slammed through the remainder of the roof, bits of lumber and debris coming down with him as he landed a few feet behind her. He folded his wings swiftly and moved toward her.

She sat absolutely still, and her eyes focused on him, on the knife in his hand, as he stepped in front of her. "Decided to do it yourself?" she said in a voice that didn't hide her fear. The Lilith was afraid of nothing, not even death. Could he have been wrong about her?

The groans and grunts of the Nephilim as they converged on the house were chilling, and their stench preceded them, the filth of decomposing flesh and ancient blood and maggot-ridden organs. She could hear them as well as he could, and she was trembling.

He slid the knife through the ropes. He looked out the empty frame of the window and could see them approaching. He would be no defense against so many, and he could simply stand there, wait for the monsters to take both of them.

There was no time to find the key to the lock that held her chains. He yanked, shredding the chains, pulled her out of the chair, and shot upward into the night sky, the howls of the Nephilim following them into the darkness.

HE LANDED LIGHTLY ON THE deserted highway, her body limp in his arms. The car was where he'd left it, the metal roof peeled back as if a firecracker had exploded inside. He angled her into the backseat and quickly ripped away the shackles he hadn't managed to unlock. Her slender wrists and ankles were raw and bleeding—she must have struggled after he left her. It wouldn't have done her any good—he'd used iron chains on purpose. Only iron could chain a demon, and she would have been helpless.

But supposedly she didn't know that. She claimed she knew nothing about who and what she was, and the torn and bleeding flesh almost seemed proof of that. He closed his hands around her ankles, so delicate that he easily encircled them. He released her, and they were smooth and unmarred once more.

He paused. There'd been times in history, when women wore layers upon layers of clothing, that ankles had been considered one of the most erotic parts of a woman's body. Nowadays, when everything was on display, one forgot about ankles, but hers were well shaped and surprisingly arousing.

This was the Lilith, he reminded himself, reaching for her bloody wrists. She was the original siren, luring men to their doom.

The warm, earthy scent of her blood hit him then. He pulled back, leaving her wrists healed, and squatted down, staring at her limp body, absently licking his fingers. And then he realized what he was doing.

He jumped away, spitting, gagging, trying to drive the taste and the smell and the lure of her blood from his body. He struggled to the ditch beside the road and threw up.

It hurt. His body fought him, craving the soothing balm of her; but he had always been in control of this strange human flesh of his, and he emptied himself of every trace of her. And then he rose, wiping his mouth, and went back to her.

He had no idea whether the Grace of forgetting would work on a demon, but he put his hand over her face, not touching her, and let it sink in. There was dried blood on his long fingers, her blood, and he cursed.

He shoved her all the way in and closed the door, then climbed into the front seat. He grabbed his bottle of water, swished his mouth out, and spat again, then poured the rest of it over his hands, rubbing away every trace of her blood. It wasn't his fault that he could still feel it there.

The car started easily enough, ignoring its ill treatment, and he pulled onto the road again. He could hear the muted noise of the Nephilim, screaming with rage at being denied their prey. They would follow, and he couldn't afford to linger. He could always move faster than they could, but having *her* with him would slow him down. He needed bright lights; he needed people.

But most of all he needed time and space to figure out why the fuck he'd just made the most stupid mistake of thousands of years of his endless life.

I HEARD THE SCREAM. IT tore from my throat as I was slammed into consciousness, the sound deafening, and I wanted to stop, I did, but I couldn't. Only for a moment, to suck in a deep, rasping gasp of breath, and then I screamed again, the sound sickening in the pure terror that had infused my very bones.

And then it stopped, this involuntary anguish, by his voice simply saying, "Stop."

For a moment I didn't move. I was lying stretched out on the seat of a moving vehicle. Logic dictated that it was the car Azazel had used to drive me out into the bush, but this one had a moonroof, and the stars overhead were oddly calming. I wondered if he'd frozen me as he had in the restaurant, but I found I could move, slowly, carefully, as if my bones might shake apart. I managed to pull myself into a sitting position.

It was almost full dark. I rubbed my tender wrists, but they were whole, no marks left by those damned ropes, which shocked me. I'd struggled like a madwoman when he left me in the muffled darkness, and I thought I'd felt the wetness of blood. I reached down to my ankles, but they were smooth and undamaged as well.

I had no idea whether he was going to let me talk or not, but I had to try.

"Why did you come back?" I didn't mean for my voice to sound accusing. He'd changed his mind about killing me, for God's sake. Why should I complain?

He didn't glance back at me. Fresh air came from the open roof, blowing his hair away from the elegant bone structure of his cold, emotionless face. "I have no idea," he said finally. "If I were you, I wouldn't question it. I may recover my sanity long enough to take you back there and dump you, so I suggest you just sit back and keep quiet."

I was smart enough to do just that. I was so cold, after the blisteringly hot day, and I shivered. I remembered the howls coming closer, the horrible smell that had assailed my nostrils, and I felt my body tremble almost imperceptibly. I decided to push my luck.

"Could you close the moonroof? I'm freezing. It must get very cold once the sun sets."

He hesitated. "It isn't that cold," he said finally.

"But I'm—"

"Deal with it."

Okay. I wrapped my arms around me, trying to get warm. He was probably right—it was just as likely shock and fear as anything else. I wanted to ask him where he was taking me, but he'd warned me not to ask questions, and I didn't want him changing his mind. I curled my legs up under me and huddled in the corner of the seat, as far from the open roof as I could get. The stars were very bright in the inky black sky overhead, and I realized I would probably be able to see the Southern Cross for the first time in my life. I had always had a secret weakness for astronomy, for the stars and constellations and the way they seemed to rotate in the sky. This might be my only chance to actually see the Southern Cross, and I hoped the sky stayed clear for as long as we were here. Unless he planned to abandon me here, which would suit me very well indeed. I could disappear into a new name and new identity here as easily as in the Northern Hemisphere. I'd had lots of practice.

I could tell by the dimming of the stars that we were approaching what looked like a small city. The electric lights were warring with nature, and electricity was winning. Light pollution, they called it. I thought I'd grown used to it, but that brief period without it had simply reminded me how much I loved the vast, endless sky.

I could smell the sea, which surprised me. I'd assumed we'd spent the day driving directly inland, so the proximity of the ocean was disturbing. I hated the ocean. It terrified me, the waves, the swells, the ebb and flow. I forced myself to take a deep breath of the rich salt smell, licking the taste off my mouth. Then I realized he was watching me in the rearview mirror, his gaze fastened on my mouth, and his deep-blue eyes were burning.

I ducked back into the darkness, unnerved. Remembering that I had reached out to touch him

mouth on mine, and if he'd stripped off my clothes and taken me there by the docks I wouldn't have protested.

I put my arms around his neck, kissing him back, my tongue sliding against his, and he pulled me up, up against him. I wrapped my legs around his hips, trying to get closer, shutting out my mind and my doubts, sinking into the hot wet cloud of need that enveloped us both.

Common sense hit him first. He pulled his mouth away, and I lowered my legs to the ground, letting them slide against his, slowly. He reached up and pulled my arms from his neck, stepping back, his eyes hooded, his expression as cool and unyielding as if the last few moments hadn't existed.

"I'm letting you go," he said in a voice only slightly roughened by what we'd been doing. "I would suggest you run before I change my mind."

I stared at him in disbelief. It was as if the kiss had never happened. Maybe I'd dreamed it. In the end, it didn't matter—what mattered was he was letting me go. "Just like that?" I said.

"Just like that," he said. "I have decided killing you is more trouble than you're worth."

I could happily agree with that. But I couldn't move. I still felt that strange, magnetic draw, still wanted to put my hands on him, to feel his body tight against mine, his skin sliding against me. I stayed motionless until his voice lashed out: "I told you to run."

And then I ran. Into the midnight-dark streets. No purse, no money, no passport. No name, no past, and no future. I didn't care. I was alive, and I was free. I'd figure out the rest later.

THE DARK CITY

Chapter Four

Azazel perched on the edge of the cliff, looking out over the roiling ocean, letting the cool sea breeze blow his overlong hair away from his face. He closed his eyes, drinking in the feel of it. In an empty existence, the feel of the wind, the smell of the sea, were among the few pleasures he could experience.

He opened his eyes again, sensing Raziel's approach. In the year and a half since Azazel had rejoined the Fallen, Raziel had repeatedly tried to hand the leadership of Sheol back to him, and he'd steadfastly refused. Raziel as the Alpha and his unconventional wife made a good ruling pair. Raziel had more compassion than Azazel was capable of feeling, and his wife, even though she'd shaken things up a bit, was proving to be a warm and caring Source.

He could look at her now without wanting to kill her, even hold short conversations with her. Because Sarah had liked her. He suspected his wife had known her death was coming—Sarah had often had unexpected visions—and she had already set the stage for Allegra Watson to take her place. If Sarah approved of her, he couldn't very well despise her.

Everyone had left him alone since he'd returned from his self-imposed exile, knowing that when he was ready to fully rejoin the ranks of the Fallen, he'd tell them. In the meantime, he'd spent the days poring over the old texts, searching for some hint, some clue, to Lucifer's whereabouts.

The first of them, the Bringer of Light, the most favored of God's angels, had been the first to be punished, imprisoned somewhere deep below the earth in an unending silence. Until they found him, they were helpless against the tyranny of the only archangel never to have been tempted. Uriel, bloody, ruthless, and completely without mercy, had been left in charge when the Supreme Being had given the human race free will and then withdrawn, leaving them on their own. Uriel had been charged with watching over things, but he'd followed through on the most horrific of the Supreme Being's punishments. Plagues that wiped out two-thirds of the world's populations—the Spanish influenza, smallpox, cholera—were successive gifts for the unrighteous. Uriel's particular favorites were syphilis and AIDS. The punishment for sin was death, and fornication was the worst sin of all in Uriel's eyes.

And no one could touch him, no one could stop him, as scourge followed scourge and mankind fell into wars and famine. Only the Fallen had any chance of halting his inexorable march toward human extermination, and time was growing shorter as Uriel's power grew.

Raziel settled beside Azazel, folding his wings about him as he stared out at the sea. "You have to go after her, you know."

"No." One didn't refuse the Alpha when he made a request or issued an order, but Azazel didn't hesitate.

He and Raziel had been the next to fall after Lucifer, with Tamlel and twenty others, and had been damned for eternity for the crime of loving human women. Neither humans nor angels, they were simply the Fallen, cursed to live out eternity with an unstoppable need for blood. The wretched Nephilim were the flesh-eaters, the darker side, the creatures of filth and decay.

"You were the one who found the link in the

old texts," Raziel said in his calm, patient voice. "You can't deny that she alone holds the key. We're just lucky you didn't let the Nephilim destroy her before you found the connection."

"She remembers nothing," he said stubbornly. "It would have made no difference."

"Did you bestow the Grace . . . ?"

"It would have failed. I could do very little with her. I could read her, just a bit, but it was all confusion. She didn't know who or what she was; she had no memory of her past life. If she cannot even recognize that she's the Lilith, how will she remember some minor bit of information that we've only just discovered could lead us to Lucifer?"

"We don't have any other choice. His voice is growing fainter, Uriel is growing stronger, and it won't be long before he finally abandons restraint and comes after us. We must find Lucifer, and I would consort with the foulest creatures in existence, even the remaining Nephilim, if it would help us."

He knew Raziel was right. He'd known the moment he'd come across that obscure reference: *The She-Demon who devours men and infants and lies with the Filth shall be entombed near the Bringer of Light, and bring forth the means of his deliverance.* Of course, it was only one line in a relatively obscure text, and its provenance was questionable. And it didn't begin to say how she might help them find Lucifer, only that she'd show them the way to do it. Which did them no good when she couldn't remember anything.

He thought back to the demon. The demon with the shape and smell and feel of a woman, who had only to look at him to stir feelings that should have been dead. He'd kissed her. That kiss had been burned into his body and his brain, tormenting him. What insanity had made him reach for her? No one else had managed to touch him in the nearly seven years since Sarah died, further proving just how dangerous the Lilith was. If she could arouse his dead soul, then she had strong powers indeed.

"I haven't kept track of her," he said, only half a lie. He'd stopped looking after her six months ago, once she'd gotten in bed with the young doctor. But he had little doubt she was still in Brisbane, still in that strange apartment that looked out over the Brisbane River. It would take him very little time to collect her.

But he would have to touch her, hold her, carry her. Breathe in the seductive scent of her skin. He would have to bring her into the safety and protection of Sheol. The very last place he wanted her.

For that one line from an obscure text that hinted she held the answer to Lucifer, there were dozens of other references to Lilith, queen of demons, and her marriage to the king of the Fallen. It didn't matter that Raziel now ruled the Fallen as the Alpha. Azazel had led them in their disastrous fall; Azazel was decreed to mate with the Lilith and reign over hell with her by his side.

Of course, those same sources equated the Fallen with a mythical Satan, a force of evil as powerful as God. In Azazel's endless experience, the only creature who came close to that description was Uriel, the one remaining archangel.

"You know where she is," Raziel said, unmoved.

"She cannot belong in Sheol. She is a demon." Was there a tinge of desperation in his voice? No, he simply sounded pigheaded.

"I know she doesn't. I know the prophecies. If you won't bring her here, you can take her to the Dark City and find the Truth Breakers. If there are answers to be found, they are the ones to do it."

He froze. He'd barely managed to survive his time with the brutal Truth Breakers long ago. And he was a lot stronger than the body the Lilith had taken. "Why me? Michael could—" He stopped. Michael had brute strength, the ultimate warrior.

He would destroy her, whether by accident or design.

Which would solve his problem, but bring them no closer to Lucifer. He racked his mind for anyone else among the Fallen who could take on the task, disposing of the demon once the information was garnered. There was no one. The strong ones would kill her; the gentle ones would be in danger once she regained her true self. He was the only one who knew enough to confine her without killing her. At least before her usefulness was past.

If she was brought into the sanctuary of Sheol, he might not be able to stop the prophecies from coming true. No matter how fierce his determination not to fall prey to the succubus, once she had breached the walls there would be no stopping her. He wasn't convinced that she had forgotten everything; but even if she had, sooner or later it would all come back to her. Prophecies had a vicious habit of coming true, particularly the ugly ones.

Though if they were to rule in the everlasting torment of hell, Uriel's favorite place, then he might embrace it. Embrace the pain as an alternative to the cold emptiness that filled him. Better to feel torment than nothing at all. Maybe.

"Take her to the Dark City," Raziel said, already

knowing he would give in. "If you find what we need, you can always leave her there. It would take her centuries to escape."

Azazel didn't move. The tide was coming in, and the wind had picked up, sending whitecaps scudding across the surface. A storm was coming. And he would be riding the wind.

Chapter Five

I zipped up my duffel bag and slung it on the floor, trying to ignore the cloud that lingered in the back of my mind. I glanced out the window at the Brisbane River. It was a bright day, sunlight glinting off the water, and there was a strong breeze blowing through the open window. It was no day for portents of disaster.

I lived on the third floor of an old colonial mansion that had been rehabbed into quirky apartments. The raucous birds had woken me every morning of the year and a half I had lived there, and I wouldn't have had it any other way. I loved birds—the noisy ones and the demure. There was something about watching them in flight that left me breathless and awestruck.

Not that I wanted to fly. I hated heights.

Hated flying, I expected, because I had no interest in leaving Australia to find out more about my clouded past. I liked being safe in my top-floor apartment with its tiny bathroom stuck under the eaves. I liked my job and my friends and my boyfriend, Rolf. I didn't want the changes I sensed on the wind.

I heard the footsteps from a distance, coming up the three flights of stairs, and an odd sense of apprehension filled me. Rolf was early. He hadn't phoned or texted me to be down on the wide porch that surrounded the building, though I knew he disliked the old house and the climb to my aerie. And suddenly I didn't want to answer the rapping on my door, afraid of who would be on the other side.

The knock came again, more peremptory, and I glanced out my open window, wondering whether I could climb out. . . . I was being ridiculous, I chided myself. Who did I think was lurking behind my door—the Grim Reaper?

I crossed the room and flung the door open, trying to ignore my relief at seeing Rolf standing there, looking hot and rumpled and bad-tempered. "Why didn't you answer your phone?" he demanded. "I've been calling you for hours,"

I picked up my cell phone, glancing at the screen. There were no missed calls—no calls at all, in fact, which in itself was unusual. Though my friends knew I was going out of town, so there was a reasonable explanation for that. But no sign of Rolf's multiple calls.

"Are you sure it was me you were calling? My phone says otherwise."

"Then your phone's broken," he said in a disgruntled voice. "I can't go."

I should have been disappointed at the very least. Instead I felt reprieved. I did my best to look upset. "Why not?"

"Last-minute emergency. I need to fill in for another doctor on the ob-gyn floor. Everyone's decided to deliver at the same time, and they're shorthanded. I don't really have a choice."

"Of course you don't," I said in a practical tone. "Can you get a refund on our travel?"

"Already taken care of," he said. "I called the resort before I tried you, so I know my phone is working. It must be yours." In fact, if anything was ever wrong in our relationship, it was usually my fault. And it was typical of Rolf to safeguard his money before he tried to reach me. He was a very careful man.

Really, there were times when I couldn't figure out why I put up with him, but then when I went out I remembered. For some reason, Australian men seemed to think I was irresistible. There was nothing that special about me—my curly red hair was more of a curse than an enticement, and I wore loose clothes and no makeup—yet for some reason men kept hitting on me. Having Rolf at my side kept them at bay.

Which meant my heart wasn't broken when he had to cancel our plans. I plastered an understanding smile on my face. "When are you due at work?"

He glanced at his watch impatiently. "I should be there now."

"Then go ahead. Don't waste your time talking to me," I said, shooing him toward the door. "I'll be fine." Of course, he hadn't asked me if I minded. Perhaps it was time to give up on good Dr. Rolf. Surely I could find someone else to provide a buffer, though I couldn't understand why I needed one.

I listened to him clatter down the stairs, secure in the belief that all was right in his world, then glanced at my packed bag. I moved back to the big open window, looking down into the garden, and for a moment I thought I saw a shadow near the hedge, something dark and narrow and threatening. Then it was gone, blending with the tall brush. I was getting squirrelly.

Well, if Rolf didn't want to go anywhere, that didn't mean I couldn't. My bags were packed, I had time off from work, and if I stayed I'd start seeing shadows in my own rooms. I was absolutely free for the next four days—much as I loved my strange little apartment, the walls were starting to close in on me.

I grabbed my duffel and backpack and left, trotting down the stairs that Rolf hated and I loved. I always felt like a princess climbing to my turret when I headed up those narrowing stairs. I let my hand brush the dark mahogany handrail in a strange kind of caress. It was almost as if I were saying good-bye.

My tiny Holden was parked in the shade, and I climbed in, tossing both bags into the backseat. I started to back out, then turned to glance in front of me. Something was standing there, something dark and shimmering like a heat mirage, and without thinking I stomped on the gas, shooting into the street and narrowly missing my landlord's parked car. I shoved the car into drive and took off, not looking back. Afraid to.

My heart was slamming in my chest, sweat on my forehead and palms. I didn't want to, but I glanced in the rearview mirror. The street was empty—there was no shadowy figure following me. No slippery horror-movie creatures looming up to take my soul. I slowly eased my foot off the accelerator as I headed down the hill toward the traffic, stopping carefully. And then, like a complete idiot, I suddenly forgot I was in Australia, and I took a right turn directly into oncoming traffic.

I heard the screech of tires, the slam of metal on metal, the grinding noise of cars crumpling. Oily smoke billowed into the air. Somehow the EMTs were already there, and I watched as they rushed to my tiny car, the driver's-side door crushed in.

"No one here!" one of the paramedics shouted. "Someone must have forgotten to put on the parking brake."

Odd. I didn't remember getting out of the crushed car. And no one was paying the slightest bit of attention to me, when I would have thought everyone would be screaming at me for being such a stupid American.

They were working on getting a woman out of the car I'd hit, but she was talking and looking relatively unscathed, so some of my guilt faded. I turned to the man standing behind me. "She looks okay." And then I froze.

I had turned to him automatically, knowing he was there, comfortable with it. Ugly reality came roaring back as I looked up into his cold blue eyes. "Azazel," I said.

He said nothing, simply watching me. I turned

and looked at the accident scene as they pulled the woman from the wrecked car. Maybe I could run for it once more. Where the hell was Rolf when I needed him?

And how had I gotten out of the car? I finally turned my back on the accident. "Am I dead?" I asked, matter-of-fact.

"Why should you think that?" His deep voice sent shivers through my body. I remembered that voice. I'd heard it in my dreams. The erotic, embarrassing dreams I'd rejected in the daylight.

"You're here again."

"You remember. That surprises me." He didn't look particularly surprised. Then again, he had never seemed to react to anything when we were together the last time.

Strange way to put it. When he'd kidnapped me and tried to kill me, the son of a bitch.

I glanced toward the police, who were now directing traffic, wondering if I had time to reach them, to scream for help. His gaze followed mine, but he didn't move. "It won't do you any good. They can't see or hear you."

I think I knew that. I just didn't want to believe it. I looked back at him. "I'll ask you again—am I dead?"

"It is not that easy to kill the Lilith."

"Don't call me that," I snapped as someone

walked right through me as if I weren't standing there. "I'm Rachel."

His eyes narrowed. "It is not that easy to kill *you*."

"I remember." I was standing too close to him. Odd that I could feel his presence, practically feel his body heat, yet people were walking through us to get to the accident. I took a surreptitious step back from him. "Have you changed your mind again?"

"It was not a permanent reprieve. But I'm here for another reason."

I took one more longing look at the police wandering around the accident, then turned back to him. Another step away. "Then explain."

"We have need of you." He looked as if he were eating an unpleasant bug as he said it. "I'm taking you out of here. It is against my better judgment."

"I'm not going anywhere with you."

"You have no say in the matter." He looked bored. "Come."

I'd managed to move a good five feet from him in small increments. "I don't think so." He could probably will me over there, but I wasn't going under my own steam.

"Come. Now." His rich voice was soft and deadly.

I still managed not to move. I wanted to, God,

how I wanted to. I wanted to cross that careful space I'd managed to give myself and press my body up against his. Against the man who wanted to kill me. I fought it, fought the need to move, glaring at him. It was a battle, one I was determined not to lose. He didn't fight fair—I believed his claim that he was something other than human, even though he was flat-out insane when he said I was a demon. But despite all his efforts, I wasn't going to let him control me. The illogical, powerful attraction I felt was probably just one more of his tricks.

I don't know how long we stood there. He didn't ask again. He stared at me out of those deep-blue eyes, so vivid in his calm face, and I fought the chill that swept over me. If I gave in there'd be no hope, though I couldn't begin to define what I was hoping for.

"You are wiser than this," he said finally. "You know I am your enemy, and it would take very little to kill you. Instead of antagonizing me, you should be trying to soften me up."

Soft was never a word I would use for Azazel. He was lean, strong, all harsh planes and angles. I didn't think he'd ever be soft at the wrong time.

Color flooded my face at the thought. Why was I thinking of sex when I looked at this man? If he wasn't human, he might not even be sexual.

And even if he was, it had nothing to do with me. I wasn't turned on by someone who wanted me dead.

But unfortunately, he had a point. I shouldn't be antagonizing him. I should be meek and submissive and maybe he'd let me go again. But I didn't move. Not this time.

To my shock, the merest glimmer of a smile danced across his mouth and then was gone as soon as it appeared. "Your choice."

And everything went dark.

I had felt this before: being crushed in an unbreakable hold, the scent of warm male and the ocean surrounding me. I didn't struggle—I remembered it would hurt more if I fought. I held still in the dark, blinding embrace, trying to register everything.

It was crazy, but it felt as if I were flying. Soaring through clouds and space and time, and it felt glorious. Ridiculous, because I hated the very idea of flying. Right now I was simply cocooned in something, my imagination going wild. But I breathed in deeply, the scent of his skin and the sea breeze in my nostrils, and I gave in to the pleasure of it, letting my will dissolve.

HE SOARED UPWARD, THE DEMON wrapped tight against him. She didn't fight him this time, which made things more difficult. He was better off fighting her. He could feel her head tucked against his shoulder, feel her warm, moist breath against his skin. If she struggled he could drop her, forget about her, and who knew where and when she would surface? But surface she would. Killing a demon wasn't that easy, even for him.

It hadn't taken long to find her—in truth, he'd always been aware of her, ready for the day when he could finish what he'd started. Letting her live was unacceptable.

He still didn't know why he'd changed his mind, gone back for her a year and a half ago. Maybe it was the simple fact that Sarah would have hated what he'd done. Even so long after her death, her gentle influence fought against his more bloody-minded instincts.

And *bloody-minded* was the term. The Lilith could bleed—he remembered that. Remembered the torn flesh of her wrists and ankles, which he'd healed after he pulled her out of there. He could make her bleed again, and this time no misguided charity would stop him. He wouldn't have thought there was a charitable bone in his body.

He would take her to the Dark City and, if it came to that, hand her over to the Truth Breakers to find out all her secrets. He would have no choice but to expose himself to her temptation, and he would prove to himself that he could resist her. He would mourn Sarah forever. She was the wife of his eternal banishment. The Lilith was a murderous whore.

No matter what she believed, he couldn't afford to let himself forget that essential truth.

Chapter Six

I OPENED MY EYES, BLINKED, THEN closed them tightly again. There was something wrong with my vision. Something wrong with my mind as well. My heart raced with remembered fear, and I took deep, slow breaths, willing calm back. I was lying on a bed, and déjà vu swept over me. This had all happened before. Where was Azazel?

I opened my eyes again, slowly, then sat up and looked around me. I was in a bedroom, large, luxurious, with a high ceiling, heavy old furniture, and what looked like a marble floor. I couldn't be sure, because the room was leached of color. Everything was a strange sepia tone, like an ancient photograph. I looked down at my body, and breathed a sigh of relief. I was in full color, my jeans the same faded indigo as when I'd put them on, my sneakers a dirty white, my arms their normal lightly tanned skin color. Some odd memory made me reach up to my hair. It was the same, long and thick, and I pulled a strand into sight. The same red I'd become accustomed to.

I stroked the coverlet beneath me. It was thick and velvety, despite its gray-brown appearance. Someone must have a really strange decorating sense, to have chosen everything in these colorless shades. Even the marble. I slid off the high bed, and the floor was hard beneath my feet. Was there such a thing as brown marble, or had they painted it?

But I knew paint was too easy an answer. I knew what I'd find when I opened the door, when I pushed the heavy beige curtains away from the tall windows, beige curtains that something told me ought to be pure white.

I turned the knob, hoping for some *Wizard of Oz* effect of the bright colors of Munchkinland beyond the door. Instead it was another sepia-toned room. No sign of Azazel, and I breathed an involuntary sigh of relief. There were the same tall windows covered with heavy curtains, and I didn't want to go look. But I was made of tougher stuff than that, and if I was here I might as well know what I was facing. I crossed the room and pushed the curtains aside, then stood there, frozen, staring out into the city.

I had no idea where I was—it looked like a cross between New York in the 1930s and London in the 1890s, mixed with some early German filmmaker's notions of a dystopian future. And it was all the same monochromatic chiaroscuro. A sort of grayish brown, like an old movie. I held my arm out in front of the cityscape. Still normal, a shock of color against the dark, shadowy lines of the strange place. I let the curtain drop, turning away, and then let out a little shriek. Azazel stood there, watching me.

At least he was in color, or as much color as he had in him. He was dressed in black as always, black jeans and a black shirt, and his long, ink-black hair framed a pale face, his dark blue eyes and high cheekbones uncomfortably familiar. But even his pale skin held a healthier color than the room, and his mouth had color. I stared at it, not sure I wanted to examine my own thoughts, and that mouth twisted into an unpleasant smile.

"So what kind of hell have you brought me to?" I managed to sound no more than casually interested. "Is this purgatory?"

"Purgatory is a mythical construction. This is the Dark City."

"You could have fooled me." I looked around me. "So why are we here?"

He didn't answer, his unsettling eyes moving over me with what I knew was cool contempt. I still couldn't figure out what I'd done to merit this, why he was so certain I was some kind of demon, but I wasn't going to ask him. I already knew that he wouldn't tell me anything.

"Are you hungry?" he said instead, which surprised me. So far he hadn't shown any particular interest in my well-being.

And I realized I was starving. "Yes."

He nodded, turning toward the door, and I stared at him speculatively. He was tall, maybe six two, and lean, with wiry strength that was oddly elegant. He wasn't quite as gaunt as he had been the last time I'd seen him—clearly he'd gotten a meal or two in the interim, though he still could have used a few more pounds. I couldn't rid myself of the peculiar sense that there was something missing when he turned his back on me. It was a strong back, broad shoulders, and muscled arms. But there should have been something else there.

He glanced back. "What are you looking at?" He sounded wary, irritated. The irritation was nothing new, the wariness a small triumph for me when I was feeling weaponless.

"Nothing," I said. "We going someplace?"

"You said you were hungry, and I'm certainly not about to cook for you. I know a restaurant."

"We're eating in a restaurant like normal people?" I scoffed. "Don't tell me—we're on our first date."

"We are not people, demon. Neither of us. You know that, whether you wish to face it or not."

"*You're* not people," I shot back. "If anyone's a demon, it's you. You swoop down and carry me off to impossible places, places that make no sense. So far I've seen nothing to prove I'm anything more than a normal human being who's attracted a supernatural stalker."

"Not even when you look in the mirror?"

I'd forgotten about that. The red hair, the warm brown eyes, the secretive set of my mouth, my determined jaw. It still felt strange, even after well over a year, yet oddly familiar. But I wasn't about to give up without a fight. "I figure that's you clouding my mind."

"'Clouding your mind?'" he echoed. "If only it were that simple. Are you coming?" He was holding the door open, and I could see a hallway beyond it.

Maybe he'd be more forthcoming when we were eating. I'd been mocking him about the date, but in fact people tended to relax when they were eating. With luck, he'd start answering at least a few harmless questions.

Though he hadn't done so in that diner in the bush, I remembered suddenly. He'd simply made sure I couldn't talk and proceeded to eat, giving me no choice but to follow suit.

We were on the second floor. I followed him into the formal hallway of what looked like a movie set, down the stairs, through the heavy front door, into the street. Gray cars and trucks drove by; gray-faced people filled the streets, with their gray clothes and their gray souls. Azazel seemed like an absolute rainbow as he walked among them in his stark black, but none of the inhabitants seemed to notice that both of us were different.

I could think of a dozen different movies of people living in black and white in a Technicolor universe, and I tried to remember what they'd done to break the spell. Dorothy had traveled in a house and landed on a witch in Oz. I could only wish a house would fall and splatter bits of Technicolor Azazel over the landscape.

Pleasantville? Hadn't people fallen in love and broken the black-and-white curse? Unfortunately there was no one for me to fall in love with, only my mortal enemy. Besides, I was pretty certain I'd never been in love in my entire life, even during those vast blank periods that made up most of it.

I certainly hadn't loved Rolf. He'd filled a need, imperfectly, and I'd already let go. I wouldn't miss him.

I rushed to keep up with Azazel. He was barely paying any attention to me. He must have known escape was pretty much out of the question.

"Do those creatures live here as well?"

That managed to get his attention. He glanced back at me. "Which creatures?"

"You know perfectly well which creatures—the ones you were serving me up to last time you kidnapped me. I never actually saw them, thank God, but—"

"The Nephilim."

I shuddered, my memory still imperfect, my instinctive horror very real. "The what?"

"You heard me. They're called the Nephilim. Creatures as old as time, angels who fell from heaven and went mad in the process. We have managed to wipe out most of them, but a few remain in Australia, others in Asia."

"I don't believe in angels."

He kept walking ahead of me, but I somehow got the impression he was smiling. Which was flat-out impossible—Azazel didn't smile. "Nevertheless," he said in a neutral tone, "that is what they once were. Now they are simply abominations, feasting on human flesh."

A shiver washed over me. "And who is this 'we'?"

At that he did glance back at me, raising an eyebrow.

"You said, 'We have managed to wipe out most of them,'" I said. "Who is 'we'?"

"The rest of my kind."

"And your kind is . . . ?"

"None of your business." He'd stopped outside a gray restaurant, the heavy drapes in the windows making it look like a café out of last-century Europe. He opened the door, his hand looking strange on the sepia knob, and gestured me inside.

This odd city might be devoid of color but the smells in the restaurant were rich and strong, spicy. The maître d' who led us to a table was very old-school in shades of gray—he was dressed in formal wear, his manner punctilious as he held the chair for me. He glanced over at Azazel. "Will you be wanting to see him tonight, my lord?"

That managed to startle me. Why the hell was he calling Azazel "my lord"? A flash of annoyance crossed Azazel's face. "I have yet to decide, Edgar. I will let you know."

"Very good, my lord," he said, bowing himself away from us. I watched with interest. I'd never seen someone actually try to move in that position, but clearly Edgar had a great deal of experience.

I turned back to . . . to Azazel. There were other guests in the restaurant, speaking in muted voices, but no one even glanced in our direction. I assumed that to them we looked as gray as they did; otherwise they would surely be staring at us. In fact, anytime other diners glanced our way, they quickly averted their gazes, as if they'd looked at something they weren't supposed to see.

They all looked beaten down and depressed. Well, if I lived a monochromatic life in a place called the Dark City, I'd be depressed too. I wondered if they were here because they wanted to be, or if, like me, they'd been dragged here against their wills. Not that Azazel would tell me if I asked.

It couldn't hurt to try. "What is this place?"

"A restaurant."

I gave up. It was a waste of time to ask. I sat back, biting my lip in annoyance, and again an expression flitted across his austere face that in someone more human might almost be a smile. "That is much better," he murmured. "I prefer not to have you yammering at me. Your questions will be answered when the time is right."

"And I don't give a good goddamn what you

prefer," I replied in my sweetest tones. Again he looked almost amused. "And what's so damned funny?"

"Your phrasing."

"Do you want to explain?"

"No."

I contented myself with a low growl. I didn't even ask if he was going to let me order for myself this time. I doubted it. It probably only made him feel superior to shut me down, and I was mortally tired of it. I could be just as taciturn as he could, even if it didn't come naturally to me. Then again, I didn't know what *did* come naturally to me.

"I am not convinced that *mortally* is the right word."

I jumped. "Don't tell me you read minds."

"Occasionally." He said it as if it were merely a boring incidental. "You are ridiculously easy to read." Then he added, "You know you're not mortal."

I stared at him in astonishment, then remembered I was supposed to be some kind of demon. "I gather so-called demons are immortal. Then how could you kill me?"

"Immortals can be killed only by other immortals. Not by human means or natural occurrences. You cannot drown unless I am the one holding you under."

"Doubtless a fond wish on your part," I said. At least I had seen no water around this dark, depressing city.

He didn't reply as a waiter appeared, laden with plates that as far as I could tell hadn't been ordered. The food was horrible-looking—gray meat in gray gravy, pale potatoes, and taupe-colored vegetables. Even the wine looked muddy. But it smelled good, and that was all that mattered. I had a choice. I could let him cow me, refuse to eat, sit there in sullen silence. Or I could eat.

I ate. It tasted heavenly, so good I closed my eyes and moaned in pleasure. Normally I wasn't a big fan of heavy German cooking, but this was so wonderful I'd risk a thousand clogged arteries for it. I glanced at his plate. Not much on it, and I had the sudden horrifying suspicion that they'd given me the wrong plate. His looked much more like the diet plates I'd been subsisting on for most of my life. Whatever life I could remember.

I set down my fork. "Did they give me the wrong plate?"

"No. You said you were hungry. I never eat much."

I was going to ask him how they knew what to bring, then picked up my fork and shoveled more food into my mouth instead. Two could play this game.

I ate in silence, slowly, savoring every bite, trying not to notice as he picked at his meager food. He wasn't as thin as the first time I'd seen him. He'd filled out a bit, and there was definition to the muscles of his arms. Strong arms. But I knew that—he'd carried me effortlessly, flown with me . . .

No, that was wrong. I had no idea where that notion had come from, but it was ridiculous. Just as I finished the heavy meal, feeling not quite sated, coffee and a raspberry pastry arrived in front of me. I glanced up at him. "No chocolate bribes?"

It was a test. "You have never liked chocolate," he said, giving me another piece of information. I was strongly tempted to demand a hot fudge sundae, but he was, as always, correct. I didn't like chocolate. I had no idea how he knew these things, the minor details of a human life, but he did. It wouldn't do to underestimate him.

The maître d' appeared at our table when we were done, and I expected to see a discreet bill placed at Azazel's elbow. There was no neat folder in Edgar's hand. "He knows you're here," the man said in an undertone. "He wants to see her."

An annoyed expression crossed my companion's face. "She needs time."

"It wasn't a suggestion, my lord."

Azazel tossed his heavy linen napkin on the table. Another man would have sighed in frustration. Azazel simply looked colder, if that were possible. He rose, glancing down at me. "Come."

I was beginning to hate that word in his cold, commanding voice. "I'm not finished." In fact, I was too full to eat much more, but I was determined to fight him at every step.

"Yes, you are." He reached down for me, but I managed to keep out of his way, rising and almost knocking the chair over in my hurry to keep out of his grasp. The other customers were watching now, surreptitiously, and I wondered if it was good manners or something about Azazel in particular that made them circumspect. Or perhaps they were just so beaten down they didn't really care.

I took a quick look around, wondering if there was anyone I could turn to for help. But the moment I tried to catch someone's eyes, the person turned away as if I were unclean. I huffed with annoyance. I was on my own, but that was no novelty. I'd survived thousands . . . decades . . .

No, that wasn't right. I'd survived years without anyone's help, and I'd survive this. After all, I'd managed to get out of the last trap he'd laid for me. Granted, it had been by his good graces, though I hated to call it that. His guilty conscience.

This new situation wasn't nearly as desperate. He wasn't threatening to kill me, at least not so far. Things had to be looking up.

We made a strange procession, the maître d' leading the way through a door in the back of the dining room into a maze of dark, narrow hallways, Azazel behind me to keep me from bolting. It was scarcely necessary—where would I go? I tried to ignore my growing panic as we went deeper and deeper into the bowels of the building. If I was about to confront someone who could bend the intimidating Azazel to his will, then this creature must be terrifying indeed.

We finally stopped in front of a large, unprepossessing door. Our guide knocked, then pushed it open, and a none-too-gentle nudge from Azazel propelled me forward.

I found myself in a cozy room with comfortable furniture scattered about, a fire blazing in the fireplace, piles of books on most surfaces. The kind of place one would want to spend a rainy afternoon, I thought, looking around me for the inhabitant.

I hadn't seen him at first, sitting in an overstuffed chair, at one with the cozy room. He was very old, with silky pale hair covering his scalp and drifting over his ears. He was as colorless as everyone else in this place, and I wondered if the same thing would happen to me and my captor, assuming we stayed long enough. He wore some kind of robe, and there was the comforting scent of pipe smoke in the air. Odd, how cigarettes and cigars smelled nasty but pipe smoke seemed dignified and comforting.

The old man gazed at me out of milky eyes, a pleasant expression on his lined face. "There you are, my dear," he said, and his accent was British. No surprise—it fit perfectly with the ambience of old books and older brandy. His eyes narrowed as he saw Azazel behind me, and he was patently displeased. "Azazel."

"Beloch," Azazel murmured in return with the merest inclination of his head. "This is not a good time."

"It's a good time for me," the man called Beloch said in a sharp tone. "You'll have to adapt." He turned back to me, and his smile was both charming and avuncular. If he and Azazel were enemies, then he was clearly my new best friend. "My dear, why don't you have a seat across from me? It's been a long time since I've had such a lovely young woman visit me in my old bachelor quarters. This is quite a treat. Azazel, pour us both a glass of brandy. Pour one for yourself while you're at it."

I'd been right about the brandy. I considered refusing—the idea of drinking anything stronger than wine was not appealing—but I didn't want this distinguished old gentleman looking at me with the scarcely veiled contempt he directed at Azazel. A moment later Azazel placed a brandy snifter in my cold hand, and I reflexively closed my fingers around the stem, brushing against his skin.

He jerked back, and the brandy sloshed a little.

Beloch made a deprecating sound at such clumsiness. "You may leave us."

"No." Azazel's short, unemotional response wasn't reserved for me alone, I was glad to see.

Beloch's mouth tightened. "Then sit in a corner and be quiet." He must have noticed my worried glance at Azazel, for he continued in a warm voice, "Don't worry about him, Rachel. He has a very controlling nature, and he doesn't like bowing to the will of others. Unfortunately for him, I outrank him when he's in this place, and he's sworn to do as I command."

At last, a champion, or at the very least a cohort. Someone with the power and ability to stand up to Azazel's high-handed ways. I gave Beloch a brilliant smile as I sank down on the ottoman.

"So tell me, young lady," he said, leaning back and surveying me out of those wintry eyes. "What brings you here to the Dark City? Besides our unpleasant friend over there?"

"I have no idea." I took a tentative sip of the brandy. Again, the taste more than made up for the lack of color, and the richness of it burned my tongue.

"There is no need for games, Beloch," Azazel snapped. "You know as well as I just why I brought her here. We need answers."

"And how do you intend to get those answers if you're terrified of her?"

Azazel's snort conveyed his contempt for such a suggestion. "Terrified? Hardly. Even at full strength she would never be a match for me. She insists that she has no knowledge of her powers, but even if she did I'm well equipped to counter any of them."

"Now, why don't I believe you?" Beloch said in a silky voice.

I sat very still, cradling the brandy I didn't want to drink, observing. While they were ostensibly talking about me, they almost seemed to have forgotten my existence, an ancient enmity surfacing instead. Which was fine with me—I had my own skin to worry about. As long as they were fighting, I could stay beneath the radar and try to figure out how to escape.

"You're terrified the prophecy will come true," Beloch continued, "so terrified you might have destroyed her before you found out what the Fallen are so desperate to discover. You won't find out what secrets she holds until you face your fears."

"Do not be tiresome, Beloch," Azazel said, unmoved. "I am far older than you are—I never let human fears and frailties affect me."

This was enough to startle me. If hunky, gorgeous Azazel was much older than the wizened Beloch, then the rules had really gone out the window. But then, I knew that. There was a great deal I knew, simmering just beneath my consciousness, things I didn't want to remember. Was afraid to remember. It could all stayed buried as far as I was concerned.

Beloch snorted in amusement. "You may be older, Azazel, but you are scarcely wiser. I give you a choice. Take her back and test the prophecy and your resistance to it. Once you know the answer to that, bring her back and I'll find the answers you need. That, or she stays here with me."

Azazel's expression didn't change, but his hooded glance darted my way, and he couldn't miss my watchfulness. He didn't argue, however, rising from his seat and tossing back the brandy with a gesture that brought a disapproving sniff from Beloch. And then he looked at me. "Come."

God, I hated that word in his deep, cold voice. Everything about him was icy, and I glanced back at Beloch's avuncular expression, wondering if it would do any good to throw myself on his mercy.

But I wasn't that naïve. Beloch might seem like a kindly old professor, but there was a hardness in his eyes that he might reserve simply for an old enemy like Azazel, or that might be a clue to his real nature. Either way, I knew enough to think before I jumped from one trap into another.

I rose, setting my barely touched snifter of brandy down and giving Beloch a smile. "It was so nice to meet you."

For some reason, my words amused him. "I look forward to continuing our association. Don't let Azazel intimidate you. You have more power than you realize, if you only decide to acknowledge it. I expect it will be very interesting to discover just how susceptible our friend is."

Not exactly my friend, but I said nothing as Azazel muttered something unflattering, took my arm in his hard grip, and pulled me out of the room. A few minutes later we were out in the dark streets of the strange city, emerging on a lower level from the restaurant near a black, fast-flowing river. Earlier, in what had passed for daylight, the city had been shrouded with shadow. Now it was pitch-dark, and I was suddenly ready to drop. Had it been only this morning that I'd been packing for a trip to the Great Barrier Reef and bright, endless sunshine? And now I was in some strange, colorless universe, once more a prisoner, and the fight went out of me as exhaustion swept in. All I wanted to do was find some quiet place to figure out what the hell I was going to do.

"We haven't far to go," Azazel said, and if it had been anyone else, I might have thought he had read my exhaustion and was offering respite. Both things were impossible—he didn't care what I was feeling, and he would never volunteer comfort. He was my enemy, and I couldn't afford to forget it.

I didn't say anything, letting him steer me down the street, past the gray inhabitants with their soft voices and disinterested eyes. I had no idea what Beloch wanted him to do, and I didn't care. As long as I could collapse in a bed for twenty-four hours, I'd be just fine. I stole a glance at my hard-eyed companion. He'd leave me alone, wouldn't he? In the past he'd wanted nothing more than to keep his distance, as if I were unclean.

But he hadn't released my arm, and I made no effort to break his hold as he guided me along the street, back toward the brownstone we'd exited a few hours earlier. There was a strange, perverse comfort in his touch. He was my enemy.

But he was the only familiar thing in this strange world. And for that reason, I wasn't willing to let him go.

Chapter Seven

Azazel kept his pace measured, determined not to give in to the fury that had swept over his body. He despised Beloch and always had, and the feeling was mutual. It wasn't simply that Beloch was one of the strange, quasi-mortal inhabitants of the unknowable world of the Dark City. Azazel routinely disliked all of the inhabitants—they were like the Nephilim without the appetite. Empty, unreadable creatures, not human nor Fallen nor sanctified, and Beloch, as ruler and high mayor of the Dark City, was the worst of them.

But his power was undeniable for all that it was incomprehensible. He was the one to deal with if you needed to use any of the Dark City's unpleasant assets. Such as the Truth Breakers. The Truth Breakers were the only beings in existence who could extract the truth from anyone, though their methods ranged from painful to shattering. The most stubborn never survived, and Azazel had seen more than one body explode into countless pieces as the process reached its conclusion, and the memory still haunted him.

He had survived his own encounter with them countless years ago, and so would the Lilith. She was too epic and powerful a demon to be destroyed by them, no matter how brutal the Truth Breakers were. They would extract the truth from her, and he could leave her here in this bleak, empty world, where she could do no harm and he would never have to see her again.

The Dark City had existed for almost as long as Azazel could remember, a mysterious, floating place of supposed sanctuary and peace, though in truth he had no knowledge of who and what came here. He only knew that those who'd been brought were usually broken in the end. But he expected most of them had been human, unable to withstand the rigors the place offered. He'd been called there centuries ago for both punishment and questioning, when he'd refused Uriel's demands one too many times. He'd survived. Just as she would.

Beloch oversaw the Truth Breakers, as well as everything in the Dark City, and he'd always taken special pleasure in the more brutal methods his underlings employed. He sat in his quarters looking like a kindly wizard while he engineered atrocities that sickened Azazel, who had seen the worst that the creatures could offer.

He was convinced Beloch had wanted to take the Lilith immediately, and he'd known an odd regret. Azazel would have forced her to admit the truth eventually, without turning her bones to jelly and her skin to flakes of mold. He could only hope it wouldn't have to go that far. Physically she was just a girl. Evidently she could no longer shift into the ancient forms she'd once used, of Lamia, the snake woman who devoured children, or the wind demon with raptor's talons. No matter how hard he'd pushed her when he first took her to Australia, she'd stayed in this form, even facing death. Clearly she no longer had the gift of transformation. Because she was physically as frail as most humans, she would give up her secrets quickly. He could have gotten them out of her, but in bringing her to the Dark City he had no choice but to do as Beloch commanded.

Now he almost wished Beloch had taken her, gotten it over with. The old man's sadistic alternative made him furious. He despised the Lilith for the vicious, murdering creature she was, for her power and her wickedness, her cruelty over millennia. But Beloch was right about one thing. He despised her most for the prophecy that held them both, and until he could let go of that rage, a rage he refused to call fear, she would still have power over him.

She'd stopped with her infernal questions, at least for now. She was silent as he force-marched her down the street, no more whats or wheres or whys. He would take her back to the house, shove her into a bedroom, and proceed to get drunk. Beloch had thrown down a challenge, but he was in no hurry to pick it up. And in no mood to test himself.

He loathed the Dark City. It was depressing. Not that that surprised him—not much in creation didn't depress him nowadays. The raw, screaming pain of Sarah's death had dimmed to a constant ache, and when he thought of her, which he did often, he did his best to let go of her. She'd hate his mourning. He'd known her so well—if she'd lived out her life normally, she would have had time to prepare him for her loss. Instead, she'd been ripped away by the Nephilim, and Raziel's wife had taken her place.

At the thought of Raziel's wife, cold anger stirred inside him. There was nothing he could do about it, and he knew that what had happened wasn't her fault. He'd even gone so far as to accept blood from her, though he'd refused to use her wrist, insisting that one of the healers remove the blood from her body first. He'd been starving, close to death, when he'd finally returned to Sheol. He would have welcomed eternal darkness, but that wasn't his fate. Once he died, he'd continue in everlasting torment, judgment for the sin of falling from grace, for loving a human woman.

Over the thousands of years, he'd often regretted that first impulsive reaching for what he wanted. But not since Sarah had appeared in his life. Sarah had made everything worth it.

And this . . . this *thing* walking beside him. It was foretold that she would take Sarah's place by his side, in his bed, to be his consort and wife and rule the darkness with him. But the prophecy was wrong.

She was trying to ensnare him, he knew that much. He could feel the power of her sexuality, the sexuality that had crept into good men's dreams and seduced them, the sexuality that had filled the beds and pallets of a thousand demons. She was the Lilith, irresistible to most, and it was no wonder he looked at her and thought of sex. No wonder he'd given in to temptation and kissed her when he'd left her in Brisbane. It wouldn't happen again.

Beloch underestimated him. Azazel had been the Alpha since the fall until Raziel took over seven years ago, and as such he'd chosen the Source, the woman whose blood sustained those who had no wives. He had never thought about finding the perfect mate. When the time came, the right woman had always been there. He'd recognized them, taken them, mated with them, ruled with them. And when one died, he'd simply choose another, loving each one as best he could.

But Sarah had been different from the very beginning. He wasn't going to think about her, he reminded himself. He just needed to remember that he'd bedded countless women, icy ones, shy ones, hot-blooded sexual ones. He'd performed as he'd needed to, as he wanted to, with tenderness, with passion, with love; but never had one of them held any power over him. Not until Sarah.

The Lilith would hold no power either. He would prove to Beloch and himself that her body was simply a tool he could use and discard, that he would never fall prey to her siren's lure. He had for a brief moment. He never would again.

The house was just as they'd left it. He hadn't bothered to lock the place—most of the inhabitants of the Dark City steered clear of him. He frightened them, he knew it. Presumably they looked at him and saw garish color and eternal damnation, and they wanted neither. The denizens of the Dark City worshipped truth and moderation, attraction rather than desire, appetite rather than hunger. He and his kind were anathema to the curbed needs of the Dark City.

He had never stopped to question who and what populated this drab and sorrowful place. It was Beloch's kingdom, a place out of time, and the shadows who moved here seemed more like lost souls than human or demon. He didn't care. They were no threat to him or his kind—not even the Truth Breakers or Beloch's police force, the Nightmen. They couldn't leave this place; they simply existed. But even here they couldn't touch him. They could only touch her, because he'd brought her here for their cruel services.

He could smell her. He'd known her scent the moment she'd walked out her apartment building door that morning, the subtle fragrance of her skin. He wondered if she emitted a mating scent, if that was how she'd doomed so many. If so, he was mostly immune to it. He looked at her and wanted her. He knew that. Beloch must think him a fool not to have accepted that simple fact. Everyone should want the Lilith, even a dried-up husk of a man such as Beloch.

But while he wanted her, he hadn't been tempted to touch her or take her, and he could have, so many times. It would go no further than desire, not action. He wanted her and he ignored it, as he ignored so many of his appetites. Beloch was a fool to think he'd be no match for her or his own needs.

He pushed the buttons on the old-fashioned wall switch in the front hallway, turning on the dim lights that only made the shadows deepen. She looked around her nervously, as if worried about what might be hiding in the shadows. She was foolish. The only thing she had to fear was standing right next to her. At least, until he handed her over.

"Go to bed," he said gruffly as he released her. His fingers felt warm, almost stinging.

He expected her to scamper away, and indeed, she moved back, out of his reach. But then she paused, and he groaned inwardly. "What did Beloch mean? Why should you be frightened of me?"

"Do you think I'm frightened of you?"

"Of course not," she said, sounding annoyed. "I'm depressingly harmless. Still, he made it sound like there's some history between us."

"There isn't," he said, only half a lie. "Until last year we had never spoken, never met. Most people think you are the stuff of myths."

"Like demons and the Nephilim."

He glared at her. She was so very different from what he'd expected. Her protective coloring hadn't fooled him when he'd first taken her, but even in her real form, she was a far cry from a sex goddess. Her breasts were on the small side, the curves of her hips subtle; her chin was stubborn, her mouth tight, her eyes filled with either anger or fear. He'd known sirens—demons and humans, creatures who tried to lure any man into their clutches—and he'd even given in a time or two, for the sheer pleasure of it.

But the Lilith was like no siren or demon he knew. Her clothes were plain and baggy, her face free of paint; she wore no adornment of any kind. It was almost as if sex were simply not a part of her life.

But he knew otherwise. He knew that beneath her drab exterior the heart of a raptor existed, a predator who was ready to claw a man to pieces once she'd mated with him. Lamia, cursed shriek owl; Lilitu, the wind demon, monster of storms. And he was drawn to her anyway.

"Your bedroom is at the end of the hall," he reminded her. He needed her gone. The scent of her was maddening, elusive, bewitching.

"I'm not tired anymore." She moved into the formal parlor, taking a seat and looking at him out of those warm brown eyes. "I want to know what

Beloch meant. What kind of test is he expecting you to perform?"

He let his eyes drift over her, slowly. He knew what Beloch was ordering, challenging him to do. He wanted Azazel to touch her, taste her, bed her. Azazel was supposed to fuck her and then prove he could walk away from her, turn her over to the shattering destructiveness of the Truth Breakers and then celebrate the destruction of one more demon.

He could no longer fool himself. They would destroy her. She might have demon blood, but she no longer had the ability to change form. She had the frail human body of a woman now, one that would break under the Truth Breakers' hands. And he would have no choice but to give her to them.

He looked at her and his body stirred, and he despised her—and himself. Every reaction was a betrayal of who he was. He could tell himself it was simply her wiles, her powers, that were doing this to him. But he wasn't asleep, he wasn't drugged.

And he wasn't going to do it. Not tonight, when need vibrated through his body and he wanted to shove her up against a wall and take her. By tomorrow he'd be back in control. By then he could take her to his bed and then walk away, untouched, unchanged. He could expose the demon the only way possible, through the act of sex. And she could no longer pretend she didn't know what she was.

What *it* was. "Go to bed," he said gruffly. "Or you'll wish you had."

She simply raised an eyebrow, the foolish creature. It was unwise to underestimate him. He could squeeze the life out of her in moment, break her neck, end her as he'd come so close to doing, more times than he could remember. He could end this farce.

She must have read some of the violence in his eyes. She rose, shoving her hair away from her face, and sighed melodramatically. She came up to him, pausing in the doorway. "I'm not afraid of you."

"You should be," he said. Just a taste, just a warning, he told himself through a haze of desire. So she knew what was coming. And before she knew what was happening, he shoved her up against the door and slammed his mouth down on hers.

I FROZE, IN SHOCK, OUT of necessity. His hands were on my arms, imprisoning me. His body crowded me against the doorjamb, and his mouth was hard, angry, punishing.

I would have kneed him in the balls, but he

was too close, trapping me between his hard body and the wall. I kept my mouth shut, wondering whether I could bite him hard enough to draw blood, wondering why my breath was coming fast and my heart was racing. It wasn't fear. I'd told the truth—I was no longer afraid of him. I remembered his kiss from the dockside, the rush of desire that had suffused my body.

As it did now. My pulse raced, my skin heated; I was wet and ready. I thought, *Fuck it,* and opened my mouth for him, taking the sweet invasion of his tongue with a shock of pleasure, and I knew I'd been waiting for this, longing for this without knowing it. Longing for him, my enemy.

His hands slid down my arms to the hem of my loose T-shirt and then up underneath, cupping my breasts in the thin bra I wore. I could feel my nipples harden at his rough touch, and I hated it, hated that I wanted him, that I needed him so badly my legs shook and my hands trembled, and he was hurting me. . . .

And then, just as I was about to struggle, he gentled, and the kiss became a sweet wooing, a delicious temptation, and his long fingers slid beneath the flimsy bra, pushing it up and out of the way, and I wanted to gasp with the sharp pleasure of those fingers against my pebbled flesh.

He brought his hands up to cradle my head,

as impossibly the kiss deepened, and I wanted my clothes off—now. I wanted to strip him naked and feel him inside of me, pulsing and thrusting. I could sense it, anticipate it, feel the thick push of him, and I cried out against his mouth as a small climax startled me.

And then I was shoved away, roughly, and I almost fell. My legs felt weak, rubbery, and I wanted more, wanted to reach out and beg him, wanted everything wicked and impossible and glorious. For the first time in my memory, in any of my twisted memories, I wanted sex and darkness and lust. His push had knocked my head against the doorjamb, but I hid it. I stared up into his eyes and saw the contempt and hatred there, and the desire, the need, vanished. I wanted to shrivel up and die.

"Quite lovely," he said in an acid voice. "You have the reserved-virgin thing down pat. If we wanted to kick it up a notch, you could try to summon the Nightmen and I could disappear, but I don't think they'll come. You have no choice."

I stared at him. He was doing a damned good job of controlling his breathing, but I had felt him against my stomach, hard. I wasn't going to look at his crotch, I wasn't going to look anywhere but his hard, furious face, and his coldness reached into me so that I wanted to shake and shiver. I pressed back against the wooden doorjamb to keep my body still, lifted my chin, and found a cool smile to answer him with.

"No choice?" I echoed, taking the salient phrase from his biting attack. "No choice in what?"

"You are a *whore*," he said. "You exist to corrupt mankind."

I didn't flinch. It was another of his lies. My memory might be damaged, but my body had known with Rolf—known the frustration, the emptiness. Sex was a necessity for men and a trial for women. "But you said you're not a man," I shot back, uncowed. "Therefore you're incorruptible."

"That's what Beloch wants me to prove."

"Prove that you're resistant to my so-called wiles?" I laughed, just slightly shaky. "You've already proven that." I ignored the memory of his erection against me. "It's hardly a great accomplishment. I'm no great beauty, no seductress. It should be fairly easy to resist me."

He made no effort to come closer, and my heartbeat was beginning to slow. My mouth burned from his, and I wanted to get away from him. "You know that you are impossible to resist. To deny it is a waste of time."

I couldn't help it, I laughed again. The idea was patently absurd. "Oh, yeah? Why is that?"

"You know as well as I do. You are not simply

some ordinary demon. You are the Lilith, the first wife, the consort of monsters, the succubus who enters men's dream, the one who smothers newborn babies for pleasure. You're a monster."

His words chilled me. His ice finally covered me, trapping me, and I couldn't speak, couldn't move, couldn't cry out that he was lying when I knew that beneath it all there was truth there, somewhere amidst all the great lies.

He didn't expect any response. He could see the shock in my eyes, knew that he'd managed to reach me. "Go to bed," he said. "Or I'll take you there."

The threat shouldn't have astonished me, not after that kiss. But it did, it shook me to my soul. Because I despised him. And I would have gone with him, willingly.

Without another word, I left him staring after me. I went, and I hid. From him. And from the creature I was afraid I was.

Chapter Eight

I didn't believe him. Of course I didn't. He could just as well have said I was Jack the Ripper. I might have an impaired memory, but I would know if I were the epitome of female evil.

Because oddly enough, I remembered all the stories. The sources of the Lilith myth, and myth it was. Lilitu, the Mesopotamian storm demon. Lamia, the screech owl who devoured children and drove men to distraction, the queen of infertility and predatory sexuality, the queen of the night and the wind. Lamia, the raptor. As well as Adam's first wife, the one who was cursed and banished to lie with demons and kill children.

I was shivering now, and I didn't have to hide it. I managed to get back to my room, slamming the door behind me. I leaned back against it, staring around the grayness with numb horror. It wasn't true. It couldn't be true.

But . . . I had run from babies, certain they would die if I stayed near them. It had made no sense, but in the snippets of my various lives I could remember what had precipitated my flight. A sick infant. Or the return of the shadows. Of Azazel, watching, waiting to take me. Just how long had he stalked me? How long had he waited before taking me?

I slid down onto the floor, wishing I could weep. I'd never been one to cry—could demons cry? *But I'm human!* I wanted to scream. I bled, I loved, I hated. I hated Azazel with such a fierce passion that I could burn through the ice that encased him. But surely demons could hate.

There was little else average about me. I had no family, no history. I kept away from men in general, even though they tended to pay me too much attention. If I were some eternal seductress, surely I would have a better sex life to show for it, not the unsatisfying couplings Rolf had provided.

But that was another clue, wasn't it? Why couldn't I remember more of the mythology of the first wife? Why had she been banished? It wasn't eating the apple. That was the crime of the second wife, the usurper, the—

Christ, what was wrong with me? Though as

a feminist icon Eve had left a lot to be desired, my cold contempt felt . . . personal. There was no way this absurd story could be true. If I remembered clearly, those stories ended up contradicting themselves. Some sources saw Lilith as a goddess figure, ripe and loving and powerful, while others saw the devouring demon. Those sources were likely divided along gender lines—patriarchal historians never liked a strong woman.

But why did I know so much about this? Early myths were hardly common knowledge. What had driven me to study these things? If, in fact, it was study and not some ancient memory.

No, he was wrong. I knew that. It was no wonder he hated me, treated me with such contempt. No wonder he thought I deserved execution and nothing more. But he was wrong. He had me confused with someone else.

The more I fought it, the more the truth pushed back. His kiss had awoken something, some hidden memory that I was still refusing to examine. I'd felt it, along with the rush of desire. The truth had come with it, a nagging, hated hitchhiker that I was still avoiding.

The bed across the room looked too big, too far away, too high to climb into. I made an effort to stand, but it was too much. Everything was too much. I curled up on the rug, my hand beneath my face. My eyes were dry, when surely this was a time for tears. But I couldn't remember crying, not ever. I squeezed my eyes tight, willing them to come, but they stayed dry. And then I simply closed them. If I couldn't force tears, I could at least force sleep, and I did, giving in to the darkness.

AZAZEL LOOKED DOWN AT THE demon, curled up on the hard floor. She didn't look like a fabled monster. She looked like a woman, a human being with all the frailties and astonishing strengths of her kind. Love for a human woman had caused him to fall, brought about his hideous curse. The loss of a human woman had brought him to his knees. Women were as dangerous to him as demons, perhaps more so. A sad, lost female could get beneath his armor, touch him when he wanted to be untouchable. He could fight power with power. Vulnerability was a greater danger.

He leaned down and scooped her up effortlessly, settling the Grace of sleep over her when she stirred. He had no idea how his powers would work with her. For all he knew, the Grace would jar her into hyperactivity. But she sank against him, deep asleep as the Grace moved over her, and he carried her to the bed, setting her down carefully.

Nothing he did would wake her now, not for at least eight hours. He worked efficiently, stripping off her clothes, looking over her all-too-human body for signs of the Lilith. Her breasts were small but perfectly formed, and they'd peaked beneath his hands as he'd known they would. The soft curls between her legs were the same red-gold as her hair, and her legs were long, her hips slightly rounded. She had the body of a young woman, not a temptress, and he wondered if he'd been wrong.

He put her in one of the nightgowns provided, fastening the row of tiny buttons up to her chin. Her red hair blazed against the soft gray room, a shock of color, and he brushed a lock of it away from her face.

No. He'd known the moment he tasted her that she was his nemesis, his curse, his doom, his redemption. If he bested her power over him, then he would prove that there was hope. That prophecies could lie, or be changed. He would do as Beloch told him, because he had no choice. He would bed the demon, and he would turn his back on her with no regrets.

And he would be free.

I DREAMED. I FLOATED INTO sleep, wrapped in safety, and I embraced its soft richness, wanting to burrow into the wordless comfort. As long as

I stayed there, no one could harm me. Enemies would step back, hard hearts would soften. Ice would melt.

I could feel hands on me. His hands, and I knew those hands had never touched me before. They were hard and cool on my skin, and I wanted to reach out to him, to open my arms and my legs and draw him in, hold him as tightly as I could, to keep the darkness at bay.

And then I drifted further, deeper into the abyss, and I could feel the children, the babies, in my arms. Sweet newborns, sleeping toddlers, helpless infants wrapped in my gentle, protective arms and smiling up at me. I would coo at them, tickle them under the chin, kiss their soft, sweet foreheads and tiny noses, and breath in the sweet baby smell of them.

And I would carry them, oh so carefully, to the same place on the mountaintop, and hand them over into the waiting arms of the mother goddess who had many names, and in my dream I wept for them, the tears that were denied me in life.

I hadn't killed them, smothered them, stolen their breath. The cruelty of nature and an unreachable god had done that. I had merely been there to comfort them, sing to them, bring them home to the mother goddess until they were ready to be reborn again, this time living out a full life.

Relief swept through me, even in the depths of sleep. I was innocent of the worst of the crimes thrown in my face. The one that had the ring of truth.

I was no temptress, seductress, wizard of sexuality and delight. That truth was twisted as well. I was the essence of desire that could never be fulfilled. I was always searching, searching, for what should be mine. What would be mine for the rest of eternity, though I had no idea what it was. Time was meaningless. Hour followed upon hour, century upon century, and I wandered, looking for what evaded me. A winged creature who would be joined to me, body and soul.

Because I had a soul. No matter what my enemies said, my soul was strong and good, even as I worked out an age-old penance, though my crimes were still lost in the mists of memory. I had been strong against the curses that had pressed down on me. I would continue to stay strong in the face of my enemies.

I stirred, moving in my sleep, and once more I could feel hands on me. They weren't real this time, though they were the same hands, cool and hard and impersonal as they brushed my body. Then they slowed as his fingertips responded to the rushing heat of my skin, and they slid down the curve of my side, almost absently, as they circled my waist, his palms against me, cupping my hips.

And his mouth followed, his face pressed against my belly, worshipping me, and I arched my back, accepting him, my arms around his neck, my fingers in his long black hair. I drew him up to me and kissed him with the fullness of my heart, and he moved my legs apart, and I was wet and hot and ready, wanting him, needing him.

And then he rolled me over so that I was above him, straddling him, and I took him, sinking down onto the hard thick delight of him, making soft little sounds of hushed pleasure as he filled me. This was what I had spent eternity searching for. This was what made me whole. This man. And the climax shook me, startled me out of the deepest layers of sleep, and I knew I was alone and always had been.

I tried to move against the smooth, soft sheets, but I was trapped beneath a weight of sleep. I couldn't reach out to him—he wasn't there. All I could do was lie there and feel the tears burn and evaporate in my dry eyes.

"Lilith," he whispered against my ear, but I ignored him, even though I wanted to turn and pull him to me. "Lilith."

And with the sound of my name in my ear, I sank deeper into a dreamless sleep.

WHEN I AWOKE, A FAINT light was coming through the drab curtains, and I could hear the noise of cars outside. There were too few of them to even call them traffic, but the muted sounds of motors were unmistakable. I was still in the Dark City. I was still Rachel.

My crazy dreams were only to be expected. He'd kissed me. I could still feel the heat and pressure of his mouth, taste him. It felt as if I'd somehow taken part of him inside me and there was no way to get rid of him.

The night, his words, were a jumble in my head. A test, he'd said? His harsh kiss had made no more sense than his words—he hated me, he wanted me dead. Why in God's name had he kissed me?

And then I remembered the feel of his erection, hard against my stomach. I knew there had to be some other meaning. Maybe he'd simply needed sex and was responding to the only female in the house. Maybe he'd managed to convince himself that I was some kind of sex goddess, though that would have taken quite a stretch of his imagination. I could remember his long fingers on my breasts, teasing the nipples into fierce arousal. A sex goddess didn't wear 34B.

I had dreamed about her. Dreamed about the demon goddess who inspired fear and hatred among men. I had known her in my dreams, a lost woman of strength and anger, a mother and a lover and a goddess and a . . . was she a whore? Or was that simply part of the lies men told?

The lies that Azazel believed. But then, he was a man, wasn't he? For all that he said he wasn't human. He had a dick, one that got hard. He was a man, with all men's frailties and lies.

The dream was fading now, like mist in bright sunlight, burned away, and I couldn't recapture it. It seemed to be what passed for late afternoon here, and the room was filled with shadows. I sat up and turned on the bedside lamp, but the shadows and gloom remained despite the glow of the light. I looked down at my body, just to reassure myself that I was still in living color, and I froze. I was wearing a stark white Victorian nightgown, all eyelet and ruffles, buttoned primly up to the neck. Those hands had been no dream, and I skittered up to the top of the bed, wrapping my arms around myself protectively, as if I could belatedly keep his hands away.

Azazel had come into this room and stripped the clothes off me, dressed me in this absurd thing, and put me in the bed. I didn't imagine for a moment that anyone else had come in to perform these services. He wouldn't care that stripping me would be humiliating. Then again, why should he care whether I slept on the floor or in the bed? He would be happier throwing me in a dungeon.

He believed I was Lilith. And he said Beloch had sent us back so Azazel could prove he could resist me, and then he'd said I was irresistible. Clearly that wasn't true. He'd kissed me, kissed me more deeply than I'd ever been kissed before, and then shoved me away, even with the proof of his body pressed against mine. He could have had me, easily. For all that I thought sex was no pleasure for women, I would have stripped off my clothes and lain beneath him without a word of protest.

But he hadn't wanted me. Despite the stiff cock against my belly, despite the hunger of his mouth, he hadn't wanted me. So much for being an irresistible siren.

And then when he'd stripped me, I'd been asleep, but I could almost see his steady, efficient hands as they'd removed my clothes. His cool, assessing gaze as he looked at my naked body. And then covered it up, from my chin to my toes, in this enveloping nightgown.

I was no threat to him. Hadn't he already proven that? That he could kiss me and walk away, that he could strip me and cover me again with no more concern than a eunuch? But he wasn't a eunuch.

We should be done by now. Whether or not he still believed I was Lilith, he knew that he wasn't affected by my so-called seductive powers. He looked at me and saw Rachel, ordinary except for the flame-red hair. He looked at me and turned away.

I slid down off the high bed and went searching for my clothes. They weren't there—just a pile of gray-brown jeans and T-shirts, the usual. I didn't want to dress like the ghosts of the Dark City. I didn't want to turn into them.

But I couldn't wander around in a Victorian nightgown, and nudity was no option. I reached for the clothes in the huge wardrobe, the underwear in my size, the jeans that fit perfectly. And saw, to my relief, that once they were on my body the color slowly leached into them. They soaked up color like a paper towel set next to paint—the jeans were sand-washed indigo, the T-shirt a deep rose that oddly enough didn't clash with my hair. I pulled the neckline out to look down at the bra next to my body. Pale lavender, with delicate lace. O-kay.

I headed for the door. It wasn't as if I had any choice. I was starving, and staying holed up in this room got nothing accomplished. I left the room, and safety, behind.

He was in the outer room waiting for me, as if he'd known I was about to emerge. I felt color rise to my face, the memory of that searing kiss between us. But then, he'd pushed me away from him, passing whatever test he'd given himself, and I should be able to meet his gaze with no embarrassment.

I straightened my shoulders, waiting for him to say something. He looked at me out of hooded eyes, and I couldn't read his reaction. And then he spoke.

"Come."

I ground my teeth. "Where?"

"You slept a long time. You must be hungry. I was planning to feed you."

"Are you taking me back to Beloch?" I tried to keep the hopefulness out of my voice. Pleasing me was the last thing on his agenda.

He shook his head. "The time has not yet come. There's food in the dining room."

"And where is that? Oh, I know. 'Come,'" I mocked him. "Lead on. I'll put up with you for the sake of food."

"You have little choice in the matter, demon."

"Don't call me that!" I snapped.

"What do you expect me to call you? A made-up name for a made-up human?"

I didn't bother arguing. "Yes. My name is Rachel." I pushed past him, anything to keep him from that one sepulchral word that made me crazy.

"Second door on the left."

I halted, not daring to hope. "You're not coming with me?"

"I expect you can manage to feed yourself without my help."

"And then do we go to Beloch?"

He hesitated, and I had the strange thought that there was something ugly that he didn't want to tell me. But then, he was my enemy. Almost everything he told me was ugly. "Nothing has been proven yet."

"Oh, come on! I think it's more than clear you find me eminently resistible, as do most men. And for your information, I can do without them, and sex, quite happily. So you've got the wrong girl for your sex demon."

He made no flattering protest, of course. He simply turned away, and I watched him go, aware of a strange sense of desolation. It was illogical and had nothing to do with the reality of the situation. I wanted him gone.

The food on the sideboard in the dining room was abundant, brown, and horrible-looking, but I managed to use my sense of smell to choose what I wanted. I wondered if there actually was a kitchen in this house, or whether some caterer had brought all this food. For that matter, were we alone in the house? I'd heard no footsteps, no voices. If only Azazel and I were in residence, there would be a lot of food going to waste.

It wasn't my problem. I ate slowly, knowing that once I was done I'd have to face Azazel again. When finally I could eat no more, I pushed away from the table and went looking for him.

He was nowhere to be found. It took me long enough to search the place—it was large and rambling, with living rooms and parlors and a library, dining rooms and breakfast rooms, and upstairs half a dozen large bedrooms, including my own. As far as I could tell, Azazel hadn't set foot in any of them.

Fine, I thought, heading for the front door. It was already afternoon and I was damned if I was going to sit around waiting for him.

The front door was locked. I shook it, beat against it, but nothing helped. Enraged, I headed for one of the tall windows, but they were locked as well. For one moment I considered throwing a chair through the glass and escaping that way, but I didn't quite have the nerve. I would sit and wait, and when he came back I'd tear into him.

If he came back. Maybe he was planning on being gone a long time. There was too much food in the dining room—maybe it was supposed to last for days. Maybe he wasn't coming back at all, and I'd slowly starve to death. No, I could throw a chair through a window before that happened. Assuming the glass wasn't some kind of bulletproof composite that would resist being smashed by an angry woman.

I headed back into the library. The walls were floor-to-ceiling bookcases, filled with colorless texts of every shape and size. I moved closer, and started reading the titles. Maybe I could find a mystery to keep me occupied. Though it looked as if there was nothing from the current century and very little from the last.

It was in plain sight: *Angels and Demons.* I grabbed it, hoping for Dan Brown. Instead it was a heavy tome, ancient and thick, with an engraved cover. I almost shoved it back, then thought better of it. Maybe I could do a little more research on Lilith.

It opened to the right page. Someone else had been reading this, but the pages were too worn for it to have been caused only by Azazel. Maybe they'd been bringing hapless women here for decades, convinced each one was Lilith.

If so, what did they do when they discovered the women were simply human? Would it be any better than what they planned for the real Lilith?

I curled up on one of the sofas, pulling my knees up under me as I opened the huge volume in my lap. I started reading, pleased to discover my dreaming memory had been correct. The Lilith myth originated in Sumer, and had been found in some shape or other in most religions, up to and including Christianity. For some sources, she'd been a benevolent mother goddess, to others an all-devouring Kali-esque demon. And everything in between.

But nothing sounded right. None of the citations had the ring of truth, though a bit here and a bit there sounded reasonable. Still, history and mythology were written by men. It was no wonder they got it wrong.

Lilith was fated to wed the demon Asmodeus, and together they would rule a secret place and bring forth many demon children. Great. If they thought they were marrying me to a demon, they had another thing coming. Though they were probably not looking for a happily-ever-after for the monster they imagined me to be.

But why in hell weren't they out looking for this Asmodeus character? If Lilith's future was to pop forth tiny demons, wouldn't getting rid of the prophesied father take care of the problem?

Men, I thought with disgust. Typical that they'd go after the woman.

I was about to turn to the front of the book, to read about the demon Asmodeus, when I heard the front door open, and I knew he'd returned.

He walked past the open library door, heading up the stairs without a word to me. I shot out of the room, catching up with him halfway up the stairs. "I don't like being locked in."

He paused, then turned back to look down on me. Mistake, I thought. If I accosted him on the stairs, I should somehow make it to a higher step. He already had a tendency to loom over me; giving him the added advantage of the stairs made it worse.

"It's not safe for you outside," he said.

"And you're concerned about my safety? Since when?"

He considered it. "Point taken. It won't be locked again. Go wherever you wish."

I looked up into his pale, set face. "Good," I said.

A moment later I was gone, into the night, into the Dark City, without a glance behind me.

Chapter Nine

Azazel heard the door slam, and he cursed, slowly and savagely. He needed to let her go. If she ran afoul of the Truth Breakers or the Nightmen, then so be it. He didn't want to be looking out for her. It was bad enough that she still lived, though he had no one to blame but himself for that one. He wasn't going out into the night, chasing after her, protecting her from all the midnight horrors of the Dark City.

And there were many. The rules were strict in this shadowed place, and the demi-souls who lived here couldn't stray far without earning punishment.

He couldn't decide whether she really was as innocent as a newborn lamb or simply stupid. She had no idea just how lethal Beloch was, or she would keep her distance. She had no idea that the man she thought of as her worst enemy was, in fact, her only hope of putting off the inevitable. If it were up to him, he would see that she didn't suffer, though he wasn't sure why. She'd made countless souls suffer over the endless years she'd lived. She deserved some rough justice. He just didn't want to be around to witness it, and he was beginning to realize that there would be no escape from the Dark City. Not for her.

He would have believed her last night, that she was a far cry from a sexual icon, if she hadn't kissed him back. If the feel of her hadn't sunk into his very bones, shaking him to the core. He wanted her and he despised himself for it. Beloch was right. He might be a sadist, overseeing the Dark City with the same cruel implacability with which the archangel Uriel oversaw the whole of creation, but he was indisputably wise. As long as Azazel ignored her siren call, he would never be certain that the prophecy was a lie, that he was invulnerable to her mythic allure. Resisting the seduction of a simple kiss wasn't proof enough.

Maybe the Nightmen would take care of her. Those savage creatures, who scoured the streets of the Dark City and wiped them clean with the blood of those who displeased them, would show no mercy. Even Beloch's demands might have no influence.

Or the Truth Breakers might find her and bring her before Beloch. He hated to think of her reaction when she discovered the scholarly old man was a torturer par excellence. He had no intention of being around when that happened.

He had no idea how far they'd go in extracting the truth from her. For all her fierce, hidden spirit, her body would break quite easily—they would barely have to hurt her to get what they needed. But he realized now that they wouldn't be likely to let her go once they were done with her.

He paused at the top of the stairs. He ought to go back down and lock the door. There were things crawling in the alleys of the Dark City that he didn't want entering the house, but a simple lock was enough to keep them out. He started back down, walking through a faint drift of scent, her skin, her hair, and he cursed again. He moved faster, racing down the stairs, and a moment later he was out into the night, going after her.

Could she see the sickness and decay beneath the gray-brown of everything? Or would she take things at face value? Wouldn't she wonder why she still had a healthy color?

The Nightmen were lurking by the sluggish black river that flowed through the center of the city. He could sense them, hear them, and he knew that she couldn't have made it that far. He heard a faint scream of agony, but it came from a man's throat and he dismissed it. At least she was safe from them—by her scent, he could tell she'd headed in the opposite direction. She was smart enough to avoid danger. The problem was, danger came at you from every angle here in the Dark City.

He turned his back on the screams and sobs of the dying man and followed her. He'd find her. And when he did, he'd drag her back to the house and handcuff her to the bedpost until Beloch was ready to send for her.

IT SHOULD HAVE BEEN A nice night for a walk. The air was warm with just the faint hint of crispness that presaged autumn, and a soft breeze brushed against my skin. If only the shadows didn't lie so heavily on everything, leaching the color from the buildings I passed, from the trees overhead, the cars, and, most of all, the people. They were sepia ghosts of another time, and no one met my eyes or responded to my tentative greetings. It was almost as if they were afraid of me, but that was impossible. I was harmless. Wasn't I?

Because if I held any latent power, if I were the monstrous demon that Azazel declared me to be and the mythology books described, then surely I would have wreaked vengeance on everyone and everything in my path, including Azazel. I would have ripped him apart if I'd had the ability.

But the people I passed scuttled by me in their gray ghostliness, heads down, and finally I caught a young woman by the arm, forcing her to look at me. "Excuse me, but do you know where there's a public park?" I had the sudden longing to kick off my shoes and feel grass beneath my feet, even if the grass was gray.

She'd frozen at my touch, her eyes wide with fear, and I wondered if she'd been struck dumb. If I hadn't been holding her gently, I think she might have run.

"We don't have parks," she said finally, her voice low and totally without inflection. Almost like a computer-generated voice.

"Then is there a place outside where I could sit for a while?" I persisted.

"It wouldn't be a good idea." There was just a trace more life in her voice, something that sounded like concern. "We don't . . . you shouldn't . . ." She stopped, clearly frustrated. "You should go home. You should leave here. You don't belong here."

Curiosity had always been my besetting sin—after all, I'd been a reporter in Brisbane and, I suspected, elsewhere as well. "Who *does* belong here? Who are you?"

She looked startled, and even more wary. "We earned our places here. It is our reward."

"Doesn't look like much of a reward," I said with my usual lack of tact.

"You should go away. I mustn't be seen talking to you."

"Why not?"

"Because you're a stranger. The only reasons strangers come here are bad." She tugged at her arm, and I released her.

"But—"

"I can't help you," she said. "I shouldn't even warn you."

"Warn me?"

"Leave the Dark City if you can. If you cannot, stay in your house and don't wander the streets at night. Whatever you do, keep away from the Nightmen."

"Who are the Nightmen?" I was trying to hold on to her with questions, but she was edging away.

"The police. Keep away from the river."

"What—"

But she'd already gone. I stared after her, one more gray person shuffling through the city streets. She'd been young, but her eyes were empty, her clothes shapeless and drab. Instead of finding answers, I was left with even more questions .

Keep away from the river, she'd said. I could do that. In fact, if I had any sense, I'd turn around and head back to the huge old house and my unpleasant companion.

The problem was, he wasn't unpleasant. For all his cool, cynical reserve, a fierce bond of heat and longing flowed between us, set free by his mouth on mine, his body pressed up against me. He felt it as well as I did, and it made no sense. We hated each other.

But even so, I was horribly afraid that if I went back there, if I went back to him, we would be past kissing. I would lie with him, I would take him inside me, I would . . .

No. I'd written about women who fell in love with their abusers. I wasn't going to let errant hormones get in the way of reason. I wasn't going to let him touch me again. And the longer I stayed away from him, the stronger my resolve would be.

Stay away from the river, she'd said. It wasn't that far away—I could smell the water on the night air. I'd turned around to head in the opposite direction when I heard the screams.

The sound was horrifying, chilling me to the bone, the raw, terrified sound of a man in such horrible pain that I wanted to cover my ears. The few people still out on the streets seemed totally unconcerned, unaware of the fact that someone was being murdered, and I wanted to grab them and shake them.

I seized an elderly man's arm in a punishing grip, surprised at my own strength. "Do you have a cell phone? We need to call nine-one-one! Someone's being murdered."

The man was looking at me in terror. "Leave me alone!" he cried. "Go away!" And he managed to pull free, taking off down the street.

"Son of a bitch," I muttered under my breath. So it was up to me. I started running in the direction of those screams, which had now moved on to sobbing pleas for mercy, racing past the gray people out for an evening walk, totally oblivious to the horror going on.

I was furious, and I shoved more than one out of my way in my desperation to reach the poor man in time. The sound was getting closer, and there was another noise beneath the screams, the ominous snick of sharp metal, and I could smell blood, as thick and evocative as the food scents had been in this drab place. I could see the dark ribbon of the river up ahead, and I sprinted the last two blocks, narrowly dodging a brown taxi that looked like it came from the 1930s; the noise stopped abruptly, leaving the air thick with silence.

I came to a stop at the edge of the river. The streetlights overhead illuminated a deserted landscape. Not even the heartless city strollers had ventured this far, and the only sound was the heavy rush of the river, black in the moonlight. I'd ended up in the last place I wanted to be.

I peered around, but the victim was gone, and I knew without question that I was too late. I stood frozen, staring, as a man appeared furtively from a nearby doorway, a hose in one hand, and proceeded to spray down the dark wet pool of liquid on the cobblestone walkway before he scurried back inside. The smell of the brackish water couldn't quite wipe out the scent of blood, and the huge dinner I'd eaten threatened to make a reappearance, especially after my desperate run. I swallowed, trying to calm down.

There were benches lining the waterside, even though no one was taking advantage of them, and I sank down onto the nearest one, my legs shaking. If I'd had any doubts about the kind of place Azazel had brought me to, they had now settled into an unhappy certainty. This place was *wrong*.

I could think of only one place where I'd felt safe. Beloch's. I tried to remember the name of the restaurant, but I hadn't paid any attention when following Azazel there. And the streets had all looked the same as I'd raced through them. I'd never had a particularly strong sense of direction, and I'd be hard-pressed to find my way back to Azazel.

Not that I wanted to, of course. Except, sitting there on the bench, I had no idea where I *would* go.

I smelled them first.

An awful thought, but that sense had been heightened as my sense of sight had been depressed, and I could smell blood, and human sweat, followed by the sound of footsteps, the muffled quiet of voices drawing nearer, and I knew without question that I was in even worse trouble than I'd been before.

Someone had been killed within a few feet of me, and I'd decided to sit down and think about things in the place I'd been warned against? Some people are too stupid to live, Azazel would tell me, and for once I agreed. I glanced at the fast-flowing river, but there was no escape there—water held more terror than whoever was approaching. I jumped up, tensing to flee, but it was already too late. They'd seen me.

I'd automatically braced myself for something like the Nephilim, but the group of men who appeared looked quite ordinary. They wore dark uniforms with high-necked collars and walked in military formation, straight at me.

They carried swords and knives, not a gun in sight, and I wondered whether I could outrun them. Probably not. Besides, why would they want to hurt me? I was just a harmless young woman sitting by the river, enjoying the night air.

Of course, I was a different color than they were, drastically different, which might be reason enough. I held very still, stiffening my back, ready to offer a friendly explanation, when the huge man who was clearly the leader of the group spoke.

"Gut her."

Those swords were unsheathed in an instant, and before I could move they encircled me, blocking off all avenues of escape. I just stared at them stupidly, noticing how shiny the blades were in the moonlight. *They must have cleaned them after they killed that poor man,* I thought, and then I snapped out of it.

"How dare you." The words came from me of their own volition, in an icy, regal tone that shocked them almost as much as it shocked me. The men froze, looking to their leader for encouragement.

But the surprise lasted only for a moment, and then they were advancing on me, and it was those blades or the river. I preferred the blades. "I'm a guest of Azazel's," I said in a more normal voice, but it didn't slow their determined approach.

A sword sliced past my face, just missing me. "Beloch wouldn't like it if you hurt me!" The last came out on a tiny scream.

"Beloch." The leader spoke the name, not as a question, just a word. And this time the words worked. "We'll take you to Beloch," he said finally. He was a giant of a man, with broad shoulders, brutal hands, and empty eyes. "And if you've lied, we'll show you no mercy."

As far as I could see, they hadn't been about to show me any mercy in the first place, but I simply nodded, not wincing when two of them grabbed my upper arms and force-marched me away from the river. I felt something trickle down my face and onto my T-shirt, and I realized the saber had been closer than I'd guessed. I made an attempt to reach up and wipe the blood away, but their grip on my arms made such a move impossible. All I could do was let them march me through the now-deserted streets of the Dark City.

We approached the restaurant, now closed, of course. They took me in through the lower level, and I breathed a sigh of relief as I recognized slightly familiar ground. They pushed me into the building roughly, then shoved me into some small, dark closet, locking me in.

Okay. I was only slightly claustrophobic, and that mainly went for MRIs and caves. Not that I could remember any MRIs or caves, but I must have encountered them at some point. I leaned back against the wall, reaching up to check my face.

I was still bleeding, but the cut wasn't deep, and it wouldn't leave much of a scar. Figuring I was safe for the moment, I pulled my T-shirt over my head and carefully cleaned the wound, using the back of the shirt to soak up the blood so I wouldn't look too gory. It stopped bleeding after a while, and I pulled the T-shirt carefully back over my head. Sudden exhaustion swept over me as the last day and a half caught up with me. Humans weren't made to live at this high pitch of stress, and I was human. I was tired, tired of being afraid, tired of being brave anyway, tired of wondering what was going to happen to me. I leaned against the wall, then slid to the floor, putting my head on my knees, shaking. No tears. Why couldn't I cry? Surely I had more than enough reason to cry.

I reached up and touched my eyes. Dry. Maybe I was born without tear ducts. It was just as well—tears were a sign of weakness and I couldn't afford to show any. I leaned my head back against the wall, willing myself to relax. Staying at this high pitch of anxiety wouldn't do me any good. I took a deep, calming breath, centering myself, and felt my body relax.

"Do not tell me you've fallen asleep." An amused voice broke through my self-imposed reverie, and I opened my eyes to look up into Beloch's kindly face framed by the doorway.

I smiled back at him, relief flooding me. I yawned and rose, stretching. Everything was going to be fine. "There wasn't much to keep me occupied," I said in an unruffled voice.

"I must apologize for the Nightmen. Our crime problem is small but virulent, and you were down by the river where the criminals tend to lurk. It was a good thing you thought to mention my name. I shudder to think what might have happened otherwise." He looked over his shoulder, and there was a faintly querulous note in his voice. "And just where is Azazel? Why didn't he accompany you? He would have made certain you didn't wander where you shouldn't have, and no one would have come near you."

"I went out without telling him." I didn't stop to wonder why I was shielding him. There was already enmity between the two men, and anything I did to further that would presumably aid me.

Beloch held out a thin, gnarled hand, and I took it, propelling myself upward. He was an old man, and I figured he would topple over if I really used him to get up. There was a light of amusement in his rheumy eyes, as if he knew I'd been sparing him, but he said nothing.

"I have tea and cake waiting for us in my study, my child," he said. His fingers had caught mine in a grip that was surprisingly tight, and I wanted to pull away, but there was no polite way to do so. He led me down the utilitarian hallways, hallways I sensed ought to be painted the universal industrial green, toward the heavy wooden door of his study. He held it open, and warmth poured out, physical and emotional. Beloch fussed over me like a grandfather, settling me into a comfortable chair, covering my legs with a lap robe, and handing me a cup of Earl Grey.

I hated Earl Grey. The smell of bergamot reminded me of old women and disapproval, but I drank anyway, glad of the warmth. "What time is it?" I asked, only vaguely interested.

"We don't keep track of time here the same way people do in the outside world," Beloch said, settling in the chair opposite me. To my surprise, a cat jumped into his lap and settled there, and he stroked it absently with his strong, gnarled fingers. The cat turned to look at me for a moment, then settled back on its master's lap.

Odd. I loved cats. And yet I'd looked at this sepia-toned cat and felt an instant revulsion.

"You're admiring my lovely Lucifer, aren't

you?" he said. "He's quite beautiful, is he not? Such a sleek, lovely coat." His hand stroked the shiny fur.

"He's gorgeous," I said politely, only the truth.

"I feed him a diet of raw meat. I find it not only improves his health but it brings him more in tune with his atavistic nature. Of course, it makes him quite savage with other people. I would suggest you don't pat him—you could lose a finger."

I laughed politely, assuming he was kidding. But I looked down into the cat's face and wondered.

"I thought I might have them make up a room for you here," he continued. "I had hoped that Azazel . . . well, he has certain things he needs to work out, but since it appears he's unable to deal with them, you may as well stay here."

That was just what I wanted. So why in the world was I trying to come up with objections? I *wanted* to be here. At least, I should. I cleared my throat. "I don't think Azazel has anything in particular to work out. Apparently he needs to prove that he isn't attracted to me. He's done that in spades. I don't think he wants me dead anymore. I think he just doesn't care. As for finding me attractive, that's simply ridiculous."

A faint smile curved Beloch's mouth. "I think you underestimate your charms, my dear."

I smiled back, still feeling vaguely uneasy. "You're very kind, but as far as Azazel is concerned I might just as well be a . . . a Nephilim." I used the word deliberately, wondering if Beloch knew it.

He seemed to. "And you hate him as well?"

"Of course. He's kidnapped me twice, maybe more, if I could only remember. He tried to have me killed, he keeps me prisoner, and he never answers questions. He won't talk to me at all." The last argument sounded rather lame compared to the others, but in truth it made me crazier than all the other offenses.

Beloch said nothing for a moment, stroking his self-satisfied, finger-eating cat. "To give him his due, he's had a sad life. His wives keep dying. I believe he's still mourning his last one to an excessive degree."

I was suddenly very cold. "What happened to her?"

"To Sarah? I believe she was murdered."

Oh, shit. Was Azazel some kind of Bluebeard? He didn't seem like a serial killer, but then, how would I know what a serial killer was like? They could be quite handsome and charming, couldn't they? Azazel fit the former—when considered dispassionately, he was absolutely gorgeous. But charming he was not.

"Er . . . how many wives has he had?"

"You'd best ask him. Though he may have lost count."

I no longer bothered to hide my alarm. How could I have been so stupid? Stupid because I had felt his mouth on mine and responded, stupid because for a brief moment I had wanted him, really wanted him.

"Maybe I'll skip that."

Beloch chuckled. "But why waste our time talking about Azazel? I'd rather talk about you, my dear. About your lives and loves, your memories, your dreams."

My lives? Just how much did he know about me and my past? I had the sudden, unbidden suspicion that he knew more than I did. Yet that was impossible.

Then again, no one could know *less* about my past. "I'm surprised Azazel didn't tell you. I know almost nothing about my life. I've got some odd form of amnesia." I didn't tend to use that word for it, but it seemed like a nice, reasonable explanation for something that felt much more sinister.

"Amnesia," Beloch echoed. "My poor child. But you know, we're quite advanced here in the Dark City. We have very effective ways of helping you to remember almost anything."

I must have looked doubtful, for he laughed. "Don't look so worried, my dear. It's simply a form of biofeedback."

For some reason, a shiver ran down my backbone, but I managed a cheerful smile. "I think I'll pass. If my past is even close to what Azazel thinks it is, I'm better off not knowing."

"Don't be ridiculous. You know the old saying: 'The truth shall set you free.'"

I blinked. "That's an interesting concept. I've never heard it before. Who said that?"

"Someone after your time, child," he said with a soft laugh. "Let me order some more tea. Yours must be cold by now."

I glanced down into the tea leaves floating at the bottom of the bergamot-scented sludge. They looked like drowned tree limbs after a hurricane. I looked up and managed a smile. "I've had enough, thank you. Too much tea makes my hands shake." I set the delicate cup carefully on the table beside me.

Beloch simply nodded. "Then perhaps I'll introduce you to—"

The door opened with no warning knock, and Beloch's gentle face darkened with displeasure as he surveyed Azazel in the doorway. "You finally decided to come after your charge?" he said in an icy tone. "You're too late."

But Azazel was looking at me, and there was a blazing intensity in his eyes. Blue eyes, deep and vivid, so different from the muddy grays and rusty blacks and browns of this sepia-tinted world. "I've been looking everywhere for you," he snapped. "Where the hell have you been?"

"I love you too," I said sweetly, but the mocking words fell oddly flat, making me uncomfortable. "I went for a walk down by the river, and some people found me and brought me here."

"People?" he echoed.

"The Nightmen," Beloch supplied. "You're lucky she's still alive. If she hadn't given them my name, she would have disappeared, and you'd have a hard time explaining yourself. Apparently your name had no effect on them."

"This is your element, not mine," Azazel said.

"True enough. And my word is law."

Azazel moved between us, blocking my view of Beloch. "It is. Which means you should think carefully before you make a pronouncement. What is more important? Vanquishing me, or her?"

Silence, and I wished I could see Beloch's face. "You make an excellent point," he said finally. "And I must say, it's not an easy decision. The leader of the Fallen, or the first female . . . when, if I wait a few days, I can have you both."

"I would hardly think you would settle for less." Azazel's voice was silken, persuasive.

"What I find interesting is why you're suddenly set on keeping her, when before you wanted nothing more than to dump her. Have you already begun to lose?"

"Don't be ridiculous." There was contempt in his voice, and I wondered how Beloch would respond. Unfortunately, all I could see was Azazel's tight rear end in black jeans. Which wasn't a bad view. "I didn't wish to hand her over the first night, though I would have acquiesced if you'd insisted."

"Would you have?"

"You rule the Dark City. As you have said, your word is law. But I have my own curiosity about her, and about the prophecy. If you take her now, I will never know the truth."

"Perhaps I enjoy the idea of you spending eternity wondering," Beloch suggested in a voice far removed from that of the courtly old gentleman who'd served me tea.

"Perhaps knowing my weakness would be an even greater punishment."

Silence. "Again, I wonder why you're seeking to lose with such determination. It does seem like the wisest choice would be to deny what you're wanting so desperately."

"Hardly desperation," Azazel said in a voice devoid of emotion. "It is your choice, of course. I merely offer it as an intellectual exercise. If you take her now, I will simply return to Sheol and forget about her. Perhaps that might be the best answer after all."

"Do not attempt to play games with me. You will lose." There was another silence. "Take her. And I use those words deliberately. If I were you, I wouldn't let her out of your sight. If she were to run afoul of the Nightmen again, I expect everyone would be very distressed, in particular your friends back home."

"She won't escape again." He turned, and I could see Beloch's face now, looking as sulky as a child deprived of a toy. And then he caught my eye and smiled.

"Don't worry, my child. Azazel won't hurt you. He wouldn't dare. He has something to prove to himself where you're concerned, and I know you have a generous spirit, enough to allow him to find the answers to what's troubling him."

I wasn't sure of any such thing, but I didn't argue, rising gracefully. Azazel hadn't moved away, and he was too close, intoxicatingly so. God, if anyone was a sex demon, it was Azazel. I only had to look at him and I felt my insides melt.

He took my arm in a hard grip, and I wondered

if I'd end up with bruises. If I had any sense I'd throw myself on Beloch's mercy—the comfort and safety of the library versus Azazel's dangerous presence. But I knew I wouldn't. I knew I would follow Azazel wherever he led me, and I didn't know why.

We were at the door when Beloch spoke again, and his words sent ice into my veins. "Don't look so worried, my dear Rachel. Azazel won't hurt you. In fact, you should consider yourself lucky. It's not every women who gets to fuck a fallen angel."

Chapter Ten

"What was he talking about?" I demanded as he led me from the building.

"Be quiet. We will discuss this when we get home."

"We don't have a home," I snapped. "And I'm not going anywhere with you until you explain this."

"Yes, you are." He was right. His grip on my arm was unbreakable, and I'd already had experience with his iron will. He would knock me out, cast some weird spell over me, do anything within his power to make me comply, and his power was impressive.

He led me past the uniformed men, who were clustered near the river as if waiting, and I could feel them watching us. We came to an abrupt halt when their massive leader moved in front of us.

It should have been ridiculous—compared to Azazel's lean, wiry frame, he was huge, overpowering. He should have frightened me more than Azazel ever had. But there were different kinds of fear.

"Where are you taking her, my lord?" The honorific sounded sarcastic to my ears, and Azazel's fingers tightened even more around the soft flesh above my elbow.

"To the house on Cedar Street. Beloch has put her in my custody. I regret having to disappoint you." Sarcasm dripped from his words, and the man's eyebrows snapped together.

"Why would he do that? She was promised to us."

"You'd best ask him, hadn't you?" Azazel said, but I could see the alarm in his blue eyes. "Besides, wasn't she to go to the Truth Breakers first?"

"We would have her when they finished with her."

"You know as well as I that there's usually not much left after the Truth Breakers finish." He seemed to have no idea what effect those words were having on me.

"An excellent point. Hence my concern that he's letting her go with you. She should stay here."

"Again, discuss it with Beloch."

"You know I won't do that."

"Then stand aside."

For a moment the large man seemed to vibrate with rage, looming before us. And then he nodded curtly and backed off. "I'll set a guard outside the house," he said. "So you don't run the risk of losing her again."

"Very kind," Azazel murmured. "But unnecessary. She won't be going anywhere without me."

"Until you hand her to the Truth Breakers."

I could feel his hesitation, though I doubted the captain noticed it. "Until I hand her to the Truth Breakers," he agreed smoothly. And with a none-too-gentle tug he pulled me into the endless night of the Dark City as shadows closed down around us.

Until he handed me to the Truth Breakers, who didn't leave much when they finished with you. Had he rescued me from the Nephilim simply to turn me over to the Dark City equivalent? As he ushered me through the deserted streets, I glanced around for any possible avenue of escape. If I got away from him, I was no longer sure where I'd go. I already knew the people who lived here would be no help, and I was beginning to have the strong, if belated, suspicion that Beloch wasn't the cozy, absentminded professor he appeared to be.

"Don't even bother," Azazel said beneath his breath. "You wouldn't get ten feet. There are Nightmen stationed all around, watching us, and I expect they will be there from now on."

I jerked, startled both by the thought of them watching and by the knowledge that Azazel, again, had read my mind. Though I supposed it would be easy enough to guess what I was thinking as my head swiveled back and forth. I dug in my heels when we reached the old brownstone, but it did me no good. He simply hauled me up the steps, shoved me inside, and slammed the door after us, locking it.

"Not that it will do any good," he muttered. "Enoch can get in anytime he wants to."

"Enoch?"

"Your new admirer. The captain of the Nightmen. He's not the best enemy to make."

"He hates you."

"Yes. And now he hates you as well."

I sighed. "Well, aren't things going just swimmingly. So tell me, what the hell did Beloch mean?"

"We're better off talking upstairs." His hand was no longer clamped on my arm, and I wondered if he'd continue to force me if I held back. I had no intention of it. I wanted answers, and this time he was going to give them to me, though I thought he was about as much an angel as I was a prehistoric sex goddess.

He started up the stairs and I followed him. I could always kick him in the head and escape, no matter how many Nightmen were lurking around the house.

One of the doors was open, and the high bed, similar to mine, was rumpled. This had to be his room, and I tried very hard not to show any reluctance as I walked in. After all, we were both adults—we could hold a discussion in a bedroom as well as in a library.

There was an uncomfortable-looking Victorian sofa at one side of the huge room, and I went and took a seat, perfectly ready to cross-examine him.

He raised an eyebrow, and I almost thought I saw a quirk of amusement at his formerly stern mouth. I had the sudden feeling that he didn't hate me as much as he had, though I had no idea what had changed his mind. He settled into a wingback chair that stood at a right angle to the sofa.

"Why did he call you an angel?" I launched right into it, not waiting for him to control the conversation. "You're not my idea of a gentle cherub watching over people."

"I'm not," he said flatly. "I'm fallen."

For a moment I didn't move. This I could

almost believe, looking at the unearthly beauty of his pale face, the cold anger in his tightly wired body. "When?"

"Before time was calculated."

I racked my brain for the snippets I'd read. "Are you Lucifer?"

I'd managed to startle him. "What do you know of Lucifer?"

"Not much. He was the first fallen angel, wasn't he? God's favorite angel, who became too arrogant and fell from heaven to become Satan."

I could practically see the wheels turning behind his cold eyes as he decided just how much to tell me. "Yes and no," he said finally. "He was God's favorite, and his name means Bringer of Light. As for being arrogant, that arrogance was simply questioning God's choice to destroy men, women, and children for one man's sin, as God had done so often. Lucifer asked questions, and for that he was banished to eternal torment. As for Satan, he is simply an artificial construct used by men to explain the actions of God and the archangel Uriel."

"You're telling me God is Satan?"

He sighed, clearly annoyed. "I am telling you Satan doesn't exist. He's made-up."

"So are fallen angels," I shot back.

"I'm far too real," he said. "Touch me."

I tried not to jerk away at the thought. I'd touched him already, and the feel of his smooth, supple skin beneath my hands was disturbing. "Never mind. I believe you."

"So aren't you going to ask me about the other part of what Beloch said?"

"I don't remember." A complete lie. I remembered exactly what he'd said, and his words had sent a shiver through my body, though not, I had to admit, a shiver of revulsion.

"He said it's not everyone who gets to fuck an angel."

That same heated shiver sliced through me. I chose my words carefully. "I presumed he was being facetious."

"And yet you didn't think he was being facetious about the angel part."

I leaned back, summoning every ounce of control to appear relaxed and faintly curious, when my entire body was tingling. This wasn't an intellectual discussion. This was going somewhere, and I wasn't sure that I wanted to go along. Then again, I might not have a choice. "Why don't you explain it to me? Everything. Such as why you're planning on handing me over to people who aren't going to leave anything when they're done with me."

He didn't even blink. "I wish I weren't forced

to give you to the Truth Breakers. I'd much rather find out what I need to know without bringing them into it."

"What do you need to know?"

"It's really quite simple. I need to know what you know about Lucifer."

"I already told you—"

He shook his head, and his silky black hair danced against his pale face. "I'm not talking about the tired mythology you've parroted to me. The Lilith knows where Lucifer has been interred. You were imprisoned nearby, as a punishment for questioning the word of God."

"I guess there was a lot of that going around. Is that why you fell?"

He didn't even blink. "No. I was the second to fall, along with twenty of my friends. We had been sent to earth to teach humans about metals and farming, and we made the dire mistake of falling in love with human females. The God of that time was an angry, vengeful entity, and we ended with eternal damnation."

I stared at him, dumbfounded. "That was the last thing I expected," I said finally. "I would have guessed you didn't even know the meaning of love."

He looked at me, and for a moment I couldn't move, caught in the deep, fiery longing in his rich blue gaze. Yearning, sorrow, and the pure dark heat of sex flamed in his long, slow look, and I felt shaken inside, my assumptions shot to hell. His expression seared me, and for a moment I could feel my body quicken in response.

And then sanity returned as his lids lowered and his expression grew cool and distant. I quickly tried to change the subject. "What do you mean, 'the God of that time'? Are you going to try to convince me there's more than one?"

"There are as many gods as people can envision, but in the end they're all the same, the Supreme Being who finally granted humankind free will and then stepped back to let them flounder on their own."

"That's not so bad, is it?"

"No, not compared to the harsh taskmaster who created the world. But he left the archangel Uriel in charge to enforce his word, and the results have been . . . less than optimal. There is no chance of forgiveness or redemption, merely eternal damnation."

"So you're damned?"

"As are you. Raziel leads the Fallen now, and he bade me bring you here to the Dark City to find out what you know. I have no power in this place. Sooner or later I will be forced to hand you over to the Truth Breakers, and there's nothing

I can do about it. They're ruthless and unstoppable."

I stared at him in surprise. "Why would you want to do anything about it? I thought you wanted me dead."

He looked uncomfortable. "I have my reasons. But in truth, as long as you lived far away and your life didn't come in contact with mine, I was willing to wait a few hundred years."

"I'm not going to live a few hundred years. I'm human."

He made a sound of disgust. "There's no hope for you as long as you keep up this game. You're not human, and haven't been for millennia, not since you defied God and were cursed. By the end of the week, the Truth Breakers will take you and you will be destroyed, and I can't change it."

"So why are we even having this discussion?"

He leaned back against the chair and closed his eyes, and I watched the still, elegant planes of his face, the high cheekbones, the narrow nose, the angry, tempting mouth. "There may be a way out." He spoke so softly I almost didn't hear him.

"Which is?"

"If you tell me what you know, I might be able to find a way to sneak you out of here. You could go back to Australia, or anywhere you want to go, as long as you keep out of my life."

"Being part of your life has never been a priority of mine," I said, my voice icy. "*You're* the one who was stalking *me*, remember?" I sat up, running a hand through my tangled hair. "And I don't know anything. You keep insisting I'm an ancient sex demon, and you won't believe me when I tell you you're wrong. I have no idea where they buried Satan—"

"Lucifer," he corrected sharply.

"I have no idea where they buried him. I can't help you."

"Then *I* cannot help *you*."

We sat in silence, neither of us willing to break it. Finally I couldn't stand it any longer. "Why did Beloch think we were going to have sex?"

"Beloch is not the kindly old gentleman you seem to think he is."

"I've begun to figure that out. Why did he say . . . what he said?"

"It's all part of his little game. He wants me to fall prey to your powers. In that way he can defeat me as well as you."

"Why would he want to defeat either of us?"

"You're the Lilith, the embodiment of female power and rebellion. Of course he wants you destroyed. And he hates me because I was once beloved of God and he never was."

"Beloch isn't a fallen angel?"

He hesitated. "It's not clear exactly what he is. I expect he's a demon."

"Goddamn it!" I snapped. "Why the hell are you so set on wiping me out when you've got a demon right there, ready to be smited? Or smote, or whatever."

"Not all demons are evil."

"But I am." I didn't even bother to phrase it as a question, and he didn't bother to answer.

"So I'm not sleeping with you," I said finally. "You can tell Beloch he can just forget about it."

"Then he'll hand you over to the Truth Breakers without further delay."

"And if I did sleep with you? Not that I would, but I'm curious. Does that mean I don't get handed over to his minions? You'd become my willing slave?" It was an appealing thought. I liked the idea of him being on his knees around me.

"Of course not. Beloch is wagering that you would vanquish me. I know that's impossible. Bedding you would mean nothing to me."

"Ditto," I snapped. "The answer to our problem is simple. We'll just tell them that we did it. That we're doing it. Doing the wild thing all night long, and you aren't quite sure whether you're going to succumb or not but you'll need more time to figure it out. Which would give you enough time to come up with an escape plan."

"There are two fatal flaws in that plan," he said. "One, you have yet to give me one reason to rescue you. I need that information, and the Truth Breakers will get it for me."

I wanted to scream at him that I didn't have any information, but I bit my lip. I hadn't given up hope of convincing him to save me. He'd saved me once already, when he'd been the one to arrange my death. Beneath his cool exterior beat an actual heart. If angels had hearts. If he really was an angel. "You said there were two fatal flaws," I said instead. "What's the other one?"

"He'll know if we lie."

"How? Does he have cameras? Microphones?"

"Stop thinking that you're dealing with mortals, Rachel. Trust me, he would know."

The sound of my name on his lips was strange, almost sweet, though he didn't seem to notice he'd used it. "How would he know?"

He bit back a sigh of irritation. "He would smell it."

"Ew! Does he think we wouldn't take showers?"

"I'm not talking about semen and sweat and vaginal secretions," he said with far too much frankness, and I felt my skin heat. "He would smell the changes in your body, in your skin, in your veins. He would know."

"I've had sex before, and trust me, there were no changes that I couldn't wash away."

"That's part of your curse. To drive men mad with desire and feel no pleasure."

"Great," I muttered. "And all this time I thought I was frigid."

He looked at me sharply then, but I couldn't read the expression in his eyes. Blue eyes in the black-and-white universe. I was coming to treasure that small bit of color when I knew I shouldn't. Shouldn't treasure anything about him.

But the ridiculous fact was, I did. I had, from the moment I'd woken up in that dingy hotel room in Australia and looked into his bleak eyes and recognized something. I didn't know whether it was déjà vu, or shock, or the fastest case of Stockholm syndrome on record. All I knew was that I'd looked into his eyes and seen a . . . I wanted to say a soul mate, but that was preposterous. But I'd seen a bond, a connection, that existed no matter what he tried to do to me. And part of that bond was a totally unexpected desire.

"So what do you suggest we do?" If he didn't like my ideas, he could come up with one of his own.

"He will give us one week if he thinks we're following his orders. If he believes you're destroying me. If he knows we've refused he'll take you immediately, and he'll win."

"As will you, for refusing to play his game."

"But you won't. You'll be dead."

It shouldn't have come as a surprise. I'd always known that was waiting for me in the end.

"And why would you care?" I asked. What a stupid, whiny question, I thought, wishing I could call it back. He'd tried to kill me; he'd told me any number of times he believed I was a monster who should be terminated. I was entirely dispensable.

Of course he said nothing. I didn't think Azazel was capable of a polite, reassuring lie. "It's your decision," he said.

I roused myself from contemplating my imminent death. "What do you mean?"

"Beloch will send someone here tomorrow, and if he doesn't find us in bed together, he'll take you."

I sat back, looking into his beautiful face. Certain, painful death, or being forced to have sex with a man who drew me more than anyone ever had? Oh, twist my arm. "I'll take sex."

He didn't look particularly happy about my noble sacrifice. In fact, he looked dismayed, and I considered taking it back. "You don't like the idea? You can always lie back and think of England."

"Why on earth would I do that?" His voice was even, unmoved.

I shrugged, irritated. "It's a saying. Mothers in Victorian England told their daughters that sex was horrible, but it was their duty and they should lie back and think of England."

"It's not my duty."

"Don't be so damned literal."

Silence. I waited for him to approach me, but he didn't move from the chair. He simply watched me out of those bright blue eyes. In the distance I heard a clock chime one, and my stomach tightened. I was actually going to have sex with this supposedly nonhuman male who looked at me with no emotion whatsoever. Or, I could die.

I waited as long as I could, but patience had never been one of my virtues. "So . . . what do we do next?"

He didn't answer. He didn't need to. I rose, nervous. "I think I'll go take a shower before we—er—do this. Where do you want to meet?"

He simply looked up at me. "I'll find you."

Oh. My. God. What the hell was I doing? The only thing I could do, I reminded myself. Maybe I was the one who had to close my eyes and think of England. He seemed totally uninterested in our upcoming sex. I only hoped he could perform on command, because I certainly wasn't the seductive type. "All right, then," I said, unable to hide my nervousness. "I'll see you."

"Yes."

Crap. I practically ran from the room, ran from him. What the hell had I just agreed to do?

SHE RAN FROM HIM. HE wasn't sure why. Probably because she knew her true self would be revealed once their clothes were off. Not that there was any trace of the demon on her smooth, lovely skin. He'd examined her carefully, and she had the body of a human woman. No sign at all of her demon origin. At least for now. He had no idea what would happen in the midst of coitus. She might turn into a snake or a dragon and devour him. The idea seemed faintly comical.

He should have known she'd say yes eventually. It was her only chance. He wondered why she was nervous. In fact, she was as skittish as a virgin. Possibly because she knew that once she was naked and on top of him, she'd no longer be able to hide her true nature.

And on top she would be. She'd been banished for a reason as stupid as the one he'd been damned for. She had refused to submit, refused to be physically dominated. Refused to lie beneath her husband. And there was no room for a rebellious female in the world in which she'd been created.

He could feel his blood pounding through him. He'd been counting on her refusal, and he would have dealt with it. He'd been a fool not to realize he'd been bringing her to a certain death. Not that he'd had a choice. He'd survived the Truth Breakers, but she was weaker. She would indeed be broken, and Beloch was not big on mercy.

If she'd said no, he would have come up with a plan to get her out of there, though he had no idea how, or whether he even could. He had to remember that the truth was more important than one small female. So he would take her body. Her agreement was reluctant, which helped. She hated and feared him—he'd done his best to foster that. He had no doubt that her seductive nature would emerge, and he simply had to do his best to resist her siren lure. No man could resist her, but he wasn't a man. He could take her, fuck her, and there'd be no tie, no bond. His body could do what it had to do, and he could take his release as a physical act, nothing more. The Lilith wanted total capitulation, but he would never give her that. It wasn't in his nature. He refused to accept the prophecy. He would kill her himself before that came to pass.

But it wouldn't. He rose, went into his bathroom, and took a cold shower, the icy pellets pounding his skin. It did nothing to cool the desire that curled in the pit of his gut. Real triumph would be not to want her. Not to grow hard at the thought of being inside her.

But that triumph was out of reach. He could no more control his physical reaction than he could bring Sarah back. But he could control everything else.

He wasn't going to dress, but if he went to her naked she'd see his arousal, and it would give her too much of an advantage. He pulled on his jeans, carefully, and went in search of her.

It was time.

CHAPTER ELEVEN

I STAYED IN THE SHOWER UNTIL THE skin on my fingers puckered and the steamy water started to turn cold, and even then I considered putting up with it for another half hour rather than face what was waiting for me. I couldn't remember sex, except for the relatively unsatisfying times with Rolf. Surely I must have enjoyed it at some point in my life, but if I had, those memories were lost. I couldn't even remember much about Rolf, except that I was always on top. And it didn't help.

But it was like riding a bicycle, I expected. Once you learned, it was easy enough to go through the motions. Besides, most of it would be up to Azazel.

But I was nervous enough, and the cold water was making me ready to jump out of my skin, so reluctantly I turned off the faucet and stepped from the shower, which was surprisingly modern for a house better suited to the nineteenth century.

There were big, enveloping towels, and I wrapped myself tightly and tried to do something with my ridiculously tangled hair. It was a pain in the butt trying to wash it, especially when the saber cut on my face had started to bleed again under the hot water, seeping across my scalp when I tilted my head back. In Brisbane I'd used half a cup of conditioner in an effort to force it into submission, but the fabulous shower here didn't come with anything but lavender shampoo. Great. I was going to scare the pants off him. I managed a nervous giggle. That was the point, wasn't it? And he shouldn't be surprised if I looked like a crazy woman—he was expecting to bed a demon. At least I could comply as far as looks went.

Unless he did this in total darkness. That would make the entire thing easier. After all, I'd had sex with Rolf and it had been no big whoop. And Rolf's increasingly limp response was one more sign that I was a far cry from the irresistible siren Azazel believed me to be. In fact, he was going to be pretty disappointed if he expected fireworks and acrobatics. I didn't know any. I had every intention of simply doing it and getting it over with as quickly as possible.

I walked into my room, planning to find the voluminous nightgown I'd worn the night before. Maybe I wouldn't even have to take it off—I could just raise it demurely and avert my eyes.

I stopped short. He was lying on my bed, wearing a pair of jeans and nothing else. I should have known he'd be gorgeous without a shirt. His skin was luminous white-gold against the colorless sheets, and his black hair was damp, pushed away from his starkly beautiful face. He was watching me intently, and my panic blossomed.

But there was no place to run. I could do this. I'd done this countless times before, hadn't I? I looked at him. "Could we turn off the lights?"

"No."

I bit my lip. "Do you know where my nightgown is?"

"You don't need it. Come." He gestured to the bed beside him. That blasted command again. I moved a couple steps closer.

"Can't you do something?" I said nervously. "Say something nice to me? Hold out your hand?"

"So you can pretend this is not what it is? I doubt it. Remove the towel and get on the bed, and stop pretending you haven't been doing this for tens of thousands of years. You can use your skills—they won't have any effect on me."

"I don't have skills," I said, frustrated. "And if they won't make any difference, why should I try?"

"It is not beyond the realm of possibility that they might speed things up, which we would both appreciate. Take off the towel and get on the bed."

I got on the bed, keeping the towel clamped around me. He lay back against the pillows, the color of him a striking contrast against the drabness of this world. He was waiting for me to do something, to take charge.

Well, I certainly understood the basics. Tab A fit into slot B and all that. I pulled my legs up underneath me and stared at him. "What if I'm not your mythical baby-eating demon?" I said suddenly. "What if you're wrong, if you scooped up the wrong person?"

"There is no mistake."

"How do you know?"

"Because of my reaction to you."

That gave me pause. And then I rallied. "Oh, I bet you hate a lot more people than just me, and you don't go around thinking they're Lilith."

"I have already told you I do not hate you. And that is not the reaction I'm talking about."

"Then what are you talking about?" I demanded, frustrated.

On anyone else, that glimmer might signal

amusement. Not on Azazel, of course. But he didn't answer my question. Instead, he said, "You can stop trying to put this off with meaningless questions."

"That's right," I said, unable to keep the anger out of my voice. "The sooner we do it, the sooner it's over."

"Exactly. Go ahead."

Go ahead? Shit, and do what? And why was I getting so upset? I wanted it over and done with as much as he did. Clinging to the knot that held the towel together, I moved over to him, careful to keep my lower half covered, which was no mean feat, given that the towel seemed determined to split apart and flash him.

I reached out and put a tentative hand on his chest, and almost yanked it back again. His skin was warm. For some reason I expected him to feel cool beneath my hand. I let my fingers slide up tentatively to his shoulder. "Shouldn't angels have wings?" I whispered.

"I have them when I need them."

"Magic?"

"Miracle," he said, not moving beneath the gentle explorations. His nipples were dark circles against his pale skin, and I wanted to put my mouth on them. The thought was so random and unexpected that I ignored it, moving my fingers across his collarbone to the other shoulder.

"You know," he said in a conversational tone, "you'd be better off moving your hand lower down. All the interesting parts are below the waist."

I yanked my hand back, suddenly embarrassed. I was doing this wrong. Why the hell hadn't I ever learned to come on to a man?

The answer was simple. I had never wanted to. Sex had been the price I paid for companionship, something men wanted, not me. It was about bringing pleasure to a man, not about my pleasure. But this time was different.

I wanted this man, despite the fear and coercion. I wanted to feel his warm skin against my breasts, feel him inside me. I wanted his mouth all over me, kissing me, tasting me. *Good luck with that,* I thought, disgruntled.

"What do you want?" I said, suddenly angry at his lack of interest.

"What do you mean?"

"Clearly you're expecting to be serviced, and despite your insistence that I'm a whore, I don't have any idea how to go about it. Is there anything special you require?"

His eyes narrowed as he watched me. "What are you offering?"

"Do you want me to perform oral sex?" I didn't

stumble over the words. I'd tried it once with Rolf, in an effort to stimulate him, but neither of us had liked it very much. "I gather it can be effective in getting someone aroused."

"I'm aroused."

I blinked. "Then what do you want?"

"It's up to you."

Crap. If it was up to me, I'd run my tongue up his chest and—no, I couldn't do that. Instead I leaned over and pressed my lips against his, briefly, then drew back. No reaction. Just those vivid blue eyes, watching me. Okay. I was going to have to do a better job of it. I got up on my knees, placed my hands on the smooth, hard skin of his shoulders, and kissed him again, softening my lips against his firm, unyielding ones, then pulled back. What was the problem? He'd kissed me yesterday, kissed me more thoroughly than I'd ever been kissed before.

His eyes narrowed, and he suddenly touched my face, pushing my hair away from the narrow cut. "How did that happen?"

"Your friend Enoch," I said, trying to sound offhand.

"Not my friend." There was a look on his face, one that I might have thought was dangerous. "Does it hurt?"

I shrugged, clinging to the towel. "It's okay. It

bled a bit, but I think it's stopped. It's just lucky I ducked."

"Lucky for Enoch," he said in a grim voice. His hand felt almost gentle on my face, like the whisper of a caress. And then he dropped it. "Take off the towel."

Okay, I could do that. I would have to sooner or later. I reached for the knot between my breasts and hesitated.

He caught my hand, pulled it away, and yanked the towel off before I realized what he was doing. I was kneeling stark naked on the bed, feeling horribly exposed. I wasn't used to this. I fought the temptation to try to cover myself, but I felt my skin heat with embarrassment.

He wasn't looking at my body, he was looking at my face. "Are you blushing?"

"No," I mumbled. I dipped my head, not wanting to meet his gaze. I would have pushed the hair away from my face, but that would have required movement, and I figured if I stayed very still—

The feel of his hand on my face once again was a shock. It was surprisingly gentle, sliding against my cheek and into my hair, his thumb brushing across my lips, and I shot a tentative glance at him. Slowly, very slowly, he pulled me toward him, bringing my mouth against his, kissing me with great sweetness, such sweetness that I wanted to cry. If only I could.

He pulled me closer so that my breasts pressed against his firmly muscled chest, and I felt my nipples harden, suddenly pinched and sensitive. His hands slid up my naked back, drawing me closer still as his lips moved down my jaw, the side of my neck, and he breathed in deeply, as if he were inhaling the scent of my skin. His mouth opened against the vein throbbing at the base of my neck, his tongue tasting me, and I heard a distant groan that must have come from me.

I felt his teeth then, a small bite against my skin, barely painful, and my muffled arousal was suddenly full-force, sweeping over my body. I put my hands on him, on his damp, silky hair, pressing him against me. The room wasn't dark the way I wanted, but it didn't matter. It was all right to want him, all right to feel overwhelming desire. There were no witnesses, and he didn't care what I was feeling. We were doing this, it was out of my control, and his mouth was wonderful against me.

I had a sudden, strange fantasy: I wanted his teeth to break the skin, to lick the blood from me like some old-school vampire. But he moved his mouth downward, his hands encircling my waist, and with seemingly no effort he pulled me over him, lifting me up, and his tongue touched my breast.

"Oh, God," I whispered as he licked me gently, carefully, teasing me until I wanted to scream at him. And then his mouth fastened on me with such deep, drawing hunger that I felt a hot spasm between my legs and, straddling him, pressed my naked body against his. He hadn't lied. He was most definitely aroused, and I rocked against him instinctively, feeling him against my sensitive flesh.

I was overwhelmed by sensation. At first everything seemed centered on the slow, deliberate pull of his mouth at my breast as his long fingers cupped the other one, teasing the nipple as he sucked. But the hardness between my legs as I straddled him was equally astonishing, and I wanted more. I wanted complete possession, and I felt helpless, unsure what to do about it.

I slid my hands down to the fastening of his jeans, wanting to tear them off him, but he let out a little hiss of pain as I inadvertently hurt him. I yanked my hands away. He caught them and put them back again, and I couldn't believe how iron hard he was. I was wet between my legs and self-conscious all over again, wanting to pull away, but then he put his hand there and I stopped thinking. I needed him to touch me, stroke me, slide against the dampness, and I struggled to get closer to him. When he pushed his fingers inside me I groaned in frustrated need, trying to get more. Suddenly desperate, I reached down to find the tab to his zipper, when he jerked and cursed again as I hurt him once more.

"I'm sorry, I'm so sorry," I whispered brokenly. "I don't know what I'm doing. I'm sorry . . ." He slid one hand behind my head, under my hair, and pulled my mouth to his, silencing me. He released himself with the other hand, the hard, hot flesh springing free, but I didn't dare touch him, afraid of my clumsiness. I trembled, helpless, unsure, so swamped with crazy desire that I could barely speak.

He didn't need words. He caught my hips in his hands, lifting me up, holding me poised over his straining erection. He'd just shoved his jeans down a bit—I could still feel the denim against my bare legs—but I didn't care.

I felt him against me, the head of his cock just resting against the emptiness that was tormenting me, and yet I was afraid to finish it, to join us, afraid I'd hurt him again. I heard his sigh of frustrated exasperation, and he took my hand and carefully wrapped it around his erection. And with his other hand at the small of my back, he started to push me down onto him.

He was so big. A huge, hard invasion that even my sleek flesh fought; but he simply moved me, teasing our bodies until the desire flowed slick and sweet between us, and I moved my hand and finally sank down onto the full length of him, my body shuddering in response.

I looked down between us, at the joining. I could see my nipples, tight and hard. See him buried inside me as I felt my body grow accustomed to his. He hadn't moved, and slowly I raised my eyes to look at him.

For a moment we simply stared at each other, frozen in time, his eyes and mine, more powerfully intimate than the joining between our legs. "Move," he said, his voice raw.

I moved, rising up on my knees, just a bit, then sinking down on him again, feeling him fill me. It only took me a moment to find a rhythm, and I closed my eyes, flinging my head back as I soared, in and out, empty and full, a ride like no other, like riding a dragon through a moon-bright sky. My hands were on his shoulders, clutching them for balance, and he was slick with sweat, and his hands were on my hips, not forcing, just touching me, and I could have gone on forever, sailing on a tide of crystal-bright pleasure, when something dark erupted, something heavy and frightening. I could feel my body slipping away from me, and it terrified me. I froze, making a choked sound in my throat.

His hands tightened on my hips then, moving me, continuing the rhythm that I had lost, as I myself was lost, and he thrust up into me, hard, again and again. I dug my fingers into his shoulders, wanting to get away, but he wouldn't let me. "Do not fight it," he whispered. "Embrace it." He slid his hand down my stomach, touching where we joined, and a jolt of reaction swept through me.

I heard my own muffled cry, and he surged up into me again, and again, and he touched me once more, hard, and his voice was a growl.

"Come," he said. And I did.

I shattered into a thousand pieces, splintered darkness all around me, as I felt him climax inside me. I was gone, there was nothing left of me as I went into that dark place, drinking it in, my body frozen. And then I collapsed against him, wanting to weep, and his arms came around me with heartbreaking tenderness, holding me as I slowly returned to my body, to the bed, to the man I was straddling.

I wanted to stay like that forever. I wanted him to kiss me, to tell me he loved me; I wanted all the fairy tales people wove. But instead his arms slid back, his hands caught my body and lifted me off him, setting me down on the bed beside him.

I turned my back on him, curling up in a tight ball, hugging myself. I didn't want to see his emotionless expression, his wintry blue eyes. I was slowly coming back—if I looked at things calmly, I could admit he'd been kind. He'd held me, stroked me, guided me when I lost my way.

And I hated him for it. He was my enemy, he'd made that clear, and what we'd just done was simple biology to him. What had shattered my soul was simply instinct on his part, and I hated that it didn't matter. Hated him.

I was acutely aware of him beside me, still propped against the pillows, his jeans shoved down his hips, not moving. Not doing anything. Not reaching out to touch me, hold me. Not saying a word.

I wished I could cry. If I'd been able to burst into tears, maybe some of the conflict would have lessened, the sorrow and power of the last half hour reduced to manageable levels. But my eyes were dry, and I stared into the room, sightless, empty. And then I closed my eyes and slept.

HE DIDN'T MOVE, COULDN'T MOVE. He'd done what he was supposed to do, and he'd survived quite well, thank you. He wasn't going to turn into a demon simply because he'd fucked one. He wasn't going to lose his soul, forget about Sarah, fall in love.

It was sex. What astonished him was how honestly bad she was at it. No, that wasn't quite true. What they'd just shared—no, he didn't want to think of it that way. They hadn't shared anything. What they'd just done had had a disturbing erotic power, despite her nervousness. Even the Lilith couldn't simulate her deep blush when he'd stripped that damned towel off her; even the Lilith couldn't have made her desire-slick flesh resist his entrance like that. She really didn't know what she was doing.

Which meant her memory loss was real, and his treatment of her had been beyond cruel. He turned his head to look down at her, curled up in a tight ball. Her eyes were closed and there was no sign of tears, but that was no surprise. Demons couldn't cry.

He should say something to her, something kind. For all he knew, that might have been the very first orgasm she'd experienced, and he knew that was shattering for a woman. But he couldn't touch her.

It would be too dangerous if he pulled her into his arms. Too dangerous to murmur soothing words against her tangled hair, to kiss her creamy skin, her breasts, the hot beat of her vein against his mouth. He'd wanted her, wanted everything from her, heat and sex and blood in his mouth, and she wasn't the one. She would never be the one.

Even if she didn't remember her power, it didn't mean she didn't still wield it. Then again, he'd been celibate for seven years. It was little wonder he was feeling equally . . . shaken.

He waited until he was certain she was asleep, then slid off the bed, shoving his jeans off as he headed for the bathroom. He cleaned himself, annoyed that he grew hard again as he remembered how her body had felt; when he came back into the room, she hadn't moved. The sun was just beginning to rise on the Dark City, and he turned off the light as he slipped back into bed beside her. She made a soft sound in her sleep, almost like a muffled sob, and it felt like a blow.

He pulled the covers up around her, settling them over her gently so as not to disturb her. He slid down on the mattress and closed his eyes. He could smell the scent of her skin, the tang of sex, the scent of the ocean that always clung to him. Familiar, comfortable smells. Why should the scent of her skin be familiar?

It didn't matter. He slept.

Chapter Twelve

When Azazel awoke he was lying on his side, his body curled protectively around hers but not quite touching her. She still slept. If she'd known he was so close, his face almost buried in her hair, she would have moved.

Beloch was watching them. He knew it. Azazel inched away, slowly so as not to wake her, slowly so that Beloch wouldn't sense his anger. He turned and sat up, the covers to his waist, deliberately shielding her from Beloch's inimical gaze.

He was hovering by the door. Not there in the flesh, of course. Beloch never left the confines of his Dark City stronghold, but he could project himself almost anywhere. Azazel had known the moment Beloch came into the room, even though he'd been asleep. It was small comfort that there had been no eyes watching them in the dark hours of the morning.

He met Beloch's eyes. "It is done," he said in a low voice, hoping not to wake her. "And still I feel nothing."

"So it is," Beloch murmured in the faintly hollow voice that came when he projected his presence. "Shall I take her, then?"

This had to be played very carefully. If he showed reluctance, Beloch would pounce, and Azazel hadn't yet come up with an alternative to her certain annihilation. "If you wish," he said calmly. Beloch had moved to the left, to get a better view of Rachel as she slept, and he shifted, shielding her once more. "If you believe this has been a thorough test, then of course I acquiesce. I am relieved you haven't asked more of me. I have assured you that I am invulnerable to her lures, and bedding her has failed to change that. I'm pleased you have been convinced so quickly."

Beloch just watched him. "I cannot decide whether you're making the very unwise attempt to manipulate me, or you are truly impervious to her. Though she appears to be far removed from the Lilith, she should still retain her erotic power. You insist that you feel nothing? That her powers do not move you?"

"I climaxed inside her. Is that answer enough?"

"So you did," Beloch murmured. "The cameras were very explicit."

Azazel froze. He hadn't bothered to search the room, knowing that Beloch could simply transport himself if he wanted to watch. He should have realized that Beloch would know he would resist.

"You were watching."

"I was watching," Beloch murmured. "What I fail to understand is why you had to do all the heavy lifting, so to speak. I would have thought she'd simply shove you down and climb on top of you. It is her way, after all."

He managed to keep his rage under control. "You underestimate her. She would know I wouldn't respond well to that, that I would find shyness and uncertainty alluring."

"And did you? Find her alluring, that is?"

She was awake. He felt the sudden tension in her body, and he wondered how long she'd been listening. He'd been too angry with Beloch to notice.

There was nothing he could do about it. "She is a beautiful woman," he said in a tight voice. "And I've been celibate for too long. Of course I responded to her. It means nothing."

"It's been seven years since your beloved

Sarah died, hasn't it?" Beloch's voice was faintly mocking, and Azazel wanted to cram the words down his throat for daring to speak Sarah's name. "And now you're doomed to follow her with the greatest female demon the world has ever known. That really must sting. I'm certain you'd be happy if I took her away before you became attached to her."

He had to tread carefully, swallow his rage. "I would appreciate it," he said, and held his breath.

Beloch chuckled. "I'm sorry, but I must agree with your original assessment. It wasn't much of a test. If you're going to prove you're not susceptible, you'll have to endure more than a quick ride in the moonlight."

He didn't show his relief. He wasn't even sure why he was feeling relief. The sooner she was destroyed, the sooner she would no longer be a threat to his future. "As you wish," he said. "But you'll turn off the cameras."

"No. I quite enjoy watching you. You're both quite beautiful animals, and watching you copulate is entertaining. You would have made beautiful babies."

"Since the Fallen cannot reproduce and the Lilith smothers newborns, I would expect that's a moot point."

Beloch looked toward Rachel's motionless figure, but Azazel shifted, once more blocking his view. "Then I will leave you two to fuck like bunnies," he said with an ugly twist to his mouth. "Wear each other out if you like. And if you can still turn her over to me, then I'll be satisfied, and you'll be free of the prophecy. Everyone will be happy. Except the Lilith, of course. But by then she won't be feeling anything."

He was gone. Azazel didn't move, and neither did Rachel. She wouldn't have his awareness, wouldn't know that Beloch had left them. Left them with the cameras as silent observers.

If he could have gotten away with it, he would have slid down beside her, wrapped his body around hers, and taken her that way. Despite Beloch's intrusion, he was still hard for her, a natural reaction after so many years of celibacy. Waking next to a warm female body was a guarantee of arousal, no matter who—or what—that female was.

But he knew he didn't dare touch her. He had no idea exactly how much she had heard, but it would be enough. "He's gone now," he said in the low, cool voice he used with her, keeping the disturbing roil of emotions hidden beneath it.

She moved so fast he was startled. She leapt out of bed, ripping the sheet off with her and wrapping it around her body. Too late she realized it left him sitting on the bed naked and aroused, and she jerked her face away, once more turning that lovely shade of pink. "Do you have any idea how much I hate you?"

It shouldn't have surprised him. He'd repudiated her and what they'd done, what he wanted to do again. "I expect you do. You needn't bother to explain—you must have a dozen reasons."

"Get out of my room."

He slid off the bed. Off her side of the bed, and there wasn't much room between the bed and the wall, and the two of them were trapped. He put his hands on her shoulders, and she couldn't fend him off without letting the sheet fall, and she wasn't going to do that. He could regret that, but he had to get rid of the cameras first.

She was stiff, angry, hurt. Who would have thought the Lilith could feel hurt? But last night he'd finally realized she was no longer the Lilith. What demon had resided inside her was gone, or it would have emerged during coitus. He'd been expecting it, prepared; but when she came she'd simply been a woman lost in the magic of her first climax. She was Rachel, beautiful, angry, wounded, staring at him with such betrayal in her brown eyes that he wanted to pull her against his body and hold her.

She'd fight him if he tried it. So he contented

himself with giving her a little shake. "Stop being childish. This is hardly a matter of hurt feelings—this is life and death and eternity. Stop being so emotional."

Demons didn't have emotions. If there was anything of the demon left, there was the chance that the layers of forgetfulness and humanity might still be stripped away, showing her as the monster she was. Or would she stay this way, confused and furious, vulnerable and combative? And melting.

None of this was having the desired effect on his cock. He released her. "I'll take care of the cameras," he said in a tight voice. "Go and take a shower."

"Are there cameras in the bathroom?"

"Most likely. He'll have been watching since we arrived—you have no privacy left." He let his hands drop, because he wanted to reach for her again. "Go," he said.

She went.

IT MEANT NOTHING. HIS WORDS still stung, when they shouldn't have. I knew he was the enemy. I knew he thought I was a monster—in fact, it was amazing he'd been able to get it up, considering what he thought of me. But he had, most impressively, and he'd been hard this morning as well. I could still feel the color in my face when I'd stupidly ripped the covers off him. I would need to remember that in the future.

Not that there was going to be any future. I didn't care what Beloch said—we'd done what he'd ordered and there was no reason to do it again.

No reason but the strange longing that suffused my body. I wanted him again. Which was crazy—I didn't want sex, I didn't like it, even when I was in love. So why did my hands shake when I thought of touching him? I thought of the way our bodies joined, the feel of him inside me, the thick slide of him, and I wanted to feel it again.

I tried to lock the bathroom door, but of course it had been dismantled, and I slammed my fist against the wood, then let my forehead rest against it. I wanted to scream with fury and frustration, but it would do no good. I dropped the sheet, no longer giving a good goddamn whether any ancient pervert was watching me, and stepped into the shower. My thighs were sticky, my muscles ached, my mouth was soft and tender from his. I leaned against the marble wall and let the hot water pound down on me, washing him away.

I dried myself, then grabbed the sheet again

before I opened the door. My bedroom was deserted, the bed made with fresh sheets, and new clothes lay folded on top of the bed. I wondered who I had to thank for that. I couldn't picture Azazel making the bed, but I hadn't sensed anyone else in the house.

And then I remembered the cameras that were definitely in this room. I dressed quickly, resisting the childish impulse to flip the bird to them. Resisted it because I didn't know where the cameras were.

There was no sign of Azazel as I made my way downstairs. I was hoping there'd be something edible left of the massive buffet from last night, but to my astonishment there was fresh, warm food, including hot coffee. Everything I could have wanted.

I could have wished that my appetite had disappeared with the events of the last twelve hours, but instead I was ravenously hungry. I went back for seconds and was sitting there, my legs propped up on a nearby chair, enjoying a second cup of coffee and an almond croissant, when Azazel walked in.

I looked at him, trying not to picture him naked, the look on his face as I clutched his shoulders and rode him. . . . "There's food," I said unnecessarily.

"I already ate."

Of course he did, I thought, unreasonably miffed. At this point there was probably nothing he could do that wouldn't have annoyed me. It was late afternoon, and the sky outside was darkening. It looked like a storm was coming in.

"What prophecy?" I hadn't meant to ask him, hadn't meant to say anything that would require a response from him. He would do as he always did, ignore my questions, give me one-syllable answers. "Never mind," I said hastily. "I don't know why I bother."

He came over, took the chair my feet were propped on, and pulled it out from under me, sitting down next to me. "The prophecy is from one of the ancient scrolls found at Qumran. Better known as the Dead Sea Scrolls."

I was more shocked that he appeared to be giving me an answer than at the answer itself. "Those are fairy tales and mythology, nothing more. Written by crazy, deluded old men."

"You would be surprised," he said. "Half of it is nonsense. The rest is far too close to the truth."

"So there's a fifty percent chance this prophecy is true. What is it?"

"It doesn't matter. It happens to be part of the fifty percent that isn't true."

"Then why does it matter so much to you?"

His mouth thinned. I remembered the feel of his lips against mine, and I wanted to close my eyes and cross the small distance that separated us. I stayed where I was.

"The prophecy states that the Lilith will eventually marry Asmodeus, king of the demons, and they will reign in hell."

Okay, I thought, reaching for my coffee. It was already cold, but I needed to stall for time. I swallowed, then looked at him. "Absurd," I agreed. "Considering I'm not the mythical demon you think I am, it has nothing to do with me. But even if it were true, why is that a problem for you? You think I belong in hell anyway. Might as well rule it."

"Hell doesn't exist. I already told you that."

"Do you think I take your word as gospel?"

"In fact, I never lie. I am incapable of it."

"Is that part of the so-called angel thing?"

"Yes."

"And you're an angel." I still found that as absurd as the thought that I was a demon. "So why do you care about the prophecy? Why do you care who I marry?" It was a ridiculous, hopeful thought, but I couldn't imagine what else was troubling about the prophecy.

"Of course I don't care whom you marry. As long as it isn't me. I am called many names in the scrolls and scriptures. Azazel, Astaroth, Azael . . . and Asmodeus."

For a moment I couldn't move. And then I couldn't help it. I laughed. "Don't be ridiculous. I'm not marrying you."

"No. I intend to make sure of it."

Why did that feel so painful? I certainly didn't want to marry him. I had no idea what marriage to an angel might entail, but I imagined it wasn't pleasant. And there was no way in hell I was going to give him that much power over me. He had too much already.

I still wanted to fight back, to make him feel the pain I was feeling, the illogical, irrational pain, and I had one weapon. "Who is Sarah?"

I might have imagined that he flinched, the movement was so quick. But he didn't avoid my gaze. "My wife," he said. "She died seven years ago. And I will not replace her with you." Watching me. Always watching me out of those fierce blue eyes in the drab, empty surroundings.

I wanted to hate her. I wanted anger to fill me at the thought of the woman he loved, loved enough to spend seven years without sex, loved enough that he'd offered me up to monsters rather than risk having to marry me and contaminate her memory.

But I could find no rage. In truth, I could

almost feel her between us, a gentle presence in the room. Oh, most definitely between us, and she always would be.

But he would be gone, and I would be dead, and why should it matter? Yet it did.

"What if I promise not to marry you? I think I can manage to survive such a crushing blow to my heart." I was trying to sound cynical, but there was just a trace of vulnerability in my voice, and I wished I'd just shut the fuck up. I twisted my mouth into a semblance of a smile. "Let's just be friends with benefits."

"We are not friends and we never will be."

Damn, we were back to the terse dialogue. "Then what are we? And don't say mortal enemies—we're past that and you may as well admit it. What are we?"

"Reluctant allies. I have decided I do not want the Truth Breakers to get their hands on you."

"Then why did you bring me here in the first place?" It was a reasonable question, and I expected an answer.

"To find the truth at any cost. I changed my mind."

"Why? Because we fucked?" I used the crude word deliberately. Sex without love was fucking. "Suddenly you care about me?"

"No. Because suddenly I despise Beloch."

I'd wanted answers—it wasn't his fault if I didn't like them. Then again, I wasn't sure if I believed him. There had been a strong undercurrent of animosity between the two of them when he'd first brought me down to Beloch's deceptively cozy apartment. This was nothing new.

"So what are we going to do about it?" I asked in my most practical voice.

"I have yet to decide." He rose abruptly, glancing around the room, and I suddenly remembered the cameras. Were they throughout the house? "I'm going for a walk," he said in that take-no-prisoners tone.

I didn't like feeling like a prisoner. "Can I go with you?"

"No," he said flatly. "You've already seen what can happen when you wander around alone."

"But I'd have you to protect me," I argued.

He looked at me long and hard. "If I were you, I wouldn't count on it."

THE COOL AFTERNOON AIR WAS heavy with an approaching storm as Azazel strode toward the old restaurant and made his way into the warren of rooms beneath it. Beloch had been his enemy for as long as he could remember. He was far more powerful than he should have been. While Azazel knew that the Dark City had existed as long as the Fallen had, possibly longer, the details were unclear. The memory of his own incarceration here was impossibly vague—he could recall the pain and the despair and his determination to survive, and not much more.

He refused to ask his enemies for favors—particularly when they were like Beloch, delighting in power and torture. Yet here he stood in Beloch's lair, the supplicant. If he wanted to bring her safely out of here, he would need Beloch's agreement.

"Please," he said, and the word cost him.

Beloch looked at him and laughed. "Have you fallen in love, Azazel?" he cooed from his chair by the fire, his gnarled fingers stroking the angry cat. "How darling! I thought you were determined not to fall prey to the Lilith. In fact, earlier you insisted that you had managed to bed her without emotion. Clearly you were lying, either to me or to yourself."

Azazel stared back, keeping his face cool and blank. "Falling in love is for weak-minded humans," he said. "Besides, the Lilith has no memory of her seductive powers—she's as awkward as a schoolgirl."

"I gather schoolgirls can be quite delightful," Beloch murmured. "Though I'm afraid I wouldn't know. The lure of the flesh disgusts me. But here's the question that really interests me. Did you drink from her, blood-eater?"

"No. You know the curse as well as I do. She isn't my mate, and we only feed from our mates. I felt no desire for her blood at all." He wondered if that was the truth. He could smell her blood pulsing beneath her skin, and his fangs had begun to lengthen reflexively. He'd fought it. It was profane enough that he'd fucked her. To drink her blood in the sacrament reserved for bonded mates would be the greatest travesty.

The only reason he'd even been tempted was that he'd been away from Sheol for so long. Away from the nourishing gift of the Source. It was only natural that he should begin to react to her on a purely visceral level. Only natural that he would fight it.

"I wonder if I believe you," Beloch said meditatively.

"I don't care whether you believe me or not. I want you to let her go. We can find other ways to get the information we need from her."

"Don't be silly," Beloch said. "The moment you entered the Dark City, you placed yourselves in my hands. I don't relinquish what is mine. You brought her here for the Truth Breakers to discover the secrets she keeps hidden inside, and they will do just that."

"They'll kill her."

Beloch smiled. "Yes, they will. Very few survive the Truth Breakers. You were one of the rare ones. I'm certain they'd love another chance at you."

He didn't move. The room was stiflingly hot, and the fire crackled like a laughing witch. He could offer Beloch a trade. He had no reason to live, no desire to continue. If Beloch would send her—Rachel—back to Sheol, Azazel had complete faith that the Fallen would find out what they needed to know, sooner or later. It would simply take more time, but in the end the truth would come out. She would live, and he would die. It seemed a fair trade.

"What do the Truth Breakers want from me?" he said.

"What you refused to give them the last time, of course. You don't remember? No, of course not. I saw to that. The Truth Breakers want nothing less than the secrets of Sheol. How you survive and thrive in the face of God's disapproval. What are the walls that keep everyone out? How many are there? Who would be most likely to repent and return to the fold?"

"Like Sammael the traitor?" He knew his voice was icy and uncompromising.

"Like Sammael the martyr," Beloch returned.

"Your little girl could go free if you are willing to open yourself to the Truth Breakers."

There was something so familiar about that smooth, tempting voice. It would be so easy to give him what he wanted. "No," he said. "Those are not my secrets to reveal."

"Instead you'll see your lover ripped to pieces by the Truth Breakers?"

His face felt as cool and hard as the marble floor beneath him. "She is not my lover. And her fate is hers."

"And it has the added advantage of breaking the prophecy that terrifies you so much," Beloch pointed out. "Bring her to me tonight."

"You said she could stay—"

"I changed my mind. She weakens your resolve. The kindest thing I can do is remove temptation. You needn't have sex with her again, Azazel. Isn't that generous of me? You're released from that particular punishment."

Azazel didn't move for a moment. "When do you want her?" he said finally, and Beloch's smile widened.

"Bring her to the river by seven. The Nightmen will come and relieve you of that particular burden."

He looked at Beloch, his self-satisfied smile. He was immortal—it would do no good to break his neck, beat him to the ground. Azazel was trapped, and it shouldn't matter. But it did. "I'll bring her," he said. And walked away.

IT WAS ALMOST DUSK WHEN Azazel returned. I'd been waiting for him in the library, impatient, nervous. I'd tried to read, but my eyes would glaze over, and I would remember his hands on me, and I would end up staring into nothingness, reliving those moments. It was little wonder I was in a jumpy mood when he finally walked in.

"Are you ready?" As a greeting it left a lot to be desired, and I wondered if he was talking about going upstairs again.

"Ready for what?" I said carefully.

"I want you to show me the river walk. Where the Nightmen found you."

"Why?"

"Because."

I swallowed a growl, and rose. I didn't want to have sex with him again, and if he'd suggested it I would have flatly refused. There was no reason to feel disgruntled and disappointed. "How are we getting there?"

"We're walking. The more people who see us together, the better."

"I don't know why. Besides, they barely pay any attention to us. I tried to talk to one young woman and she practically ran away screaming."

"The people of the Dark City are watching us very closely. Everyone is a spy. The more time we're on the streets walking, the less time we're supposed to be having sex. I assume that would meet with your approval."

My stomach had jumped at his words. Again I could feel him, and again I forced myself to banish the memory. "Absolutely," I said in a firm voice.

I made the mistake of looking at him, into his pale face and his blazing blue eyes, and I knew he didn't believe me. He knew I wanted him again. Just as he wanted me.

The twilight held the promise of rain in the air. I looked up into the sky, searching for any familiar sign. I had no idea where we were, if we were in some strange, alternate world that existed in another universe. I never saw any sun overhead, only the omnipresent grayness that had spread into everything. Azazel and I were still in color, our flesh alive, our mouths red, our bodies creamy. What was this world, where every spot of color was gone?

We were halfway to the river when I heard the distant rumble of thunder, and I felt a moment's nervousness. Something was wrong. Not that that was anything new. It just felt more wrong than before, and my skin felt like ice. "There's going to be a storm," I said unnecessarily. "Maybe we should go back."

"We're unlikely to melt."

"What if we're struck by lightning?"

"It won't kill us."

Okay, I believed that. So I walked on, Azazel at my side with his hands in his pockets, occasionally brushing against me. Each time it happened my entire body reacted, suffused with warmth, and I wanted to lean against him, close my eyes and sink into him, into his bones, lose myself in his beautiful white-gold flesh.

I kept walking.

The river was in sight when the first light rain began to fall. The coat I'd found in my wardrobe had a hood, but I didn't bother with it, turning my face up to catch the drops of rain. He took my arm then, steering me across the street to the embankment along the roiling gray river, leading me toward one of the empty benches that fronted it.

He released me and sat at one end, and I understood perfectly well that he didn't want me cuddling up next to him. I sat in the middle of the bench, so as not to be too obvious, and looked at him.

"Where were the Nightmen?" His voice was as calm and dispassionate as always.

"They came from under that bridge." I gestured toward the narrow passageway that led back into the darkness. There was a door across it now, faded and probably rusty. The area was deserted—the gloomy evening was too stormy even for the dour inhabitants of the Dark City.

He turned to look at the passage, then back. "They're not anywhere around," he said.

"How do you know that?"

"I know. I'm not doubting your word. But if the Nightmen were here last night, they're now in some other part of the city." He leaned back against the cement bench, now marked and splattered with the gathering rain. "No one is going to see us."

"See us do what?"

At that moment lightning split the sky, so bright that for the first time the Dark City was bathed in crackling white light like an old *Frankenstein* movie, and then it was gone again as the sharp crack of thunder followed.

I rose. "We should get out of here."

He glanced up at me. "I couldn't find the cameras. They may not even exist—it wouldn't be unlike Beloch to lie in order to torment us. But if they're there, I can't find them and disable them."

I had no idea why he was telling me this, telling me now. Another bolt of lightning, this time so close I could hear the sizzle as it struck nearby. He rose and took my hand in a tight, unbreakable grip, dragging me across the cobbled walkway much as the Nightmen had the night before. But Azazel wasn't going to kill me.

We reached the sheltered door and he released me, reaching for the handle. It was locked. He yanked at it, hard, but it was stronger than it looked, and it didn't move. He swore beneath his breath, something foul, and looked around somewhat desperately. There was no other form of shelter.

"I guess we're doomed to get wet," I said, doing my best to sound cheerful.

"Yes," he said. And shoved me against the door.

Chapter Thirteen

The rough wood of the door was hard against my back. I stared up at Azazel in astonishment. "What are you doing?"

His body crowded mine back into the darkness as his hands slid up my neck, his thumbs stroking my throat, and I knew a brief glimpse of fear. He kissed me, and if the fear didn't leave entirely, it morphed into an instantaneous arousal. I'd wanted his hands on me, his mouth, his body pressed against mine, since I'd awoken. No, I'd wanted him since he'd lifted me off him and I'd turned away. This was what madness was—destructive need that was drowning out common sense and wisdom and self-preservation. I whimpered against his hard mouth, put my arms around his neck, and pulled him closer still, letting him kiss me with a furious desperation that I met.

This was bad, I knew it. It would only end in disaster. Yet I couldn't stop, wouldn't stop. It didn't matter what price I would end up paying—it would be worth it. Worth it to feel his hands slide down between us, slipping inside my coat, under my loose T-shirt, cupping my breasts through the lace of the bra. It had a front clasp, but he ripped it open anyway, and his fingers on the bare skin of my breasts made me cry out, aroused beyond belief.

I could feel the thickness of his erection against my stomach, and I was wet, that quickly, ready for him, needing him, not caring if he shoved me down on the cobblestones and took me there. I wanted his skin, and I pushed at his shirt, shoving it off his shoulders so that I could feel it, and I wanted so much more I could have cried. I could never have enough of this man, never in a thousand lifetimes. He was mine, he was my body and my soul and my heart, and I was caught so tightly with him I would cease to exist if someone tried to break the connection.

I kissed him back, my tongue against his, and closed my eyes, letting the delicious reactions sweep over me, the tightening of my breasts, the fluttering between my legs. He was pressed against me, hips against mine, and I could feel his long legs against the skirt I was wearing, and I momentarily cursed it, wishing I were wearing pants so I could get closer to him, wrap my legs around him. He rocked against me, and I felt a frisson of reaction, then another, as he bumped against me again, deliberately, pressing, and I remembered my fear last night of the deep blackness. I had survived and come through, wounded and yet complete, but I wasn't ready to go there again. It was too much, but he'd shoved my T-shirt up, exposing my flesh to the cool, wet air. His fingers stroked my breasts, plucking, pinching the nipples gently, and a shiver went through me, a choking gasp as a tiny explosion rocked me.

He broke the kiss, moving his mouth to my neck, and I tried to speak. "Let's go home," I gasped. "I don't care about the goddamned cameras."

"No," he said, his voice rough. His hands left my breasts, and I was afraid he was going to pull away.

"Wait," I cried, my fingers digging into his bare shoulders. "Don't stop. Not yet."

I'd never heard him laugh before. I didn't know if this was even a laugh—just a short, derisive sound. "No," he said again, his hands sliding down my waist, down my legs. Pulling the long skirt up, exposing my legs in the stormy afternoon, so that I felt the rain pelting against them, and I knew I should care whether someone was watching. I did care, just not enough. Not even when he reached for my panties and with one rough yank tore them off.

He put one hand under my butt, lifting me up, pressing me back against the door, and I heard the rasp of his zipper, his muttered curse as he freed himself, and then he pushed inside me, not waiting to see if I was ready for him.

I was. More than ready. The thick force of him made me gasp, afraid he might hurt me, but it stopped short of pain, only a faint discomfort that quickly spread into such pleasure that I felt another small orgasm hit me, a spasm of pleasure that jolted through me, and I tightened my legs around his hips, holding on tight.

Another sizzle of lightning, followed immediately by a crack of thunder. I saw something spark but I closed my eyes, the better to absorb the deep thrusts that were shaking me apart.

His hands were on my bare thighs, holding me up, and he pushed into me again and again. I could hear the wet slap of our joining, and it was another jolt of dark pleasure. He kissed me, hard, and I could taste blood, his or mine or both, it didn't matter. He couldn't get enough of me and I couldn't get enough of him.

He was going to want that final surrender, that dark explosion that frightened me. If I went into that place I might never return, and I tried to fight it, but I couldn't. Everything seemed centered between our bodies, on the powerful invasion of him into me, my unbound breasts rubbing against his chest, his mouth on mine, and holding back was no longer an option. If I went there he would be with me, he'd keep me safe as I let go of everything else.

He tore his mouth away, gasping for breath, and I rested my head on his shoulder as a dry sob was torn from my throat. The world exploded. One more crash of lightning, and the sky opened in a deluge. He slammed back into me, and I went over the edge as I felt him jerk and pulse into me. I have no idea why I did it, only knew that I needed to; my mouth opened, and my teeth sank into his strong, powerful throat, breaking the skin, tasting the rich sweetness of his blood.

I heard his deep groan, felt him swell inside me, and then nothing more as sheer sensation washed over me. I shook, convulsing, lost in a place that terrified me, with only his arms and his body supporting me as I flew.

It might have been moments, it might have been hours, before I opened my eyes, shivers still rippling through me. I lifted my head. There was blood on his neck, a faint smear, and I licked it away, feeling him jerk again in reaction. Why had I done such a thing? Why had it felt so right? As the shudders began to slow I put my arms around his neck, rested my forehead against his shoulder, and said the damnable words.

"I love you." My voice was rough, broken, as if I'd been screaming when I knew I hadn't made a sound. The rain was pounding down around us, streaming into my eyes and his as I lifted my head to meet his unreadable gaze. "That much of the prophecy must be true."

And then I heard them coming.

HE PULLED OUT OF HER, letting her feet down on the ground, still holding her against the door. He could feel the weakness of reaction still rippling through her, and he wasn't sure she'd be able to stand yet. When he thought she was steady enough, he let go of her and rearranged his clothes, pulling up his zipper, then looked up to see the raw panic in her eyes.

"We need to get out of here," she said in a shaky voice. "They're coming."

He had already felt them. Known they were

converging on this place. Known that they would sense their presence. He should feel regret, but it was too late for that. He'd known it would end this way when he'd let himself come inside her last night. When he'd been torn with desire all day. When he'd felt her teeth nip his flesh, just enough to draw blood. When he'd heard her words. "I love you," she'd said. And impossibly enough, he knew it was true. The demon loved him. For no reason. She was right, the prophecy was true.

And he had no choice whatsoever.

She was tugging at him. "We need to run."

He looked into her eyes, slowly shaking his head. And then she realized the full extent of his betrayal, and her eyes grew black with shock and pain. She tried to break away, but he was too strong. He held her, his hands wrapped around her wrists like manacles, and he knew he was hurting her, knew that in a little while the pain he was inadvertently inflicting would seem like a caress.

She fought like a madwoman, but she'd forgotten any of the powers she'd once had, except for the power over him, and there was nothing she could do. The Nightmen rounded the corner at a forced run, swords drawn, and he wondered if they would finish him as well. He could only hope so.

But this strange existence never offered an easy way out of the betrayals and cruelties and need that living brought. He stepped back when they put their hands on Rachel, and he saw Enoch's eyes glittering with pleasure. No, not Rachel, he reminded himself. The Lilith. A demon, neither male nor female, and he'd broken the laws of creation and fucked her, at Beloch's orders. It was the only way Beloch would do his part in helping them find the truths she had hidden inside her altered memories, and if Azazel paid for it with the soul he'd already lost, then so be it.

There was no pleading, no reproach, no fury, in her huge eyes. After the first shock, something had closed down over her, and she turned her head away, not looking in his direction.

She had a trace of blood on her mouth. His blood. He reached up and touched his neck. She'd barely broken the skin, and the bleeding had been minimal. He had no idea why she'd done it. But if he'd had any doubts about what he was doing, that was a sign.

They were hurting her. They'd manacled her hands, using iron to keep her lost gifts at bay. Demons were powerless against iron—he'd used it himself when he'd staked her out to die. It would have been more merciful to have left her there. It would have been over, in the past, and he would have forgotten her.

But they would never have gleaned the information she had locked in her brain, as the Truth Breakers were sworn to do. And he might have doubted his decision, with no proof that she was any danger to him.

He had that proof now. He was tied to her, part of her—his blood and his semen—and she was part of him. In the taking of his fluids, she had taken his autonomy. They were bound together, in flesh and feeling. Until they killed her.

"Take her to the Truth Breakers," he said in a harsh voice.

"We'll take her anywhere we damned well please," Enoch said, and Azazel wasn't sure which was worse: the Nightmen's random, murderous violence, or the careful sadism of the Truth Breakers' torture.

"Beloch will be displeased if you kill her," he said coldly, playing the one card he had. He wasn't doing her any favors by saving her for the Truth Breakers. But the Fallen needed the information that was buried as deeply as her demon memory.

Enoch's face darkened. "We would never disobey his orders. But he won't mind if we hurt her a little. Get a taste of what you've been enjoying. It's not every day you get a chance to fuck the Lilith."

His blood roared in protest, but he managed to keep his voice steady. "You would regret it," he said. "She's a scourge. She'll cause your man-part to shrivel and fall off. I'm immune because of the prophecy. None of you would be so lucky." The lie came easily, shocking him. He shouldn't have been able to lie.

Enoch looked properly horrified, and the men holding Rachel shifted uneasily, appalled even to be touching her. Good. He'd spared her that much, at least.

"Keep your distance, men," Enoch commanded. "I don't know if Wing-boy here is lying or not, but she's not worth taking the chance." He glanced back at Azazel. "I didn't think you had the stones to do this. You must be more like us than I thought."

Azazel didn't flinch. The rain was pouring down, drenching them, and he felt as if he were drowning. There was nothing more he could do.

They dragged her away. They'd attached an iron chain to her manacles and they dragged her, refusing to touch her. She never looked in his direction, never made a sound of protest, even when she fell on the cobbles when they jerked her too hard. She simply struggled to her feet before they could yank the chain again. And she was gone.

THEY PULLED ME THROUGH THE streets as the rain poured down on us. I could barely walk with the shackles around my ankles, and I could feel the wetness between my thighs. From him, from what we'd done. Just before he'd turned me over to the killers.

Betrayal. I couldn't think, couldn't feel, I simply plodded onward, slipping now and then, going down hard and then being hauled up again. I wouldn't see him again. They would either find out what they needed to know, whatever was hidden in the recesses of my mind, or they wouldn't. Either way, I would be dead.

I should care. I should try to escape. But the shackles were iron. Even if they'd been tin, I doubted I would be able to break them. If they'd been paper. It didn't matter. Nothing mattered. I was ready.

They pushed me, sent me sprawling, laughing at me. By the time we got to the building I was bruised and bleeding, barely able to walk as I was shoved forward. Not into the warmth and comfort of Beloch's retreat, but into a stark white room that looked more like a hospital surgery theater than anything else. There were various pieces of medical equipment and other things that I couldn't identify. I stared at them, trying to move my mind from the pain in my body and the shock of the appalling thing he'd done.

They lifted me onto the table, using new restraints even as they kept the iron shackles in place. They'd barely finished when six creatures glided in. They were dressed in enveloping, monk-like robes, the hoods drawn low over their heads, their faces in darkness. They said nothing, simply arranged themselves around me, and I knew they must be the Truth Breakers. My stoic façade began to crack, and I looked around desperately, to see Beloch standing behind them with his kindly smile, his gentle eyes.

"Help me," I said brokenly. "Don't let them do this."

He moved to the head of the table. "Dear child," he murmured, stroking my wet hair, "I'm the one who's told them to do this. I would tell you I'm sorry, but it's simply the wages of sin." He leaned forward and kissed me gently on my forehead. And then he was gone.

I stopped feeling then. Stopped hoping. They would hurt me, they would kill me, and there was nothing I could do about it. I would simply endure, until they ended me. I had no other choice. I wouldn't beg, plead, and God knew I couldn't cry. I would endure in dignified, reproachful silence. One of the Truth Breakers raised his arm, and I saw what he was holding.

And I started to scream.

CHAPTER FOURTEEN

AZAZEL DIDN'T GO BACK TO THE house. Instead he walked through the city in the rain. He was soaked through to his skin but he didn't care. He simply kept his mind a blank as he walked and walked. He couldn't leave yet. Not until he had the information he'd come to retrieve. Damn Beloch for putting him through this torture. Why hadn't the old man simply taken her that first night and been done with it?

The answer was simple. He'd seen that Azazel wasn't ready to let her go. And Beloch knew he had found fertile ground for the cruel games he loved.

He should have known he'd end up here at Beloch's headquarters below the innocuous old restaurant. More proof of her insidious power, he tried to tell himself as he entered through the lower door, but the words weren't making any sense. His mind was a deliberate blank, because his thoughts were too vicious, too harmful. Her fault, he thought again, and knew he was making excuses. He had done what he had to do. He had no regrets.

So why was he here?

He saw Enoch first, playing dice with some of his men in the foyer. He looked up at Azazel's approach, and grinned. There was blood on his uniform, and Azazel took a deep breath. He could smell it. Rachel's blood.

"I knew you'd show up sooner or later," Enoch drawled. "You look like you swam here. Didn't you notice it was raining?"

Azazel didn't bother answering him, heading toward the hallway.

Enoch moved quickly to block his path. "And what do you think you're doing?"

"Get out of my way."

"You can't change your mind, you know. It's not your decision to make, it's Beloch's. It's always been Beloch's, and you know it."

"Get—out—of—my—way." He bit the words off.

"It's too late. The Truth Breakers have had her for a long time. She stopped screaming hours ago."

Enoch stood even taller than Azazel's six feet two and outweighed him by forty pounds of muscle. Azazel didn't even hesitate. He went for him, rage filling his body with such strength that Enoch fell back in astonishment. He tried to rise, but Azazel hit him again, so hard that Enoch skidded across the room, landing in a crumpled heap against one wall, and stayed down, dazed. Azazel walked on into the building.

There was no noise, apart from the usual sound of the diners overhead, politely stuffing themselves. As he made his way down the corridor purposefully, Edgar appeared, unruffled as always.

"Were you wishing to dine with us upstairs, my lord? I'm afraid we cannot seat you dressed as you are," he murmured, unctuous as ever. "But I am certain I can find you some dry clothes to make you more presentable, and then we can most assuredly—"

"Where's Beloch?"

Edgar didn't blink. "I presume in his rooms. He's made it clear he doesn't wish for visitors tonight. He's been busy with a, er, project and doesn't want to be disturbed."

"I know what his project is. How do I get to his rooms?" The rooms and hallways in this rabbit warren of a place shifted daily, and there was never any way to tell where Beloch resided. It was part of his elaborate defense system.

"In fact, my lord, he's not in his rooms." Edgar hesitated, then leaned forward and said in a whisper, "He's spent the last few hours observing the extraction room. A particularly difficult case, I gather."

He knew the extraction room. It was where the Truth Breakers worked. Very few people had survived the extraction room. He was one of them.

"It is still on the lower level?"

"Of course, my lord," Edgar said with a disapproving sniff. "I can't have my guests' meals interrupted by screaming, can I?"

Without another word Azazel turned on his heel, ignoring Edgar's sputtered protests. He took the steps two at a time into the bowels of the building, then came to a halt. He could smell it. A thousand things. Her blood. Her fear.

He could smell the stink of death and shit, but those were older smells, not from today. He was past feeling relief. He didn't even know why he was here.

"Hello, dear boy." Beloch's voice came from behind him. He was sitting in state in a high-backed chair, a jewel-encrusted goblet in one hand. "I was expecting you to show up sooner." He waved his hand toward a less ornate chair beside him. "Sit and tell me why you've come."

As if he could. Azazel took the seat, trying to stall for time. "Have you found out her secrets?"

A smile curled Beloch's mouth. "Of course we have. Not everything, of course. She's resting while I decide her fate."

The cold knot that filled his chest seemed to expand into his gut as well. "And you discovered what she knew about Lucifer?"

"We did indeed. I must say, Uriel is very pleased with you right now. You've almost redeemed yourself."

Azazel froze. "What does Uriel have to do with this?"

Beloch shook his head. "Dear boy, when will you understand that Uriel is part of everything? Your actions have been very beneficial, and he's willing to reward you for them."

"Beneficial how?"

"He's been looking for the Lilith for hundreds upon thousands of years, yet all he had to do was wait for you to do something about the prophecy. He knew you would lead her to me, and that he could then rid the world of her foulness. If you continue to serve the archangel well, I imagine there might be redemption for you."

"There is no redemption for me." He looked into Beloch's milky eyes. There was something there, something familiar, something *wrong*, in his calm gaze, but Azazel didn't have the stomach to try to place it. "The Supreme Being cursed us. It could hardly be up to his minion to reverse that curse."

Beloch glared at him. "Uriel is not his minion!" he snapped.

Azazel was past taunting him. "What did she tell you?"

"What you already know. That she was confined near Lucifer when she refused to obey the Supreme Being and lie beneath Adam."

"But he released her."

"To rain terror on mankind. To seduce men and take their life essence so their seed is barren, to smother newborn babes and steal them from their mothers' arms."

"And why would God do that?"

"Who are you to question the Almighty's word?" Beloch thundered, and again Azazel had that eerie sense of recognition. He tried to remember where their enmity had started, but whatever had caused it was lost in the mists. It seemed as if it had always been there.

"I have never been afraid to question God's word. It was for that very transgression that I was thrown out of heaven, if you remember. For falling in love and for questioning." He sounded remarkably cool.

"If you ever want to go back, you'll have to learn acceptance. That's what faith is. Obedience without question," Beloch said in a petty voice.

"And why should I want to go back?"

Beloch looked startled. "Of course you want to. Everyone does. It's perfection, the epitome of all that is good, the pinnacle—"

"It is heaven," Azazel said flatly. "And I prefer humanity, with all its flaws."

A slow, secret smile twisted Beloch's withered lips. Azazel knew full well that Beloch could take any form he wanted, and he wondered why he'd chosen the old man this time. He probably enjoyed fooling the unsuspecting into thinking he was kindly and caring. He'd managed to fool Rachel at first.

Azazel needed to get the hell away from here before he heard her crying out. "What exactly did she tell you? We knew she was imprisoned with the First. We went through all this to find out what else she knew. She holds the secret to Lucifer's prison. What has she told you?"

"You'll have to apply to his holiness, the archangel Uriel, to discover those answers. In the meantime, there's cleanup to complete. We will make certain there's nothing else locked in the recesses of her memory, and then the Truth Breakers will finish her."

He was going to throw up. He should have known that Uriel would find a way to trick them. He stared into Beloch's oddly familiar face, and knew demands or pleas would be useless. "They will be merciful, I presume?" It wouldn't help the way his gut was twisting inside him, but it would be easier on her.

"Don't be ridiculous. The words of the dying are often their most interesting. The Truth Breakers will continue in a few hours."

Everything roiling inside him stopped. "Why are they waiting? Is any other outcome possible?"

"Of course not. This happens quite often. When the Truth Breakers are given orders to be brutal, as Uriel has decreed, then the initiate gets so covered in blood that it's hard to get the other information she might carry within her. And there is the question of her voice." Beloch gave him that smug smile.

"Her voice?"

"Her screams have left her without a voice. It should return shortly, at least enough for us to glean any final information." Beloch chuckled. "Did you wish to say good-bye to her? I'm not sure she'll be able to respond very well, and since you were the one who brought her to us I doubt she'd welcome having your face as the last thing she sees, but it's up to you."

The cadence of his voice was oddly familiar as

well. The impossible suspicion was born, and even as he told himself it was insane, it grew stronger and stronger.

"I will see her," he said.

Beloch looked startled. "I don't think—"

"I will see her."

He knew that disapproving huff, the narrowing of the familiar eyes. And suddenly he *knew.* And his rage was so powerful he was paralyzed as the man calling himself Beloch continued, "Enoch will take you."

The Nightman was walking with a limp when he appeared, and his fury was palpable. Azazel knew him as well, with a certainty that shocked him. How had he been so blind before?

He cast one last look at Beloch. At the old-man disguise, the cruelty and hatred that hid inside. The last of the archangels, hidden by the ancient flesh. He was Uriel, and always had been. Just as Enoch was his most trusted soldier.

He followed the Nightman's limping figure and rigid shoulders, down into the shadowy lowest levels of the old house, into the empty corridors, and he knew that Enoch would try for him again.

Enoch stopped outside a heavy door and turned to face him. The long dagger in his hand was no surprise. Nor was the fact that it glittered with celestial power.

"You've made your final mistake, Azazel," he said, his eyes shining. "He's ordered me to finish you. If it were up to me, I would let you see what's left of the girl, but I am one who follows orders."

"Of course you are, Metatron."

The king of the angels, ruler beneath Uriel, looked startled. "You know?"

"That this is Uriel's idea of heaven? That the charming old man is the archangel himself, playing games of pain and pleasure? Those poor, colorless people who wander these streets must be the few he considered worth saving."

"You and the girl are the ones without color, you fool. It makes killing easier when the blood isn't red."

"I do not care what color your blood is. Just that it spills."

Metatron's mouth curved in an ugly smile. "My sentiments as well. But I have the knife and you have nothing."

Azazel returned the smile with a calm one of his own. "You have fought me in years past, Metatron. You should know I don't need weapons."

"Nor do I," he snarled, dropping the glowing blade and advancing on Azazel with the cold certainty of physical superiority.

It was over quickly. A kick to the groin brought him down, fast and in shock; a hard chop on the back of the head and he went sprawling, unconscious. Luck and surprise had helped him, Azazel thought. Arrogance on Metatron's part had brought his fall. He wouldn't make that mistake the next time. And there would be a next time, Azazel knew full well.

He stepped over Metatron's body and reached for the door. She wasn't dead, he knew that much. He would know, he would feel it, if she ceased to exist. Uriel was never going to tell them the secrets that she'd unwittingly held. He'd put her through that torture for nothing.

The room was dark, but he could smell her blood, and for a moment he halted. It was unavoidable, instinctive, powerful. He wanted that blood flowing down his throat, coating his tongue. Almost as much as he wanted the source of that blood.

It took him a moment to get his fierce need under control. He switched on the light, and looked at the creature lying on the stretcher.

He knew her by the red hair, even though it was dark with blood. Her face was so battered and swollen she could be anyone. Her torso and legs were a mess, her wrists and ankles bleeding from the shackles. She must have struggled against them. They would have liked that.

He couldn't help her—she was too far beyond

his meager gifts of healing. She was near death, in truth, but when he leaned over her and unfastened her shackles, she opened her eyes through the swollen bruising and looked at him.

Her mouth moved, and he put his ear to it, but the rasp was too raw to understand. He didn't want to see the hatred in her eyes, so he concentrated on the shackles on her ankles, then undid the other restraints. There was no reason to keep her bound like that—she was too weak to fight. It must have been for their pleasure in her pain.

He slid his arms under her fragile body, and she jerked in silent agony. He had no choice—he had to get her out of there. He lifted her carefully, cradling her against his chest, and his hands were wet with her blood. He kicked open the door, stepping over Metatron's body, and headed toward the street.

He could sense it, a door to the outside that few used. He could carry her up the stairs, out past Uriel-Beloch and the other angels, but he could not kill them all without putting her down, and that he wouldn't do.

And he couldn't kill the archangel. In a battle he could hurt him, but only temporarily. Assuaging his vengeful fury and his crushing guilt wasn't important. What mattered was getting Rachel out of there. To someplace where they could find help. To Sheol.

The hallways were more like dark tunnels, but his sense of direction was infallible, and he followed the twisting path toward the exit, almost there when a shadow crossed his path. More than one. Truth Breakers.

"You think you can ignore Uriel's commands," one of them said in its hollow voice. "You are foolish. Put her down."

He didn't tighten his grip on her. He had hoped to avoid them. Beloch must have been waiting. "I'm not accountable to Uriel anymore," he said evenly. "I refuse to bow to his tyrannies. Get out of my way if you wish to live."

"You are mistaken," the Truth Breaker said. "You are the one who is going to die. Set her down, or she will die with you right now."

The Truth Breakers were gifted bringers of pain and death. But they were neutral, unfeeling. They didn't have his fury. "Gladly," he said, setting her down carefully. He had no choice. She must have lost consciousness, a small blessing for her.

Despite his fury, something had held him back from killing Metatron. He felt nothing for the shadowy torturers surrounding him, and it was over far too quickly for his taste. He was fast, brutal, and efficient; their surprise at his strength was their downfall. He refused to think about what he was doing, the rending of flesh and bone, the carnage caused by him alone. Perhaps it would haunt him late at night, perhaps it wouldn't. Within moments the six of them lay at his feet, whatever strange form of life they'd possessed now gone.

He moved back to Rachel's body and froze. Her eyes were open, and she'd watched everything, the horrific savagery he was capable of. And then she closed her eyes again, as if even looking at him was seeing an unspeakable monster.

He held her carefully. Her life force wasn't strong; she'd lost a great deal of blood, and if he didn't get her help soon she would die. And much too late, he suddenly realized that he couldn't bear it if she did.

He kicked open the door into the moonless night. The rain had stopped, but the gloom remained. How fitting that this was Uriel's idea of the perfect afterlife. Heaven, Paradise, Valhalla. The Dark City, with no sunshine, no joy, no light.

He looked down at Rachel. Yes, she was Rachel, not the demon, not the Lilith, no matter what darkness hid inside her. She was Rachel, and he'd betrayed her.

There was only one person who could save her. He would have to take her to the woman he hated, the woman who'd taken Sarah's place. He would have to take Rachel to Sheol, to Raziel's wife, the new Source. And pray to the God who had abandoned them that Allie could save her.

He spread his wings wide and surged upward, into the dark, threatening sky that surrounded this cursed place. Up toward the brilliant sun, leaving the Dark City and the archangel Uriel far behind.

Sheol

CHAPTER FIFTEEN

THE EARLY MORNING AIR WAS still and silent in their bedroom looking out over the ocean. Allie lifted her head, shoving back her thick brown hair. Over the years her senses had grown more attuned to the rhythms of Sheol, their hidden fortress in the mist, and the Fallen who lived there. She knew their comings and goings, their anguish and joys, their needs. God, she knew their needs. Right now someone needed her quite desperately, someone who wasn't there yet, and she started to roll over, but Raziel caught her arm and pulled her back on top of him.

"Where do you think you're going?" he murmured lazily. "We only just got started."

Allie laughed, burrowing against his lean, strong, deliciously naked body. "May I point out to you what we did down on the beach in the moonlight just last night? And then what we did when you carried me back to bed?"

"It's a new day," he said with a wicked gleam, rolling her underneath him. He was fully aroused, and she let out a little purr of delight.

"So it is," she whispered, reaching up and pulling his head down to hers. Their kiss was full and sweet, and she was warm and ready, tilting her hips up for his thick, gorgeous slide, closing her eyes and losing herself in the sweet dark magic of desire. The ebb and flow, thrust and withdrawal, building and building, almost to the point of pain, and then glorious release, cascading down.

Later, when she lay spent and breathless on the huge bed, she watched him rise and stretch, a man, an angel, a blood-eater well pleased with himself and his life. He cast her one salacious grin before heading into the bathroom, and she managed a weak grin back. She only wished she had his energy.

After seven years their bond had only grown stronger, so tight that nothing could break it. Not even the laws of nature, she thought with a trace of grim determination. She didn't care what the rules were. She was never going to die, never going to leave her immortal husband. She flat-out refused.

It was the way of things, she was told. The

Fallen didn't make mistakes. Once they'd chosen a partner, that connection became unbreakable. As the wife grew older and older. And the husband stayed young forever.

She was lucky, though. She was the Source, the spiritual leader of the Fallen, the mother, the nurturer. And the source of blood to sustain those without partners, even the grumpy and unaccepting Azazel, husband of Sarah.

As the Source, she would live much longer than the short human span. But after a couple of hundred years she would die, and Raziel would go on. And she couldn't bear it.

She sat up. She considered herself a practical woman, and she limited her brooding to a few minutes daily at the most. Right now there was no time for it. She had a naked husband in the huge walk-in shower, and she needed to bathe as well. And he was so good at soaping her up.

She needed to eat, and to get ready. Something was coming that would require everything from her. Something was coming that would change everything.

She needed to be ready.

IT WAS ENDLESS, FLYING THROUGH storms and dimensions, past the angry roar of a demigod, her broken body wrapped carefully in his arms.

She didn't awaken, which was a blessing. She was afraid of flying, and he'd had to knock her out the last time he carried her, or her struggles could have sent them hurtling toward the ground. He would have been fine, but a crash could have killed her, and he hadn't wanted to risk it.

Right now she was barely breathing. There was a ring of blue around her lips as she struggled for breath, and he wondered if they'd damaged her heart.

No, he was the one who'd done that. Stupid and cloying as the idea was, he'd seen the look on her face when the Nightmen arrived and known that was exactly what he'd done. He'd broken her heart.

But what choice did he have, one he'd brought her to the Dark City? He had survived his incarceration there long ago, and he'd lied to himself, told himself that she would survive as well.

He'd been an idiot not to realize the lengths to which the archangel Uriel was willing to go. An idiot not to recognize the Dark City for what it was: Uriel's perverted afterlife, a heaven made for those who had already lost their souls. And he'd delivered her straight into Uriel's bloody hands.

He was half-afraid Uriel would do something

to try to stop him; but if an angel, fallen or otherwise, chose to leave the Dark City, no one could prevent him. The laws of free will still held, no matter how Uriel despised them. He would find a way to circumvent them sooner or later; but so far he'd only been able to send the Nephilim in an abortive attack upon Sheol.

Azazel wasn't going to think about that, about the unbearable day seven years ago when Sarah had died. He had to concentrate on getting Rachel to safety, getting her the help she needed. He had to let go of mourning and concentrate on the living, at least for now.

He landed on the beach lightly. The early morning mist was rising from the sea, and the sand was deserted. He looked up at the huge, cantilevered building that housed the Fallen and their wives, its blank windows reflecting the deep blue of the sea. He would have to wake them. She hadn't moved, hadn't made a sound for the last hour, but she was still breathing. He held on to that much, and started toward the wide entrance, cradling her carefully.

She stepped out onto the lawn. She looked straight at him, clearly waiting for them, and he felt his usual anger flare up. But it was no match for his need.

She took one look at Rachel and immediately

became efficient. "The infirmary is set up for her, and I have Gabriel's wife, Gretchen, waiting. What happened?"

He followed her into the hall, responding to her businesslike tone. "She was tortured."

"The Truth Breakers?"

He was surprised she even knew of their existence, but then he'd forgotten the bond that grew between the Fallen and their mates. Raziel would have told her everything. "Yes."

"Poor child," she murmured.

"She is not a child," he said sharply. "She was once the Lilith, the first woman, and a murderous demon. Even if she has forgotten her past, she could still be dangerous."

"Then why are you holding her so carefully?" the woman shot back. "I don't care what her history is, right now she's a wounded child and she needs help."

"Yes." He didn't have to ask her, didn't even have to call her by name. She would do what he needed, because that was who she was. The Source, as his Sarah had been. The healer, the nurturer. The only person he could trust who could help her.

He laid Rachel carefully on the hospital bed, but she didn't awaken. There was a hitch in her shallow breathing; he could sense her pulse, the blood in her veins, and they were sluggish, fading. She was dying.

He turned to the woman he hated, the woman he refused to call by name. "Please," he said. "Please, Allie. Save her."

She looked at him for a long moment. "I will."

I FELT AS IF I were drowning in something thick and viscous. I couldn't fight my way out of it—the more I tried to push toward fresh air and sunlight, the more it fought me. I was dying and I knew it. I couldn't breathe, and the sun was too far away. I fought. I wasn't ready to die, but I could barely form a conscious thought. I didn't know who I was, where I was, I only knew that the pain was unbearable, and I would scream until they came and put something in a tube, and then I could rest again.

There were people around me, shadowy shapes tending to me, tending to the body I hid inside, and there was nothing I could do to stop them. I wanted to crawl off to a cave and heal myself, but I sensed that was no longer possible. I needed help, and I had no choice but to accept it as I learned to ride the pain; it ebbed and flowed, crushing me in an iron fist and then releasing me. I had to fight so hard to live through the storm. I had been through worse, I knew it instinctively, even if I couldn't remember where or when. I had survived unspeakable horrors, but those memories were locked away in a place I never had to visit again. If I could just get through this, I thought, struggling to breathe. One more minute, one more hour, one more day, and then everything would be all right.

Even in my half-conscious state, I knew that was a lie. I knew that once I worked my way through whatever torment was being visited upon me, the respite would be brief; then life would once again pull the rug out from under me. It would never be all right. It would be pain and despair and disaster, and it would be so much easier just to let go.

I tried to. I felt the soft, sinking cushion enfold me, and it was so warm, so comforting, that I wanted to release the desperate hold I had on everything and drift into it, lost forever. I let myself float, only to have a harsh voice call me back, berating me, angry and demanding. I knew that voice, knew that tone. He should have been no inducement to live, but he was. I pulled myself out of the soft darkness and went toward him, knowing instinctively that there was the light. There was why I wanted to live.

And I began to fight anew.

Azazel paced the sand, glaring at the house. Allie had banished him from the sickroom, and he couldn't blame her. Yelling at Rachel not to die wasn't going to help. He'd felt her slipping away and he'd panicked. It had been all he could do not to grab her shoulders and shake her. Instead he had told her she'd damned well better not die. He'd harangued her, threatening her with all sorts of ridiculousness, a return to the Dark City being one of them. If she died, there might be nothing left. Demons had no souls, and if Rachel had possessed one, it should be long gone by now. What happened when a demon died? Did it simply disappear?

He ran a harassed hand through his hair, staring out at the sea. He felt like the ocean, storm-tossed and angry. Its healing beauty seemed out of reach. He felt no urge to strip down and dive beneath the cool, blessed waters. His body was whole. It was his mind, his spirit, his soul, that were in torment.

Did the Fallen have souls, or were they no better than demons? They'd argued that for millennia, over campfires and by candlelight and gaslight and electricity, and there was no clear answer. God had stripped them of everything, including any possibility of redemption. There was no forgiveness for the fallen angels, only eternal damnation according to the angry God of old and his zealous administrator, Uriel.

But that God had changed. He'd granted free will to everyone, the Fallen included. Had he granted them souls at the same time?

He started pacing again, back and forth along the edge of the water. The tide was ebbing now. He'd been walking since it was coming in, splashing through water at high tide. Now it was pulling back, and there was still no word from the infirmary.

"You'll wear a rut in the sand," Raziel said, sitting down carefully, his iridescent blue wings closing around him. "No word?"

Azazel barely glanced at him. "No word. Go talk to your wife. She banished me from the sickroom."

Raziel arched a brow. "And you went? You astonish me. I wouldn't have thought Allie could get you to do anything."

"I didn't do it for her, I did it for Rachel."

Raziel looked at him. "Rachel? Do you mean the Lilith? Or have we made a mistake?"

Azazel halted his pacing. "She doesn't remember who she is. She has no powers, apart from the seductive one that pulls any man she sees into her web."

"That must have been inconvenient when you were in the Dark City. Did all the men start following you around in a pack?"

Azazel glared at him. "Don't be ridiculous."

"Because that's what would have happened if the demon Lilith had been about. No one would have been able to resist her. They would probably have tried to kill you, but you look like you're unscathed. How is that?"

"I have no idea. It took every ounce of strength I had to resist her."

"And just how much did you resist her, old friend? You seem particularly disturbed by her condition."

"Because it is our fault. My fault. I handed her over to them, knowing what they could do to her!" he said furiously.

"That's what we agreed to do. That's why you took her to the Dark City in the first place, took her to Beloch. Granted, we had no idea that Beloch was Uriel. I wonder if he always was, or if Uriel simply took over the Dark City and the demon who controlled it."

"I fail to give a rat's ass," Azazel snarled. Raziel's soft laugh didn't improve his temper.

"So you did as we agreed, and then you suddenly went in and took her back, infuriating Uriel in the process. Why?" He sounded more curious than censorious; but then, when the roles were reversed, it was hard for the former student to reprimand the master. Particularly when Raziel had contravened the law in much the same way not so many years ago.

"Because she . . ." Because she knew nothing? He had no certainty of that. Because she was someone else? He knew that wasn't true—behind those bright, curious brown eyes and that mop of red hair was Adam's first wife, the one who lay with demons and smothered infants. He knew it, when he wished he didn't. "Because I wished to," he finished lamely, trying to hide his truculence. "And I trusted my instincts."

"And you didn't consider that your instincts might be clouded by the Lilith's powerful sexual thrall? Because I hate to tell you, it's quite apparent you got sucked in, if that's the operative word, by her."

"I did not get— Damn you!" He whirled on him. "She's dying, and you dare to make prurient jokes?"

Raziel shook his head. He wore his hair longer—thanks to his wife, it was now past his shoulders—and he wore it loose, so that it swirled in the light breeze. "Allie will save her. She's not going to die, I can feel it. You could too, if you weren't so caught up in your emotions."

"I have no emotions."

Raziel let out a bark of laughter. "Then why did you sleep with her?"

"Beloch—Uriel forced me." And then he realized how totally ridiculous that sounded. Uriel hadn't forced him to do anything he hadn't wanted an excuse to do. He glared at Raziel once more. "I slept with her because I wanted to. Is that the answer you want? I told myself it was to see whether I could resist her, but we both know that is nothing but a lie. Whether I wish to admit it or not, I wanted her, and I have since . . . I'm not sure when. Since long before I offered her to the Nephilim."

"Honesty is always good for the soul," Raziel said lightly. "Trust in Allie. You trusted her enough to bring Rachel here, enough to put her in Allie's hands. I think worrying about whether Rachel lives or dies is a waste of time. She'll live. You've got something far greater to worry about."

Azazel drew back to look at him. "And what could that possibly be?"

"What the hell you're going to do about her when she does."

Chapter Sixteen

It was a very strange feeling. It was as if I were being born, for the first time, for countless times. Yet I knew this was for the last time—it was one of the few certainties I had. No more names, no more lives. Just this one.

The fog of pain was slowly lifting. The world was coming back into focus, and I could see I was in a hospital bed, with all the requisite tubes going into and out of my body. I observed them with distant interest. It was as if they were attached to somebody else. This broken body had betrayed me by giving me so much pain, and I preferred to keep myself aloof.

I could smell the sea. I had always been afraid of the ocean, the pull of the riptide, the waves that could crash over you and beat you down into the suffocating water.

Odd, because I was accused of suffocating infants.

In fact, old memories felt more real than my current state, half in and out half of a pain-infused nightmare. I knew my curse now. Not to kill innocent children. But to catch them up and cradle them and carry them to safety when something ended their lives.

The untouched ones were the hardest. It was called many things—witchcraft, crib death, SIDS. I carried them in my arms and washed them with my tears, each loss as wrenching as if it were my own child. It was a cruel and monstrous punishment, but there was more to it.

I comforted the women who were barren. I held them in my arms when they slept and sang to them. I went to their husbands and whispered to them, and they would rise up and take their wives and sometimes, just sometimes, the women's bellies would fill with the children they longed for. But too often they mourned, and the husbands went elsewhere, and I could only grieve with them.

I lay down with monsters. I had a body that was used until it wore out, and then I was given another, and then another, as the foulness of their bodies defiled my human one. Their members were misshapen, barbed, clawed, and hideous, and each night my body would tear in pain, in punishment. But that was over. Long gone, and this body was new. I remembered only the acts, not the way I had felt. I was spared that much as I slowly came alive again.

I lay down with human men, always on top of them. My sin was asking questions, and my punishment was great. I lay down with human men and used them because they wanted me to, and I felt nothing.

And I lay down with a fallen angel, and felt too much.

I kept my eyes half-closed, watching the woman as she moved around my bed. She was pretty, wearing a brightly colored dress that swirled around her ankles, and she looked happy. Had I finally found a place where people could be happy?

There was color everywhere—the blue of the sky outside, the rich brown of the woman's hair, the rainbow dresses she wore. I hadn't realized how much I'd missed color during my sojourn in the Dark City.

Day turned into night and then into day again. At times I dreamed my enemy, my betrayer, was there watching me, and I wanted to cry out. But when I opened my eyes he was gone. It was only a nightmare.

I remembered everything. I remembered him. And I remembered how to hate.

"You're awake, aren't you?" the woman said, her voice low and musical. I considered ignoring her, but she'd tended me so carefully that I knew I had to answer.

I tried to speak, but no sound came out of my throat. For a moment I wondered if my voice was gone forever, torn away by my screams, but then a rusty sound emerged. "Yes," I said, shocked at the gravelly sound.

"That's good," the woman said cheerfully. "Don't try to talk any more. You tore your vocal cords, and the best thing you can do is rest your voice. I'm Allie, and this is Sheol. Home to the Fallen."

The Fallen what? But I knew the answer. One of the fallen angels had saved me, circumvented Azazel's execution order.

"You've been sick a very long time," she continued, taking my hand in hers, the hand that didn't have an IV in it. "But I'm happy to say the worst is over, and you're well on your way to a full recovery. It will take time, but you're getting stronger every day."

Good to know, I thought hazily, sliding down in the bed. She still held my hand, and for some reason I didn't pull away. I'd never liked being touched, but this woman calmed me, soothed me. Healed me. The way I had calmed, soothed, healed the barren women of the world.

"There are about forty of us here, men and women. My husband is Raziel, the leader, and I'm sort of chief cook and bottle washer. I'm the healer, the shoulder to cry on, the voice of reason occasionally, though my husband would disagree with that. You're safe here, I promise you that. There's no way Uriel, or Beloch, or whatever he was calling himself, can get in here. This is sacred ground, and he's not allowed. And none of his nasty little bullies can get in either. No one's able to reach us unless we invite them in."

"Like vampires," I whispered.

Allie suddenly had an odd expression. "I guess you could say so. But bottom line, no one can bother you here."

I thought of Azazel. Was he still in the Dark City, enjoying the fruits of his betrayal? Or had my rescuers killed him during the attempt to free me? Come to think of it, how did they know I would need freeing? Hell, they were angels, albeit fallen ones; they could probably know anything they damned well wanted to.

I was getting tired, and I pulled my hand free, resting it on my stomach. Big mistake. I moaned in pain, snatching my hand back. My entire stomach felt like someone had carved their initials—

I had a flash of exactly what the Truth Breakers had done to me, with their blades and their hands and their fingernails, and my stomach twisted in horror. "I need to sleep," I croaked.

Allie nodded. "I understand. You don't need visitors right now."

Visitors? Who would be visiting me? I didn't know anyone here. I closed my eyes, shutting her out, the calm voice, the soothing touch, the healing presence. I wanted nothing and no one. Just sleep.

AZAZEL HAD LOST TRACK OF time. He sat by the water in the darkness, silent, knowing he could do nothing to help her. He simply had to wait, and waiting was torture.

Torture, he mocked himself. He remembered torture, remembered his time at the hands of the Truth Breakers, centuries ago. He had survived, but just barely, and he had strength and endurance far greater than mere mortals. And no matter what Rachel was, the body she inhabited was human, and therefore vulnerable.

What he'd gone through long ago would have killed a human three times over. He didn't know how Rachel had managed to survive, but it had been a close thing. Another five minutes and she would have been gone. And he didn't know how he could have borne it.

He felt her approach. The Source, Allie, the woman who had taken Sarah's place. The woman who had been Sarah's friend, even for such a short time, and had Sarah's blessing. Sarah hadn't had an angry, resentful bone in her body. She would be ashamed of him.

He started to rise, for the first time showing her that courtesy, but Allie gestured to him to sit and took the seat next to him, staring out at the sea. He held his breath. She had come to tell him that she had done her best, but that Rachel had died. Died in pain, hating him.

"She's going to be fine," she said softly. "She's sleeping now, but she was awake for a while, and even able to talk a bit."

Azazel started out of his chair, but she put her hand on his arm, her gentle touch staying him. "She's not ready for visitors," she said. "And before you see her, we need to talk."

His old animosity reared up. "What about?"

"You need to understand what kind of shape she's in. What she remembers and what she doesn't."

Her skin felt like ice, and he turned his face away to look at the dark, churning water. "Tell me."

"She remembers everything. In bits and pieces, but I'm not sure how clear she is."

"Everything?"

"She knows she's Lilith. She remembers her

curse, and what she had to do to work through her penance. Unlike the Fallen, it doesn't appear that her curse is eternal, and someone has finally released her. At least, it seems like it."

"It couldn't be Uriel. He still wanted to destroy her."

"Uriel wants to destroy anyone who has ever sinned, and that includes most of creation. After he wipes out humans, he'll probably find a way to discover sin in animals. There's nothing to stop him."

"Nothing but us," he said in a low voice. "What else does she remember?"

"She remembers her curse in fragments, and it sounds as if it's not quite what the scrolls have led us to believe. Which isn't a surprise—the scrolls were written by a bunch of misogynistic old men who used any excuse to denigrate women." She made a dismissive gesture. "And don't start giving me shit about the problem with bringing humans into Sheol and that I've got a bug up my ass about women's rights. The Judeo-Christian tradition is pretty lousy toward women, and anyone with a brain knows it."

"Are you accusing me of not having a brain?" he said in a mild voice. "I do know it."

"Oh," Allie said, deflated. And in the darkness, Azazel found he could feel amusement. "I imagine she'll tell you what she remembers, and the truth about her curse. Eventually."

" 'Eventually'?"

"Her memory of the last few years is as spotty as her memory of her ancient history. But she remembers you. She remembers that you staked her out for the Nephilim, but for some reason changed your mind. She remembers that you had sex with her, and then immediately handed her over to the creatures who almost killed her. But she doesn't remember that once again you were the one to save her. Why is that?"

"I have no idea why she doesn't remember. It's of little importance."

"Don't try to dodge me. You gave her to those butchers. Why did you save her?" In the past Allie had given him a wide berth, but the last few years had strengthened her inner power, and she was no longer afraid of him. Not afraid to challenge him, to ask the hard questions, to take him to task if need be. Things had definitely changed.

"I changed my mind." His tone made it clear that he wasn't going to discuss it further, and she shrugged.

"You'll need to give her a better reason than that. When she's ready to talk to you, that is. Shall I tell her you saved her?"

"Given our recent history, I doubt she'll be impressed. I'll tell her myself if I decide she needs to know."

Allie nodded, then lapsed into a meditative silence. Strangely enough, he felt comfortable, sitting in the darkness with Raziel's wife, watching the tide roll in. He could feel the last of his resentment slipping away. Sarah was gone, and the best way he could honor her and what they'd had together was to let go, move on.

He closed his eyes, and for a moment he could almost feel her hands on his shoulders, her lips brushing a kiss on the top of his head, her heavy silver braid brushing against him. He kept his eyes closed, soaking in the benediction, and then she was gone.

He opened his eyes, to discover they were wet and stinging. He blessed the darkness, but he knew Allie could see anyway. He cleared his throat. "Shouldn't someone be checking on her?"

"Gretchen is there. I wouldn't have left her if she hadn't stabilized. You know that, Azazel." Her voice was only faintly accusing.

He deserved it. "Yes," he said. He had to say it, and for some reason it didn't gall him. Perhaps it was Sarah's blessing. "Thank you, Allie. Thank you for saving her."

He half expected her to make light of it, but she simply said, "You're welcome."

"Raziel wonders what will happen to her."

"She belongs here. She's like a newborn—this

is her new life, her memories, old and new. We'll find a way to work her into the community."

She didn't ask him if he minded. It was no longer his decision. He'd ceded leadership to Raziel and gone on his quest, his quest to destroy the Lilith. Now he was simply one of the Fallen. And she would be here. Hating him.

"As it shall be," he said, using the old words.

"As it shall be," Allie murmured formally. She glanced over her shoulder. Raziel had come to join them, standing behind them, and the two of them shared a smile, the sort of secret communication he'd once had with Sarah, and he waited for that flash of anger, of jealousy and rage for all that he had lost.

It was gone. Washed clean. Astonishing, when it had ruled his life for so long.

Allie glanced up at Raziel, and he nodded, putting his hands on her shoulders as Sarah had once touched him, leaning down and placing a kiss on her head. The parallel should have disturbed him. Instead, it began to warm a very cold place inside him.

"You're weak, Azazel," Allie said after a moment. "I can feel it. You've been running on sheer nerves. It's been much too long for you, and you know it."

He shook his head. "I'm not ready to go up to the house or go through the ritual."

"No need," she said. And held out her slender wrist.

He glanced up at Raziel in surprise, but Raziel simply nodded. "You need it," he said.

It was against the laws of Sheol to partake of the Source without the full ritual, but now Raziel made the laws. And things were already changing, with Rachel, with him. He wanted to fight the clawing need, to reject this woman, but he couldn't. His need was too strong. He took her wrist in both hands, hesitating a moment. And then bit, delicately, as his fangs extended, and the blood was thick and sweet and healing.

He stopped before he was sated, careful not to push things, and released her arm with the traditional words of thanks.

"Are you certain you've had enough?" she asked, as both healer and Source. He nodded, feeling the strength course through him, filling him with steely power. "Then I'll go check on my patient."

As she moved back to the house, he realized that at some point she'd attained the perfect grace that went with being the Source. He could see it and admire it now.

Raziel took her abandoned seat. "I take it you don't hate her anymore. That's a good thing, brother." He followed Azazel's gaze out to the sea. "And you're at full strength now, I presume. I have a question for you. Allie has decreed that Rachel will stay here. Does that mean you will leave?"

He thought about it. She would hate him, and the sight of her would bring a deep, inexplicable pain. A pain he wasn't going to run from. He'd run from pain for long enough. "No. I will stay."

Raziel nodded. "Good. I suspect we're going to need you. I take it the Truth Breakers were unable to unearth her memories of Lucifer?"

"According to Uriel, they succeeded, for all the good it does us. We were fools to think he would actually pass the information along. And that would have been the first part of her brain they scrubbed clean."

"Naturally. It doesn't matter. She stays."

Azazel nodded, rising. "I'll be in soon."

The sky was inky dark, the moon barely a sliver. He soared upward, past the clouds and mist that always enshrouded Sheol, into the clear, cool night. The stars were pinpricks of light, and he banked and turned, feeling the wind rush past him like fingers through his hair, kissing his face, and he thought of Rachel far below. He had to let go of her, release her as he had released Sarah.

He pushed upward, higher and higher, and the air grew colder. He could see his favorite perch down below, on the edge of the cliff, but he'd sat and brooded long enough. He was pulsing with the energy Allie's blood had given him, and he wanted to glide and soar through the sweet-smelling night air, dancing on the wind.

He moved farther out over the ocean, where the waves rolled on top of the water in little ruffles of foam, and he turned, spun, and plunged downward, hitting the icy water in a smooth, clean dive that barely disturbed the surface.

He went deep into the bracing salt sea, and he felt its healing power rush through him, making him whole once more. He breathed in the water, letting it fill his body, his lungs, then moved upward to breathe in air again. He dove once more, and the dolphins were there, the ones he knew. They welcomed him as one of their own as they swam through the currents, turning over in the pleasure of the water, swimming with their friend with the odd fins.

He lost track of the time he spent in the water. The sun was coming up by the time he tired of it, and he pushed upward again, high enough into the air that the heat dried his clothes so that they were stiff and salt-encrusted, and when he landed lightly on the beach, Michael was waiting for him. Michael, the fighter, who never would have let the Truth Breakers take Rachel.

"Welcome back," he said. "Raziel says you're here to stay this time."

"I am."

Michael nodded. "We'll need you. The few Nephilim that are left are gathering. Turns out the dumb bastards finally realized they could fly."

"Wonderful," Azazel said grimly. For a moment he remembered chaining Rachel in that deserted house in the Australian bush, and he felt sick. In the end, he'd saved her, he reminded himself. He'd saved her twice.

Because he'd tried to kill her twice. He'd been so terrified of a prophecy that he'd been ready to sacrifice her without finding out who and what she really was.

"You'll be ready to fight?" Michael asked.

He thought of Rachel, lying in the hospital bed, so close to death. He thought of the guilt that smothered him. Exactly what Uriel would want. He needed a distraction, and he needed it now. "I am ready to fight," he said.

CHAPTER SEVENTEEN

THE DAYS PASSED. EACH DAY HE asked Allie if Rachel was ready to see him, and each day she said wait, until he thought he'd go mad with it. Once he faced Rachel, he could let go. The prophecy was clearly false, broken. He had been able to turn her over to the Truth Breakers with no hesitation, even if he hadn't been able to keep from coming back for her. He hadn't meant to do that. He'd had the vain hope that they would be merciful, but one look and something had cracked.

He'd feel that way toward anyone. Torture was an abomination, and it was little wonder he felt guilty for handing her over. And he had no excuse for shoving her up against a wall and having sex with her before they took her. He hadn't been able to stop himself, and he'd told himself that if he could come inside her and then give her to the Truth Breakers, then the prophecy must be a lie.

And so he had. He'd proven what he needed to prove, and whatever knowledge she had wedged in her brain about where Lucifer lay trapped had been extracted and stolen. Uriel had it now, though presumably he'd already known it in the first place. When the Supreme Being had passed the reins to the last archangel, he'd ordered him to watch over the universe he'd created. There was no telling what the details were.

Uriel had seized his new role with a vengeance, wielding ancient power to smite evil wherever he could, sending plagues and floods and fires and devastation wherever he saw fit. Some humans saw it as God's curse; more enlightened ones declared such tragedies the law of nature, to be endured with God's help. They had no idea that God's minion had visited disaster upon them.

Just as he'd fed on Azazel's own fear that he was doomed to spend eternity as the mate of a horrific demon. And Azazel had been fool enough to let him.

He was tired of waiting. He was doing his best to get along with Allie, but she was still a strong-minded female who was slowly turning the laws of Sheol upside down, while Raziel watched carefully, seldom restraining her. She ruled the infirmary; she ruled the house and the women. She was the Source for the unmated Fallen, she was omega to Raziel's alpha. But he was getting tired of her shit.

He was perched on the outcropping, high over the ocean and the vast building that housed the Fallen. The moon was shining down, mirrored by the dark sea, and he suddenly surged upward into the dark sky, then settled lightly on the damp sand. The time had come.

He didn't recognize the young girl sitting at the desk in the anteroom of the infirmary. Clearly she'd been left on duty, and he put the Grace of sleep on her lightly, so that she'd wake in a few hours. He didn't want to put Rachel at risk by knocking her caretaker out so thoroughly, but if she needed help Allie would know and leave her bed. Rachel would be in no danger.

He pushed open the door silently and slipped inside. She was asleep, as she had been those first days after he'd brought her and he wouldn't leave her bedside. He could recognize her now. Her battered face was no longer swollen, the bruising faded to an ugly yellow. She was healing, slowly but surely.

She no longer had tubes connected to her body, though she looked very small and frail in the big white bed. It wasn't right. He thought of her as strong, powerful, not a vulnerable human.

She still had bandages around her arms and legs, and her torso looked swollen under the sheet, either from bandages or her injuries. He didn't want to wake her.

He sank down in the chair Allie had banished him from and watched her, contemplating her injuries. Allie's gifts as a healer were extraordinary; such was always the case with the Source, and Rachel would be well very quickly, much faster than with normal human medicine. Raziel and Allie had decreed that she would stay. They hadn't taken her into account.

If he'd learned one thing, it was that Rachel had a mind of her own. The problem was, she wouldn't be safe anywhere else. Uriel hadn't finished with her, and only the walls of Sheol could keep him out. At least for now. Uriel had spent millennia trying to figure out how to breach them, and he'd only succeeded with the Nephilim a few years ago. Sooner or later he was going to come up with an answer, though, and there would be little they could do.

She stirred in her sleep, murmuring something, and he jerked his head up, holding his breath. She slipped back into sleep again, and he relaxed, glancing toward the monitors that kept track of her pulse and her blood pressure—only to see that they were spiking.

His eyes swiveled back to her, and she was looking at him with such complete terror that it shocked him.

"Do not scream," he said, his voice soft so as not to alert anyone.

She was shaking, and he wanted to put his arms around her and pull her against him, soothing her. Except he was the one who was frightening her. "I can't." It was barely more than a breath of sound in a raw, damaged voice, and he remembered that Uriel had said her voice had broken.

"I'm not going to hurt you," he said, starting to rise, but she shrank back, and he quickly sat down again so as not to spook her. "I wanted to see how you are."

There was no missing the flash of contemptuous disbelief in her face. "Why should you care?" she whispered.

That was one question he couldn't answer. "Allie is a very gifted healer." By now he'd gotten used to praising Allie, though it still stuck in his craw just a tiny bit. "She brought you back from the brink of death."

"No thanks to you," she whispered. He'd forgotten she didn't remember he'd saved her. It was hardly enough penance for allowing them to put her through such hell in the first place.

"No thanks to me," he agreed. "But I promise you, you have nothing to fear from me. Not ever again."

"And you lie so well." Her voice was getting weaker, and he knew he was putting a strain on it.

"I never lied to you. I am incapable of lying." It was the truth. He'd explained nothing, but he hadn't lied.

"Get out of here." The words were barely audible, but there was no missing the hatred in them.

It was no more than he'd expected. Not the fear—that had been a surprise. But the hatred and anger were normal. He'd betrayed her in every way a man can betray a woman, sent her off with torturers with his seed inside her. In truth, he was the monster.

No, he wasn't going to tell her he'd changed his mind and gone after her. Too little, too late.

He rose, and stretched out one hand to touch her, wanting the feel of her to be absolutely certain, but she shrank away in such terror and revulsion that he pulled back, knocking against the chair as he went.

"Don't come back," she whispered.

He closed the door silently behind him.

I STILL COULDN'T CRY. GOD, if ever there was a time when I needed to weep, this was it. He was the monster, not me. How could anyone make love with someone and then hand her to her executioner? Not that it was making love. In fact, it was sex, hot and rough and primal, and I'd wanted it just as much as he had. I couldn't remember much—maybe I'd even instigated it. I knew I'd been waiting, longing for him to touch me again, kiss me again.

But I couldn't remember where we'd been. There was water, and a door behind my back. It was night, but it seemed as if it was always night in the Dark City. Wasn't that what they'd called it?

Beloch had been nowhere to be seen. My memory was full of holes—he'd been kind, hadn't he? Almost fatherly, in his book-lined study with the comfortable smell of pipe tobacco. He couldn't have known that they were—

I couldn't think about that. About the things they'd done to me. I'd discovered I could refuse to allow certain things into my memory. There were too many lifetimes, too many horrors to withstand, but I could choose to banish those I couldn't bear.

I needed to banish the Truth Breakers, and the knives, and the cooing sound they made.

Gone. It was that easy. Just as I'd banished the hundreds upon hundreds of years of lying down with monsters. It wasn't this body, and it was over. Gone as well.

I could get rid of Azazel just as easily. Wipe out the memory of his strong hands touching me, his mouth against mine, the way he lifted me on top of him and pushed inside me.

I could get rid of that memory in the pouring rain, when I'd wrapped my legs around him and fought to get more of him. The memory of the climax that had shattered me, thrummed through my body in waves as he'd slowly released me.

And the Nightmen had come.

It would be the wise thing to do. I could remember other sex, unsatisfactory sex with humans, and maybe that was part of my curse. Though wasn't Lilith supposed to arouse men? And I had, but not for myself. I'd aroused them for their wives, for the babies that hadn't yet come. While I had been raped by monsters.

Gone. That was gone. And yet, in the Dark City I had only followed my natural course. I had had sex with a monster, although this one was beautiful, and he had been smooth and strong and hard.

I'd learned pleasure at his hands—maybe that was worth remembering.

Allie and Raziel would protect me from him. I hadn't asked who'd saved me—someone must have known there was trouble. I had no illusions about it: Azazel was important here. They had more than likely been watching him, and had come to save Azazel as much as to save the Lilith.

The reasons didn't matter. I was safe, and would continue to be. Azazel would never hurt me again. Never touch me again. Allie had promised me, and her word was law.

So why did I want to weep?

CHAPTER EIGHTEEN

Azazel took me at my word. I never saw him, not when I walked along the beach, soaking up the sun that somehow managed to shine through the mists that surrounded Sheol. Not at the communal meals; not in the long, spacious halls of the peculiar building. It looked like an old seaside villa from Hollywood days, part bungalow, part mission style. I couldn't remember how I knew that much. There were too many lives for me to remember, and I learned to take my arcane bits of knowledge with equanimity. I knew enough of what was important. That my curse was finally lifted. And that I didn't dare see Azazel.

I wondered if he'd been sent away. I had been welcomed by everyone, the fallen angels whose names were the stuff of legend: Gabriel and Michael, Gadrael and Tamlel, and the lesser-known ones, with names like Cassiel and Nisroc. And their wives, sweet, quiet women whom Allie was trying to drag into the twenty-first century. For the first time in my endless life, I felt safe and happy, cared for and at ease, and I couldn't help but wonder if the fact that there were no babies in Sheol had something to do with it. I wouldn't have to watch a baby die, ever again.

I could help, though. The women assured me they had willingly traded the hope of children for the rich love they shared with their husbands, and never regretted the loss. They told me this as they wept in my arms, and my heart ached for them. At least I knew I hadn't brought the curse of infertility to them—it had been a gift from an angry God, along with other curses they refused to speak of.

I worked in the infirmary alongside Allie, tending the small hurts and minor illnesses. Up until recently there hadn't been so much as a cold among the Fallen, but that had changed. It had started seven years ago, with the loss of so many in the battle with the Nephilim, and the inhabitants of Sheol were slowly becoming more vulnerable.

"I'm not sure whether that's a bad or a good

thing," Allie confided one afternoon as we sat out in the sun. For once we were doing absolutely nothing. Allie had an almost feverish energy and was seldom still, but for now we simply sat, our hands idle. "I used to call them the Stepford wives—everyone was perfect; no one gained weight or had colds or even got so much as a splinter. It was creepy. But once the Nephilim broke through, everything changed. The wives stopped being so acquiescent, the men became less autocratic. Some of the women have even told me the sex is better, though I find that hard to believe. Sex with the Fallen is . . . miraculous, no matter what the circumstances."

I felt my face heat, and I turned away to glance toward the mountains, hoping she wouldn't notice. "Do they have magic dicks or something?" I said in my raspy voice, trying to sound cynical and unconcerned. Everything about me had recovered from the trauma the Truth Breakers had inflicted, both inside and out. Everything but the wound of Azazel's betrayal, and my voice, now permanently raw and broken. Allie assured me it was very sexy. I couldn't see any particular advantage in that.

I felt her eyes on me. "Don't you know?"

So here was the question. Should I lie to her, the woman who had saved my life, and protect my tenuous peace of mind? Or did I admit to a truth she probably already knew?

But Allie was a better friend than that. She simply moved on, letting me avoid giving a direct answer. "I think it's more a case of the Fallen only taking their true mates. When they're between wives, they will sometimes indulge in casual sex, but I gather those couplings are simply enjoyable, not life-altering. That's how I knew I was supposed to be Raziel's bonded mate. It took him too damned long to admit it, of course; but then men, even the fallen-angel variety, are a pain in the ass."

Life-altering? The moments with Azazel deep inside me went far beyond enjoyable, but I refused to believe it meant anything. Besides, he was gone, banished, and I didn't have to—

"Raziel requires your presence."

I let out a little shriek. I hadn't heard him approach, had had no idea he was anywhere near. And suddenly he stood in front of us, the dark creature who'd followed me, kidnapped me, loved me, and betrayed me.

No, he hadn't loved me. He'd simply fucked me, following orders. Orders from Uriel.

Allie's worried eyes were on me. "What does he want? Tell him he can wait."

"He can't wait," Azazel said, his blue eyes boring into me. Even in this world of color they were still vivid, hard, unreadable. "There is news."

Allie hesitated, glancing at me again. "Then come with me—"

"No," Azazel said. His look was physical, like a touch on my newly healed body, like a caress, and I wanted to close my eyes and revel in it. I ignored it and him as I rose, preparing to follow Allie.

He caught my arm. Just like that, he put his hand on my arm, and I was helpless to break free as a rush of feeling swept over me. "Rachel and I have unfinished business. We'll follow in a moment."

Allie cast me an apologetic glance. "He's right. I've been keeping him at a distance, but you need to deal with it sooner or later."

"Deal with what?" I said coldly. Azazel's flinch was so brief I might have imagined it, but I knew what had caused it. My ruined voice.

So he was capable of feeling guilt. So what?

"The elephant in the room," Allie said incomprehensibly. A moment later she was gone, leaving me there on the beach, with Azazel still touching me.

"What do you want?" I rasped. In truth, it *was* a sexy bedroom voice. For what little good it did me. "If you're going to tell me you're sorry, I don't want to hear it."

"I'm not sorry."

Now, why didn't that surprise me? "Then why are we talking?"

"I did what I had to do. I had no choice, and if I had to do it over, I would do it again." His voice was cool, matter-of-fact.

"Including fucking me up against that door in the pouring rain? That was what you had to do? What you'd do over again?"

"Find me a door."

I swallowed convulsively. So I wasn't immune to him. That shouldn't surprise me. Fucking Azazel was the first sexual pleasure I had known, I told myself, deliberately crude. That was a powerful influence, no matter how epic his betrayal.

"What do you want from me?"

He said nothing, and I made the mistake of looking up into his eyes. They weren't icy cold at all, I saw with sudden shock. They were filled with heat, an earthy desire that shook me as I stared at him, and I wondered what he could see in mine.

And then I knew, as he leaned down and covered my mouth with his, and instead of pushing him away I came closer, my body drifting against his as his arm came around my waist.

He held me there, his hand on my hip, and I could feel his erection. My reaction was immediate: I was wet, longing for him, my nipples hardening in anticipation, my secret flesh quivering for his touch. His tongue pushed inside my mouth, as I wanted his cock pushing inside me, and I wanted him so desperately that everything disappeared, his betrayal, the pain, the horror. I needed him inside me; I wanted to shove him down on the sand and mount him.

I shivered, trying to fight it, but I was kissing him back, and that knowledge was a shame so great I froze.

He must have felt my sudden chill. He set me away from him, seemingly without reluctance, and his eyes were hidden by hooded lids. I didn't have to look down to know he was still hard, to know he wanted me. Though I wondered why.

He had had others, better. Women he'd loved, presumably, though the idea of Azazel and love seemed inconsistent. "Is this part of some sadistic entertainment for you?" I said in my newly husky voice. "New ways to inflict pain?"

He didn't react. "You have had ample time to deal with your ordeal in the Dark City." He was cool and even, as always. "You need to come back where you belong."

I was breathless at his gall. "And where is that?"

"In my bed."

Fury and disbelief overpowered me, and I simply stared at him in disbelief. He took my arm, and I yanked away, stumbling back.

"We need to join the Council," he said patiently. "I'm not about to ravish you on the sand."

I wanted him on the sand. I was suddenly reminded of an old children's book. In a chair, in the air, on a boat, in a coat. On the sand, with your hand. Every way I could take him. I drew myself up to my full height, hoping I was radiating dignity but knowing I probably simply looked sulky. "In your dreams," I said.

"And yours."

Had he seen my dreams? The wickedly erotic memories that woke me with mini climaxes? No, there was no way he could see inside my mind.

"I can read your thoughts," he said with horrifying frankness. "Not all of them, but enough, if I try, though you are more difficult than most. I can't see much of your dreams, but I can imagine. I have the same dreams."

I couldn't stand another moment talking to him. I started past him, heading toward the house, and if he'd touched me I would have run. But he didn't. He simply fell into step beside me, and it wasn't until we'd made our way to the door of the meeting hall that he whispered, "Mini climaxes?" in a soft voice, and I could feel the heat rise and stain my face.

They were all gathered. The Fallen were seated around the table, with one chair left for Azazel. The only woman at the table was Allie—the other wives were seated in the back, and I'd started toward them when Azazel took my hand. "She belongs at the table."

I desperately wanted to yank my hand free, but there were too many people watching, and I felt suddenly shy. "He's right," Allie said. "Someone get her a chair."

"I don't need—" I began, but Azazel overruled me.

"This is of concern to you as well."

Someone drew another chair up to the vast table beside Azazel's, and I had no choice. I sat, trying to keep apart from him in the confined space, but when he slid in next to me his thigh brushed against mine, and there was no way I could retreat, short of climbing into Michael's lap—and even I stopped short of climbing into the archangel Michael's lap, whether he'd fallen or not.

"Word has come to us," Raziel said. "Uriel has found Lucifer's tomb."

This meant nothing to me. Allie had told me the Fallen were searching for the place where the Supreme Being had imprisoned the first of the Fallen, but it had nothing to do with me.

But all eyes were upon me, an unsettling situation, and I felt Azazel's hand on my thigh, calming me, restraining me, copping a feel, I wasn't sure which. I wanted to scuttle out of the way, but Michael was too close, and with his shaven head and tattooed body he looked almost lethal. I stayed where I was.

Finally Allie said, "Stop looking at her. Don't you realize she doesn't have any idea what's going on?"

It was Raziel who spoke. "You told Uriel where Lucifer is," he said, his measured voice expressing no censure. "That's what the Truth Breakers were trying to retrieve from you."

"I should point out that my visit with the Truth Breakers wasn't my idea, it was Azazel's," I said with remarkable calm. "And if you hadn't sent someone to rescue me, I would have died."

"In fact, it was the Council's decision to send you to the Truth Breakers. We didn't know that the Dark City was part of Uriel's kingdom."

"Well, that's all right, then," I said, letting the sarcasm through. "Didn't you think there might be an easier way to get the information from me?"

"No."

God, he could be just as monosyllabic as Azazel.

"The bottom line is, if Azazel hadn't turned me

over to the torturers, they wouldn't know anything about where Lucifer is. And don't ask me—I don't remember anything but . . . pain." My ruined voice broke a little on that, despite my best effort, and I glared at Raziel. I wanted to glare at the man beside me, but that would mean I actually had to look at him, and I couldn't trust myself to do that.

"They took that memory from you," Azazel said from beside me.

"Is that why you sent someone to save me at the last minute?" I asked Raziel, ignoring him. "Because you realized they were the bad guys? Or because you figured they'd already stripped my memories of anything useful?"

I could see Azazel make some kind of gesture out of the corner of my eye, but Raziel ignored him. "I didn't send anyone to save you. You're a demon. Your well-being isn't our concern—you were expendable."

"Then who—"

"None of that matters," Azazel interrupted. "The question is, what are we going to do now?"

Raziel's eyebrows slammed together in displeasure. "I think you should answer Rachel's question."

I had the sudden idea that I wasn't going to like the answer. No one else was volunteering the information—no one was saying anything—so I turned my head to look at Azazel.

It hit me anew, my longing for him, for the monster who'd delivered me to torturers. It was crazy and wrong, and I would die before he found out. "So tell me," I said calmly.

The bright blue eyes, watching me without emotion. The gorgeously shaped mouth that had kissed me. The hands that had turned me over to the Truth Breakers without a moment's hesitation.

"I brought you back."

I froze, going through a mental litany of curses. I was just going to shut up now, before I found out anything else I didn't want to hear. What was I supposed to do, thank the son of a bitch? I couldn't move away from the insistent pressure of his thigh against mine, and knew that if I tried to leave the table, he'd simply force me back down. But I could move his restraining hand. I picked it off my thigh and deposited it on his own. He left it there.

"We have decided to follow the prophecy, since fighting it has only made things worse," Raziel was saying, though whether to me or the others I wasn't sure. "The demon Lilith will wed Asmodeus, king of demons, and together they will rule hell. They will raise Lucifer up from darkness, and they will beget a new generation of the Fallen."

"But we know that's impossible," Allie spoke

up. "For one thing, Rachel is no longer the Lilith. Her servitude is broken."

"How do you know?" her husband said.

Allie ignored him. "As for Azazel, he's only referred to as Asmodeus in a few obscure texts. Some people think he's an entirely different demon."

"I might point out that I'm not a demon." Azazel's voice beside me might almost have held humor, but I knew that was impossible. Besides, if he found anything about this funny, I'd hate him even more than I already did.

"On top of that, we can't reproduce, so how they can beget a new generation of the Fallen is beyond me. The prophecy is just one of the twisted stories Uriel put about to torment the wives of the Fallen and sow discord among us. It's wicked enough that we offered Rachel up to them in our desperation to find Lucifer. If you'll remember, I was against it in the first place. And it not only didn't help us, it gave Uriel the advantage, and in the meantime we lost our humanity."

"My love," Raziel said gently, "we're not human."

"Well, I am," Allie snapped.

"In fact, you're not."

She glared at him across the table, and a lesser man would have watched himself. "Are you suggesting we offer Rachel up as a virgin sacrifice once more, even though she no longer has anything we need?"

"That remains to be seen. Asmodeus and the Lilith will rule—"

"Enough, already. She's no longer Lilith, and we don't know if Azazel ever was Asmodeus. Come up with a better reason."

"How about this one," Azazel said from beside me. "Uriel believes that prophecy, whether it's true or not. It unnerves him, frightens him, and there's not much that can frighten the archangel. And frightened creatures make mistakes. If he believes he has something to fear from us, he'll go straight for where Lucifer is entombed, and he'll lead us there."

"So what do you suggest we do?" Michael demanded. "Sit and wait? Wait for him to uncover Lucifer and destroy him?"

"He can't do that. He can't override the Supreme Being's edicts, which is why he hasn't destroyed us. We live in the curse placed upon us by an angry and vengeful God. Uriel's not divine." Raziel's voice was measured.

"Even though he thinks he is," Allie said. There was a ripple of laughter around the table, which astonished me. I wouldn't have thought these grim creatures capable of laughter.

"So what do we do?" Michael repeated.

"The answer is obvious." Azazel's cool, deep voice almost seemed to vibrate within me, he was so close. "He will attempt to wipe out the first threat. He's already tried it and failed, which must gall him. If he believes the Lilith and Asmodeus are truly mated, he will panic. The threat of the union is at least twofold: not only that we will find Lucifer, but that we will beget children and the curse will be broken. If the Fallen can have children, then our numbers increase, and we grow stronger."

I was speechless with outrage, and by the time I found words Michael had already overridden me. "And you will reign in hell. Uriel has joined heaven and hell, so if he believes the prophecy, he will fear that you will reign over his own kingdom."

"The Dark City?" Azazel said. "He can have it."

"And if you bond, you will find Lucifer and raise him, and our army will have a leader," Michael added, his voice tight. "It sounds like a good plan."

Michael, the warrior angel—of course he'd think anything involving battle was a good plan. Once more I opened my mouth to protest, but no words came out. It was my damned voice. There still wasn't much to it, and any stress or heavy breathing shut it off entirely.

"It's not without its risks," Raziel said. "But as

far as I can see, it's our best option. Are we all agreed? Azazel and Rachel will mate?"

I pulled away, knocking my chair over as I went. Azazel could have stopped me, but he let me go, and I ended up with my back against the wall, literally and figuratively.

Finally I found my voice. "Hell, no."

Chapter Nineteen

THEY ALL JUST LOOKED AT ME AS if I'd grown a second head. "You heard me," I said fiercely. "Hell, no."

Azazel's eyes were on me, unreadable as always. "Why have you suddenly become so squeamish? We've already done most of it."

Heat flooded my face. "Yes, you fucked me on Beloch's orders. You see how far that got us."

Damn, everyone's eyes were moving between Azazel and me as if this were the world's best tennis match. That, or a soap opera.

"I disagree. I found it most instructive," he said in his cool, emotionless voice. "It proved we're physically compatible."

"Not anymore," I snarled.

Allie jumped in, thank God. "Azazel, you

haven't thought this through. You can't risk mating with her. It's too dangerous."

"He already has 'mated' with me, didn't you hear him? And why should it be dangerous? I'm not a praying mantis—I don't bite the heads off my partners once we're finished. Even if they deserve it," I added.

Allie shook her head. "You don't understand. And really, you don't need to. This is simply too dangerous for Azazel to attempt. He knows he can mate only with his chosen one. If he mates with a casual partner, he could die."

I had no idea what the hell she was talking about, but everyone else in the room seemed to understand. I stood there, wishing I hadn't jumped up. Now I felt foolish and vulnerable, the only one in the room standing. I was being too emotional—it had always been one of my failings.

"She's right," Raziel said finally. "You can't risk it."

"It is no risk," Azazel said. "I choose her."

There was dead silence in the room, shock mixed with doubt. I opened my mouth to announce that *I* sure as fuck hadn't chosen *him*, then wisely shut it again. Spouting off wasn't getting me anywhere.

"Azazel, her blood will poison you," Allie said gently.

"If I am wrong, perhaps. But I am not. Consider the prophecy."

"If you believe all the prophecies, the world should have ended a dozen times already," she said stubbornly. "You don't really believe that you and Rachel will reign in hell. Only Uriel does."

"Yes. And Uriel will know when we mate. When I take her blood. Only then will we—"

"Wait a minute." I pushed away from the wall. "What's all this about blood?"

"Sit down," Raziel said, an order, not a suggestion. I didn't want to, but Azazel took my wrist and yanked, ungently, and I was crammed in beside him again. This time his hand held both my wrists beneath the table, and there was no escape.

"I can explain this to her when we are alone," Azazel said, but Raziel made a dismissive gesture.

"Explain it to her now," he said.

Azazel was watching me, his expression impassive. "Very well. When we fell, we were sentenced to eternal damnation, with no hope of redemption. We were cursed to watch our loved ones grow old and die; there would be no children, and we would ferry the dead between this world and the next. But when the second waves of angels followed us, they became the Nephilim, abominations."

"I remember," I muttered, trying to yank my hands away. His long fingers about my wrists might as well have been manacles.

"The Supreme Being added a new punishment. The Nephilim, the abominations, could only go out in the dark, and they would survive on flesh." He hesitated for only a moment, then continued, "The Fallen are the blood-eaters. We must survive on the blood of our chosen mates, or, if one of us has recently lost a mate, the Source provides enough to keep him healthy until he mates again."

"What's the Source?" God knows why I asked that stupid question, with all the absurdity washing over me.

"I am," Allie said quietly. "I am married to the Alpha, and I provide the blood for those like Azazel and Michael, until each finds his bonded mate. It's a complicated process, and a mistake can be fatal. Only my blood and that of his chosen is safe for one of the Fallen. If he tries to drink from anyone else, he sickens and often dies."

"God," I muttered. "As if this weren't crazy enough, we get vampires too."

"Blood-eaters," Allie said gently. "From the Bible."

"Seriously?" For a moment I was genuinely

distracted, wondering where in the Old Testament the vampires lurked. Where was the Book of Twilight, between Proverbs and Psalms? And then things became clearer. "*My* blood? You think he's going to drink *my* blood? Are you out of your mind?"

"I agree," Allie said. "You're grasping at straws, Azazel. If she is your bonded mate, we all would have known it. If you agree to this, you'll kill both of you."

"Uh, explain that," I broke in, my voice sounding even rougher. "You said my blood would poison *him*."

Allie said nothing, and Azazel continued, "If you aren't my chosen mate, there's the possibility that I might drain you before I die. In some circumstances the need becomes more and more powerful, uncontrollably so. It happened a few years ago, with Ephrael."

"We can't afford to risk Azazel," Raziel concluded.

Not to mention me, I thought grimly. "No."

At the same time, Azazel said, "Yes."

"You can't make me." This came out sounding like a playground taunt, but I was past caring.

"I could," Azazel said smoothly.

Before I could protest, Raziel broke in. "No, we can't make you. Indeed, there is no question but that the body and the blood must be freely given. If you say no, the discussion is at an end."

Dead silence reigned again, making me feel guilty and edgy. "It's not as if the fate of the world is hanging on this," I protested.

The expression on Allie's face gave me the answer.

"Azazel," Raziel said, "you must find another partner. Clearly you are mistaken in thinking Rachel is your chosen one. You must look elsewhere."

"No!" I looked around me, not able to believe that protest had erupted from my damaged throat. It had nothing to do with rational thought. The idea of Azazel claiming another sent a white-hot rage through my body. Which was another surprise.

"I beg your pardon?" Raziel said.

I wouldn't look at Azazel. I knew his expression would register triumph, and I couldn't bear it. "I said no," I repeated. "You don't have time for him to find some hypothetical chosen mate. It's like looking for true love—it never shows up when you go searching."

"Rachel, a chosen mate *is* a Fallen's true love," Allie explained.

I squirmed. Nothing like digging the hole deeper. "If he goes searching, he's even more likely to find the wrong one, and he could die," and damned if my broken voice didn't crack on the word *die*.

"Then what do you suggest?" Raziel's voice dripped sarcasm. "We just wait for the world to end?"

Shit. So it was all coming down to me? I felt as if I were suffocating, all the millennia crushing me, and I couldn't breathe. "I need to get out of here," I said in a panicked voice, which of course could barely be heard. "Please. I need to think."

The hands around my wrists released me, and I moved before he could change his mind, pulling away from the table. No one tried to stop me, and I ran from the room, practically falling in my haste to get away.

The sun was shining through the eternal mist that covered Sheol. Everyone was in the council chamber—the only living things outside were the seagulls wheeling and mewing overhead. I walked down to the water's edge, staring as the waves crested and spilled toward me.

I knew now why I was afraid of the ocean: I had been drowned by a man I thought loved me, hundreds and hundreds of years ago.

I made myself sit on the sand, watching the roiling water as the tide came in, closer and closer. So the fate of the world came down to me? I would have laughed if it weren't so damnable. Why did it have to come to this?

I hadn't smothered babies. I hadn't lured men to their doom. But I had done other reprehensible things in my rage as the Lilith. I was a storm demon in ancient Mesopotamia, whipping up wind that buried towns and all their inhabitants in sand. I had brought down hurricanes and typhoons and tornadoes; I had rained destruction on those who had hurt me over the years. Once I'd escaped from my sexual servitude to the demons, my rage had been monumental, and I had visited it upon everyone.

I had penance to complete. On the one hand, the entire world might be destroyed and an evil old man would triumph. On the other hand, I could pay for my sins and save the world, simply by having sex with a creature who made my bones melt, no matter how much I hated him. I wanted him just as much as I wanted him dead, and no common sense seemed to talk me out of it. In truth, I might not be his chosen one. But whether I liked it or not, he was mine.

The answer was clear. It might kill him, which was fine with me. It might kill us both, which was, oddly, equally acceptable. But I knew it wouldn't. I knew the truth, though I refused to face it head-on.

The only thing I didn't like was the blood part.

I rose. The tide had come in far enough to touch my bare toes, and they tingled, flexing, almost drawing me in. I pulled back, though. I was afraid of the ocean, I reminded myself. Afraid of drowning.

I walked back into the house, kicking the sand off my feet as I went. I could hear their voices raised in argument, too many people talking at once. I pushed open the door, and everyone fell silent.

My eyes went to Azazel's. His face was impassive, pale, and beautiful. He already knew the answer. I looked away.

"I'll do it."

AZAZEL WATCHED THE CONFUSION ABOUT him with a calm he hadn't felt in years. He wasn't going to think about when, or how, or why. He distrusted prophecies. But he knew this was meant to be.

The assembly room had emptied quickly after Rachel's blunt announcement, with Allie and the women spiriting her away and the other Fallen heading off. Only Michael and Raziel remained. Michael, the warrior, the loner, who seldom mated and subsisted on the bare minimum of the Source's blood. He had that lean, hungry look, his hair shaved close, his muscled, tattooed arms tight with anger. Raziel was looking equally disturbed, ready for another kind of battle. Azazel knew what was coming.

"You needn't bother trying to talk me out of it," he said. "The decision has been made."

"You can change your mind," Raziel said. "We've barely made do without you for most of the last seven years. I don't know what we'd do if you died."

"You have a death wish," Michael said in a rough voice before Azazel could argue. "We've all seen it."

Denying it would be useless, even if he could. And these were the two men he trusted most in the world. "*Had* a death wish," Azazel corrected him. "And you're a fine one to talk of death wishes, Michael. You storm into any battle you can find—it's a wonder you've survived so long."

"Don't change the subject," he said. "Battle is in my nature; it's my purpose in life. Yours is to rule."

"Not any longer. Raziel rules, and rules wisely. I have another role to play, and I no longer fight it. As for my death wish—it would be useless to deny it. Sarah's death was . . . too much. I had no warning, no preparation, and I was tired of it all. But I've changed my mind."

"Because you've fallen in love with a demon?" Raziel arched an eyebrow. "Forgive me if I find that difficult to believe."

"She's no more a demon than I am. Which I suppose is a possibility, if you read certain scrolls," he added with uncharacteristic humor. He had begun to find certain things oddly amusing recently, which still managed to astonish him.

"That still begs the question. Are you telling us you're in love with the woman whose death you've been seeking for the last seven years?"

"No. Of course not. But there remains a connection, for good or ill, and it's our only hope."

"And if you die?" Michael said.

Azazel shrugged. "Then I die. I've lived an endless life; I've been on earth for millennia. I am not afraid of death, even if I no longer embrace it."

"What if death is some eternal damnation we haven't figured out?" Raziel demanded.

"Even then. But I doubt that will be the case. I think for those of us who are cursed, our fate will be an eternal nothingness. With just enough awareness to recognize it."

"It sounds like hell to me," Michael grumbled.

"It sounds peaceful," Azazel said. "But it is not my time, and won't be. We will mate and bond, and Uriel will know, and it will drive him insane with worry."

"And you're willing to put up with her being your bonded mate? Even if your feelings are, shall we say, lukewarm, you know as well as I do what bonding does to a female. She'll be tied to you, and there won't be any escape."

"I know."

"She'll be taking Sarah's place," Michael said with devastating bluntness, going straight for the heart, the warrior whose arrow was true.

"I know," Azazel said again. "But she will not serve as the Source. As far as I can tell, she has no powers left to her—she's fully human. And if we find we are not compatible, there are endless jobs I'm needed for away from Sheol. I don't anticipate her being a problem."

"All right," Raziel said finally. "Just make sure you don't drain her. It would solve my problem, but Uriel might think it would get in the way of a happy marriage."

"The corpse bride," Michael said with a dark laugh. "Why not?"

Azazel said nothing.

THE PROBLEM WITH EAVESDROPPING WAS that you never heard good stuff, like someone talking about your intelligence and beauty, or hell, even something boring like the weather. You were more than likely to hear something you'd be better off not hearing. Otherwise they would have said it to your face.

I was being ridiculous, of course. Why should I think he'd fallen in love with me, simply because he'd announced I was his chosen? I imagined a chosen mate in this clearly patriarchal society was simply whomever he fancied who would hold still long enough. The whole thing about poisoned blood was bogus. In fact, the whole thing about blood was probably bullshit. It had nothing to do with us.

Except that I remembered in the darkness, in the rain, I'd bit him, tearing his skin, licking at his blood. Why? I was no blood-eater. It apparently was a curse for the Fallen alone, yet I'd sought his out. Maybe I was simply kinky when I was so aroused that I couldn't think. Anything was possible, considering I had never been so aroused in my life.

It would serve him right if I bit him again, but I doubted he'd care. In fact, I thought, bored forbearance was the way to deal with things, since that was most likely how he'd handle it. So what if I'd experienced astonishing pleasure with his lean, beautiful body? I could control my own reactions. He could do anything he wanted, and I'd simply think about something else.

It would drive him crazy.

"What are you grinning at?" Allie demanded, coming up beside me. "You look positively wicked."

"We all have wicked thoughts," I said serenely, moving away from my listening post. In truth, it hadn't been my fault. I'd simply gone in search of some quiet, finding it in the low-slung chairs out on one of the decks. I hadn't realized it led off from the assembly room.

"Come see your rooms."

"The bed in the infirmary is just fine—"

"No, I'm talking about Azazel's rooms. And yours."

"I am not—I repeat, not—going to share rooms with Azazel. I'll mate with him, do the bonding-blood thing, but that's it. Afterward we can go our separate ways."

Allie shook her head. "No, you can't. It's permanent. A tie that can't be broken, except by death."

"Death didn't seem to break the tie between Azazel and Sarah." I hated the thought of her existence, even though she had been only one of an endless line of human wives he'd outlived.

"That was more the circumstances of her death than the tie between them," Allie said gently. "Sarah would have let him go, wanted him to let go. But Azazel can be very stubborn, and he was filled with rage and had no way to vent it."

"Except to go after a demon. Why me? Why did he suddenly decide that he had to kill me?"

"Because of the prophecy, of course. You were supposed to take Sarah's place. He wanted to make certain that was impossible." She was trying to make it reasonable, but I wasn't buying it.

"By disposing of the demon," I said.

"Yes. But you need to realize he didn't know you were no longer a demon," she said fairly. "He thought you were a monster who killed babies."

"He shouldn't believe the bad publicity."

"He wasn't thinking clearly."

"And I'm supposed to forgive him? Because he didn't know?"

"I don't know that he wants your forgiveness," Allie said. "I don't think he's there yet. He's too caught up in guilt."

"Tough," I snapped, feeling brutal. "I'm not sharing the rooms, the bed he shared with his beloved Sarah." I was horrified to realize that I sounded jealous. What was wrong with me?

"You won't be. These are new rooms. It seemed wisest—Azazel is better off without the Alpha quarters."

"But I thought Raziel was the Alpha." I was trying not to think about Saint Sarah and her sleeping arrangements. I was trying not to think about why I was feeling such resentment. But I was being eaten up with jealousy.

"Raziel has only been the Alpha since Sarah died. The only Alpha the Fallen have ever had besides Azazel. So you don't have to worry about any old memories getting in the way of your relationship."

"We don't have a relationship," I said.

Allie just smiled.

A few minutes later she pushed open the heavy wooden door to the suite and gestured me inside. I paused for a moment, taking it in.

The living room was beautiful. Almost Japanese in its simplicity, with low-slung couches and lower tables, it felt quiet and peaceful. Almost as if it were waiting for someone.

"The bedroom's just beyond," Allie said helpfully, and I couldn't avoid it.

It was beautiful as well, with a huge bed as the centerpiece. A bed I'd share with Azazel, I thought, grimacing. It was a lovely room, and the bathroom was a sybarite's dream. I could be happy in these rooms. If I didn't have to share them.

"Whose rooms were these?" I asked, running my hand along the thick silk coverlet on the bed. It was deep red, the color of wine. The color of blood, I thought absently. Maybe they wanted to hide the stains.

"Tam's last wife was into decorating, and she wanted to make a honeymoon suite. No one's used it—you won't find any memories here."

I took one last look around me, then nodded and headed back into the living room. "All right," I said. "I like it. The question is, where do I sleep until we do this mating thing?"

Allie's expression was one of grave concern. "Didn't you realize, Rachel? It's going to be tonight."

Shit, I thought, taking another look around me. "What if I'm not ready?"

"Have you changed your mind? You're allowed to."

"No, I haven't changed my mind. I just hadn't thought it would be so soon."

"We might as well get it over and done with," Azazel's voice came from the doorway.

Chapter Twenty

She looked as if she expected him to cut her throat in order to drink her blood, Azazel thought grimly. He still wasn't sure why the hell she'd agreed to this. He'd expected he'd have to spend days, weeks, breaking down her resistance. No one had been more shocked when she'd returned to the council chamber and announced she'd do it.

She had a trace of sunburn on her nose. No wonder—with her flaming hair she had very pale skin, and she'd headed straight out into the midday sun. He'd kept an eye on her through the council-room windows, watched her as she sat staring at the water. He'd known the moment she'd made up her mind, known by the squaring of her shoulders. He just hadn't known what that decision would be.

And now she was here, in the Alpha's rooms, looking at him like he was her worst nightmare. She was right. If he'd left her alone two years ago, she could have had a peaceful life. The demon inside her had probably already left her, though he wasn't intuitive enough to recognize its disappearance. He could only trust Allie's word.

But it was too late for what-ifs. She was wearing some shapeless white thing, and he hated it. He wanted to tear it off her, with his teeth if need be. He wanted Allie to get the hell out of there and leave them alone. He could smell Rachel's blood through her skin.

He smiled politely. He'd spent too much time hating both of the women before him, wanting them both dead, and it was all connected to Sarah. To missing her as if a piece of himself had been cut out.

He wasn't going to let that happen again. It was too painful, and it spilled over onto the innocent. He wasn't going to feel that obsessive love again. He would mate with Rachel, bond with her, and that would be that. Uriel would be enraged, and they could concentrate on fighting him, not worrying about wives and mates and sex and blood.

Sex and blood. He looked at Rachel and his nostrils flared. "Why don't you leave us, Allie?" he said in his even voice. He had worked eons to perfect the cool unconcern he usually displayed, and he wasn't about to give it away now.

"Why?" Rachel said nervously.

But Allie merely gave her an encouraging smile and slipped out the door, closing it behind her.

For a moment he wondered if she'd make a run for it. "You can always change your mind," he said softly.

"And have the fate of the world weighing on my shoulders? I don't think so. If all I have to do is lie back and let you do me, then I think I can manage."

"*Do* you?" he echoed, startled and amused.

"I've decided I don't like the word *fuck*," she said primly. "So, exactly how do we go about accomplishing this?"

At that point he did smile. He couldn't help it. She was not happy with the situation, and he couldn't blame her. "I think we managed well enough before."

"I mean, do you bite me before or after?"

She was nervous, which surprised him, given the sex they'd had both in her room in the Dark City and outside in the pouring rain with the Nightmen bearing down on them. It had been intense, visceral, animalistic, strong enough to shake him to his bones. He wouldn't have thought she'd retain any shyness after that. "I thought you remembered everything from before," he said. "You're acting like a scared virgin, not a succubus."

"I wasn't a succubus!"

"You bedded down with monsters."

"And I'm doing it again," she shot back. "The good thing is, I don't remember it. With luck, I'm going to forget all about you."

"No, you're not," he said. "Not ever." And he started toward her.

I HELD MY GROUND. HE probably wanted me to run, to be afraid, but I knew there was nothing to be afraid of. He wouldn't hurt me, not deliberately. I had agreed to this, and my motives weren't completely noble. I wanted to see if having sex with him was as devastating an experience as it had been before, before he'd betrayed me. I wanted to see if this time I could resist him. I wanted to see if I was the weak, useless creature I feared I was. I wanted . . . I wanted him.

He didn't pull me into his arms, as I'd expected. I was prepared to be stiff and unyielding, but he made no attempt to touch me. He simply stood there, too tall, looming over me in his dark clothes, while I was wearing the flowing white pajamas Allie had brought me. It seemed symbolic.

He reached out and undid the first button on

the front of my loose white jacket, his touch so light that I didn't feel it, just felt the button give way. He moved to the second, again that deft touch, and cool air danced against my skin.

I swallowed. My heart was hammering, and I tried to remember tricks I had learned, ways to slow my heartbeat and my breathing, ways to calm my body. I tried to picture a cool, glassy pool. Another button gone. Imagined lying in a field of green, looking up into the blue, blue sky, watching the clouds chase each other as birds sang noisily. Another button, and I didn't think there were many left. I wasn't going to look down—that would make things worse. I closed my eyes, humming in my mind, some nonsense song to try to drive away the feel of the cool air against my suddenly hot skin. He reached the last button, and it was all I could do not to jump away from him.

I could think of nothing to distract me as he pushed the jacket off my shoulders, letting it slide down my arms and onto the floor, so that I was standing there in a loose tank top, the drawstring pants, and nothing more. The Fallen didn't seem to believe in underwear, and I'd had to insist on the tank top to wear beneath the clothes, despite Allie's arguments. He surveyed me for a long moment, tilting his head slightly as his heavy-lidded gaze washed over me.

"Try counting to one hundred in Latin," he suggested affably, reaching for the hem of the tank top. "That might work."

I glared at him. I'd forgotten he could occasionally read my thoughts. "Do you know how annoying that is?" I said, trying to work up a good head of steam.

"I don't care." Before I realized what he was doing, he'd skinned me out of the tank top and tossed it on the floor, leaving me half-naked.

Okay, he'd already seen me that way. My nipples tightened instinctively in the warm room, remembering his touch on them, his mouth on them, sucking, and I—

I wasn't going to get aroused. Cool water, I thought, mentally letting it wash over my heated skin. He didn't touch my breasts, when I was expecting him to, had steeled myself against it, and somehow that was even more arousing. The anticipation was making the blood pool everywhere it needed to. Blood, I reminded myself, trying to cool the heat in me. For some reason it only made me hotter.

He was going to unfasten the drawstring next, and the pants would go sliding onto the floor and I'd be naked, and there wasn't a damned thing I could do about it. Not without going back on my word. I waited, impatient.

But he didn't. Instead he picked me up, and at his touch I froze, remembering his arms supporting me against that wooden door, remembering his strength, remembering his betrayal. Wanting to cry, when despite my lack of demonhood I still hadn't been able to summon tears, only dry, racking sobs when no one was around.

There would be no tears in front of Azazel. He carried me into the bedroom, even though I was stiff as a board, and set me down on the huge bed. A second later he followed, kneeling over me.

"Uh, don't you think we ought to pull down the covers?" I said nervously.

"Why? Do you think we'll mess them up?"

Asshole, I thought, glaring at him.

"Green fields and blue skies, Rachel," he said. "Lie back and think of England, remember?"

I lay back, more to get my breasts out of his way than for any other reason. I was still expecting him to pull off the loose pants, but he did nothing, and I wondered if he was going to bite me first.

"You didn't answer my question," I said, my broken voice edgy.

"And which question was that?"

"Are you going to bite me before or after sex?"

His bright blue eyes met mine. "During," he said, and put his hand between my legs.

I arched off the bed, surprised, aroused by his

touch through the fabric. Reflexively I tried to close my legs, but he moved one knee between them, keeping them apart, as his long fingers moved between my legs, touching me through the light cotton. "Why are you wet, demon?" he whispered. "You're not supposed to be liking this."

"I'm . . . I'm not a demon any longer," I said in a tight voice, trying to fight the insidious feelings that were sweeping through me. His touch was light, but even I could feel the dampness as he slid the cloth against me.

"No," he said, leaning forward, one hand braced on the bed, the other still between my legs. "Only to me."

I felt sorrow and disappointment begin to overtake me, but he brushed my lips with his, so softly that it felt like a benediction. "You have become my own personal demon. You haunt me, tempt me, drive me mad with wanting you, and I can no longer blame prophecies or powers or fate. It's just you. I have chosen you, because I cannot imagine ever wanting anyone else, ever again. You possess me, obsess me; you're everywhere inside me and I cannot get rid of you. And worst of all, I don't wish to."

I was breathless, staring up at him. "For a declaration of love, that leaves a lot to be desired."

"I don't love you. I won't love you," he said, and

his gently moving fingers found the center of my pleasure, and I jerked, sliding down on the bed. "But by the time I'm done with you, you won't notice the difference."

He put his hand behind my neck, drawing my mouth to his as he slid down beside me, and his tongue silenced all my useless words of protest. He was wrong. Afterward I would remember the difference. But right now the burgeoning sensations were so powerful that I couldn't fight them. Pride had gone out the window. I was starving, ravenous for him. I would take what I could get.

The wet cloth that separated his deft fingers from me was maddening. I felt him push inside me, but the fabric prevented him from all but the slightest penetration, and I made a low, moaning sound of frustration against his mouth, arching my hips in mute supplication. He lifted his mouth, and his eyes were bright blue in a room that now seemed full of shadows. "Ask me," he whispered.

I clamped my mouth shut, determined not to say the words, and he let his tongue play along the seam of my closed lips, teasing, tasting, until I wanted nothing more than to open to him. Stubbornness and frustration were warring with one another until I wanted to scream. I slid down farther on the bed, arching my hips against his hand. "Ask me," he said again, a finger brushing against me, sending sparks of desire shooting through my body.

I was panting now, and the friction of the damp cloth against the most sensitive part of my body was exquisite, almost to the point of pain. I needed so much more, I needed release, I needed it now. I closed my eyes as he leaned over me, his lips teasing mine; but as the arousal built to an almost unbearable point, I opened them to stare into his, not bothering to hide the rage and hurt that were filtering through the heat.

His own eyes had been slumberous, half-closed, but they opened and met mine, and in a different creature I might have seen regret. His hand moved from between my legs, and he hunched forward, cupping my face, his thumbs brushing my lips before he leaned forward and kissed them. "All right," he whispered. "I'm sorry."

I'd never thought to hear those words from him. I thought of my ruined voice, the scars on my body, and then I let go. Hating and loving him was tearing me apart. I could no more stop loving him than I could stop breathing. So I had to stop hating him.

His mouth moved along the line of my jaw, kissing, nipping lightly, gliding down my throat till he tasted my pulse, and I knew a moment's wonder whether he would take my blood now, but he moved past, down, and my breasts were tingling, waiting for his touch, waiting for his mouth. His hands slid down, covering them, and I cried out with the sensation, a raw, rough sound, and then I made no sound at all as his mouth closed over one taut nipple, drawing it in tightly, his tongue dancing across the beaded top as he sucked, and I wondered if I could come simply from his mouth at my breast. And then I remembered his hoarse, one-word command, "Come," and my body went rigid as a small climax caught me.

I fell back against the pillows, panting, shocked by the intensity of my response, but he'd already moved to my other breast, the climax this time almost immediate.

I tried to catch my breath as he slid the loose pants down my legs, and then his hands slid up them, up the insides of my calves, my thighs, strong hands. He was going to take me now, I thought, part of me rebelling. I didn't want him on top, controlling me; I didn't want to be mastered. His hands touched me, and I knew I was wet and ready for him, and I told myself I could do this, I could lie still for him. I waited for the sound of his zipper, the rough rustle of jeans pushed down, but he leaned down and put his mouth against me.

I knew people did this, of course I did. I had

inspired men to do this to their wives, in my demon life. But no one, absolutely no one, had ever done this to me, put his mouth between my legs and licked me, tasted me, sucked at me, until a muffled sob broke from my throat and my hands came up to his head, wanting to push him away. It was too much, I couldn't bear it; but his long hair flowed onto my hips and instead I threaded my fingers through the silky strands.

The touch of his tongue was more subtle than that of his strong fingers, luring me into a dark, strange place where such delight existed that I hovered, frightened, as his tongue circled and flicked. He slid a finger inside me, and I arched off the bed, but before I could sink back he'd withdrawn it and pushed two inside, and I could feel my toes begin to curl. And then three fingers, and I was done, a silent scream coming from deep inside me as my entire body convulsed into darkness.

He was inside me before I had even begun to come down, pushing, his cock deep inside me, and I panicked, bucking, fighting him, trying to throw him off me.

He caught my wrists easily, slamming them down on the bed, his hips pinioning me. My struggles were useless, yet I couldn't stop, terrified.

He lay on top of me, holding me down. "Stop

it," he panted in my ear. "Stop fighting it. I'm sorry, but it has to be this way. There's no other choice."

His words were barely making sense. All I knew was that I had to stop him, had to reverse him, had to be on top, not beneath him; but he was too strong, and I couldn't dislodge him. He wasn't trying to continue, merely holding me there like someone trying to break a skittish mare, I thought with sudden, almost hysterical amusement.

"No," I pleaded, my pride vanished. "Please, no."

He put his face next to mine, rubbing gently, an almost animal gesture of reassurance. "We have to, Rachel," he whispered. "Just this once, I have to take you this way, so that I can take your blood."

I kicked, trying to throw him off, but he was too strong, his possession too deep, deep inside me, filling me. "You can reach my neck if I'm on top," I managed to choke out.

"No."

"Standing up." I couldn't believe I was suggesting such a thing, after the last, devastating time that had turned into such a betrayal.

"No," he said between gritted teeth, and his body, his naked body, was slick with sweat, and for a moment I was distracted from my mindless terror, wondering when he'd taken his clothes off, wondering what he felt like, naked against me.

I tried to get my elbows between us, but his strength was unbelievable. It was like beating at a brick wall—nothing could break his hold, his possession—and slowly, slowly, I stopped struggling. I lay still, panting, my body covered with sweat, covered with Azazel. I raised my eyes to meet his, and I could see real regret in his eyes.

The shadows had leached all color from the room, the only exception being the deep blue of his eyes, and I was remembering the trap of the Dark City once more, the trap of his betrayal. He was sorry, I thought, miserable. He regretted this. He didn't want this. He was being forced—

"Shut up," he said, releasing my arms to cup my face. I had worn myself out fighting him, and I could do nothing but lie beneath him. He kissed my mouth, my eyelids, my nose. "I'm sorry that I must force you to lie beneath me. How many times do I have to tell you? My need for you is so powerful I'd agree to anything you want. But it has to be this way. Do you understand?"

To punctuate his words, he withdrew partway, the thick penetration releasing me, and then thrust back in again, hard, hard enough to push me back into the mattress, and I shivered, trying to still the panic that swamped me.

I could feel his skin against mine, warm, damp, his muscled arms around me, his mouth pressed against the side of my face. His long legs against mine, the shallow penetration, his cock inside me that wasn't enough.

Slowly, slowly, I lifted my legs to wrap them around his narrow hips. Slowly, slowly, I put my arms around his neck, pulling him closer as I let go, let go of the ancient need born out of stubbornness and transformed into a vicious curse, let go of the memory of the thousand demons who had taken me this way, night after night, tearing me, hurting me, destroying me. Gone, it was all gone, and there was only Azazel, the smell of his skin, the cool ocean scent of him, the warm flesh, the taste of him in my mouth as I licked his shoulder, the steady thrust of him, touching someplace inside me that made me wild. And I was the one who kissed him, arching up to meet him, joining him in this mad dance of lust and love; and it wasn't about him controlling me, conquering me, it wasn't about who was on top and who was on the bottom, it was just the two of us, the joining, thick and hot and wonderful; and my climax, more powerful than ever, was coming closer, and even though I wanted to hold back to prolong it, the feelings were too shattering, and I let go of the need to control, let go and simply existed in a sea of pleasure.

I could feel his own need rise, his cock swelling inside me when I would have thought that was impossible, the slamming speed of his thrusts that shook me, shook the bed, and I cried out for more, for what I wanted, needed; and as I hovered on the crest, as I felt him begin to spurt inside me, his teeth clamped down on my neck, his teeth piercing my skin, and I shattered. The pull of his mouth at my neck, sucking, drinking, lost in my taste, the sweet hot rush as he filled me were too much. I was dying, and I didn't care. We would die together, destroyed by a desire that was elementally wrong; they had warned us, and neither of us had cared. I was dying, and I was in his arms, and that was all that mattered.

There were feathers, feathers closing around me, soft and blessed, drawing in the darkness, and as I tumbled back to earth I let myself rest in their gentleness, at peace.

CHAPTER TWENTY-ONE

I OPENED MY EYES SLOWLY, NOT AT all certain what I expected to see. The flames of hell? Beloch's—no, Uriel's triumphant face? The total darkness of nothing at all? What did one see in the afterlife? I was afraid to look.

He was lying beside me on the white sheet, his black hair obscuring his face, though I didn't have any doubt as to who he was. He slept like the dead, lying on his stomach, but I could see the rise and fall of his breathing, and I knew he'd survived.

I touched my neck gingerly. There was nothing there, no mark or pain, yet a frisson of remembered reaction washed over me as I let my fingers trail against my flesh. I seemed to have developed a new and entirely unexpected erogenous zone at the base of my neck, and as I remembered the pull of his mouth, I let out a quiet moan of remembered pleasure.

I sat up, very carefully so as not to wake him. The room was filled with the odd half-light that I knew was dawn, and I stared out the French doors into the private garden with astonishment. It had been late afternoon when I entered this room. Late afternoon when Azazel and I had made love, if that's what you could call it. I doubted that was the operative word on his part, but I wasn't going to go searching for others. Yet now it was morning, and I remembered nothing after the blackness had closed around me. Except hadn't there been feathers?

He was watching me. I should have known he'd sleep like a cat, instantly alert. He rolled over onto his back, before I remembered that I'd wanted to look for signs of the wings I knew he must have. His gaze was heavy-lidded, and I looked for signs of my blood on his mouth, wondering if it would disgust me. Would he taste like blood?

"We're alive," I said, somewhat unnecessarily.

"Did you have any doubts?"

"Of course I did."

Surprise flickered in his eyes. "And you agreed anyway?"

"Yes." I could be monosyllabic as well. I wasn't going to explain myself. Explain that wanting him was a fever in my blood, driving through me, and I would have faced the Truth Breakers once more just for the chance of sharing a bed with him.

He pushed himself to a sitting position beside me, for all the world like a husband about to read the Sunday paper, and stretched, a slow, sinuous movement that made my mouth go dry. I had the top sheet pulled up to primly cover my breasts, though as far as I could remember we'd started on top of the silk coverlet that was now on the floor. The sheet was draped loosely around his hips as well, for all the world like a PG-rated romantic comedy. I wondered what would happen if I jumped him.

"We slept," I said. Another scintillating bit of conversation.

"It is to be expected. The first bonding is a powerful experience for both partners. I'm sorry if I frightened you."

There it was again, another apology. But never for the right thing, for the real betrayal. "You didn't frighten me."

He gave me a disbelieving glance, but then, he'd felt my panic when he'd pushed inside me, face-to-face. I could deny it all I wanted, but my fear had been real. It was gone now, another part of my curse broken. A part I hadn't even known remained.

But he'd known, and been prepared for my reaction. He knew too much about me.

He was still watching me, and I was suddenly unwilling to meet his gaze. I slid down in the bed once more, turning my back to him. I was unwilling to get up and go in search of clothing, but his steady gaze made me desperately uncomfortable. "I'm going to sleep some more," I mumbled.

I hoped he'd take the hint and leave the bed, leave me; for a minute he didn't move. And then he did, sliding down, turning and curving his body around mine in a gesture I might have thought was protective if it weren't for the hard ridge of flesh at my back.

His arms went around me, pulling me back against him, his hands sliding up to cover my breasts. I made a hissing noise, only squirming for an instant, and then settling back against his protective warmth. I don't know why I felt I needed protection—he had proven to be my greatest danger. But for some reason he felt like my greatest safety, and I closed my eyes and slept.

LYING IN BED WITH RACHEL wrapped in his arms was pure hell, and it was only the beginning of his penance. If he could bring her at least a small portion of peace, then he would, no matter what the price. A raging hard-on was minor torment, right?

How had he come to such a place in his limitless existence? He'd prided himself on being cold and controlled with everyone but Sarah, and her loss had scoured away the last bit of gentleness he owned. It had taken too long to realize he'd become a monster, what he despised most. He might not have been Uriel's bitch, but he'd come close enough, and it had taken Rachel's near death to make him realize it.

He could still taste her—the sweetness of her desire, the richness of her blood—and he wanted to groan. He didn't dare fall asleep; he'd probably end up with a wet dream, thoroughly horrifying her.

He couldn't stop thinking about it: how she'd finally accepted him, wrapping her legs around him and drawing him in tighter; the soft sounds of need that came from her throat when he thrust; the way she'd thrown her head back and arched her neck into the pulling of his mouth as he'd sucked the nourishing, strengthening blood from her.

Hell, who was he kidding? The taking of blood was ritual, deliberate, a holy act and one of healing and strength. It was also the most erotic thing the Fallen were capable of doing, and it had sealed him to her.

God, he thought, shaken. And yet he'd known. Known that it would come to this, that they were bound together whether she hated him or not. She knew it too, even if she refused to admit it. He expected she'd keep fighting it. And he would let her, up to a point. He would have given her more time if he'd had the option, but Uriel was getting too close. Azazel had had no choice but to throw his own doubts and hesitation to the wind. He'd allow her to keep hers for as long as feasible. One more thing he owed her.

His face was in her hair, and it should have tickled. Instead it felt like silk against his skin. He remembered what it was like to feel this way about a woman, the physical connection that never left. And he knew the guilt that had ridden him hard. Guilt that had nothing to do with Sarah and everything to do with him and his own anger. Sarah had let him go, long ago. Now it was time for him to finish releasing her.

Rachel settled deeper into sleep, clearly exhausted. He hadn't taken enough of her blood to make a difference—in fact, he'd deliberately denied himself as much as he wanted, all that would have been acceptable, in his urgency to protect her. But the power of the first real mating was bone-shattering, and she might sleep all day.

It didn't matter. They had a war to plan. She could sleep, and he would come back to her.

She could sleep.

IT LOOKED LIKE LATE AFTERNOON when I finally woke, alone in the big bed. I was suffused with the strangest feelings: delight and dread, luxurious lassitude and the certainty that I needed to be rushing around, intense physical satisfaction and deep sexual longing. I wanted him again. I wanted him between my legs, leaning over me, sweating, pushing. I wanted his mouth on my neck, drinking what only I could give him.

I forced myself out of bed and headed toward the bathroom. I was in such a fog I could barely appreciate its elegance; but after a few minutes under a shower that felt like a gentle rainfall, I felt much more alive.

I found my discarded clothes neatly folded on a chair, and I wondered who had done it. The thought of Azazel tending to me was too bizarre to contemplate, yet I thought I would have known if someone else had come into the room. It had to have been him.

I dressed quickly, trying not to think about how those clothes had come off me. The one thing I couldn't find was the camisole, and I remembered his disapproval and found a brief smile curving my mouth.

I went through the living room, not even bothering to look for something as civilized as a note, and opened the door to the hall. I could hear the arguments from there. Men's voices, furious and demanding, behind the closed door of the council room. Immediately I turned around and went back in, closing the door behind me. I wasn't interested in their curious eyes. They would know exactly what Azazel and I had done, and how we had done it, and right then it felt agonizingly personal. I didn't want anyone else intruding.

So I was starving to death. Big deal—I'd survive.

The sun was already beginning to set. I opened the French doors and stepped out onto the secluded patio, letting the soft breeze dance around me. The smell of the ocean on the air was soothing, which was odd, considering that the sight of it terrified me. And thank the gods and goddesses, there was a tray on the low table, with fresh fruit and croissants and iced tea, the ice still fresh.

I glanced around for another entrance to the patio, but I could see none. Whoever had brought the food was a magician, and I didn't care. I sank down into one of the wicker chairs and began to eat.

I could still hear the angry voices, but at a distance, and I closed my eyes, letting myself drift back into the memory of last night. I was immediately wet, and disgusted with myself.

I wasn't going to worry about it. That's what I felt like; and when he finally returned to these rooms, he'd sense my arousal and—

What if he didn't return to these rooms? What if the initial bonding was all that was needed? He'd made it clear he didn't want to have feelings about me. I didn't doubt that he did—I wasn't that insecure—but I knew he was more than willing to fight them. Just as I was.

Except that I wasn't. I needed him, I needed him now. I leaned back and closed my eyes, letting my fingers drift to my mouth, down to my breasts, then up to the invisible brand on my neck, and I wondered if I could will him to come to me. If I called to him, would he hear me?

A shadow passed between me and the sun, and I opened my eyes in instant, unguarded delight. And then froze, looking up into the cloaked face of a stranger.

"Who are you?" I croaked. By now I knew every inhabitant of Sheol, by face if not by name, and this was no man I had ever seen before. I looked into his eyes and they were empty, as if there were no one there, and I had seen eyes like that before. When I'd been strapped to a table in a dark room in a dark city, out of my mind with pain.

I tried to scream, but no noise came out. They'd already taken my voice, and this time they would finish me. I scrambled to my feet, knocking over the chair in my hurry, but the creature didn't move, simply following me with those empty eyes.

I tried again for my voice, and found a husking remnant of it. "Go away. You don't belong here. I don't have any more information for you. I've told you everything—you don't need to hurt me anymore."

He spoke then, in an eerie, disembodied voice that sounded mechanical. "We are not here to hurt you."

We? I looked around and saw there was another one to my left, watching me with the same soulless intent. I stood a fighting chance against one of them. Two—impossible.

I still tried to back away, toward the French doors I'd stupidly closed. If I got inside I could lock the door, slowing them down while I ran for help. "Then why are you here?" I asked.

"To kill you," the creature said, his voice expressionless.

"Why?" I was edging closer and closer to the door, and neither of them had moved. There was just the slightest chance I could make it.

"So it has been decreed, and so it shall be," he said, moving toward me, and I saw his hands, hands that were more like claws, and for one crucial moment I froze in remembered terror.

My panic broke, and I whirled around just before he touched me, making a dash toward the door; but he caught me, talons ripping through the white cotton into my shoulders, and I felt the spurt of blood as I screamed once more, in deathly silence, knowing they would kill me, praying that death would be quick and merciful.

I didn't want to die. Not now. I wanted to lie in bed with Azazel and explore all the pleasures of the flesh. I wanted to walk in the bright sunlight beside the water that frightened me. I wanted to talk with Allie and laugh with the others, and I wanted to do what I did best. I wanted to heal the loss, make certain there were babies for these women to hold in their arms.

I felt a strange frisson ripple through my body, almost as if I were changing form; and instead of running, I lashed out at the Truth Breaker nearest me, watching in shock as the talons of a night bird ripped across his face, and he screamed in pain.

A second later the French doors exploded in a hail of glass shards, and Azazel stood there, rage on his pale face, his wings, his beautiful wings, unfurled. They were a deep blue-black, seeming to fill the space with a righteous fury, and then he was a blur of movement, ripping the Truth Breaker away from me and slamming him against the wall. I could hear the crunch of bones, the creature's high-pitched squeal of pain as I dropped to the ground, clutching my torn shoulders. I must have imagined that temporary shift, the lashing out with a raptor's talons.

Someone had followed Azazel and was making quick, efficient work of the second one, breaking his neck and dropping him to the ground, but Azazel was horrifyingly merciless. He tore the pincerlike hands off the first creature as it shrieked and babbled, and then, with a quick twist, broke his neck and ripped his head from his body.

I should have been sick, horrified. Instead, if I'd had a voice, I would have cheered him. I was on my knees on the stone patio, blood streaming down my arms, my hands making no progress in trying to stanch it. Feeling dizzy, I swayed, thinking I could just lie down for a moment; then he was beside me, scooping me up in his arms, an unreadable expression on his face as he cradled me against him.

And then we went up, up, into the twilight sky, my blood soaking into his clothes as it soaked into mine; and I felt light-headed, though I wasn't sure if it was from blood loss or being flown in the arms of an angel. And then I saw where he was heading.

I began to struggle, desperate to escape his grip. Allie had explained to me one afternoon how the sea had healing powers for the people of Sheol, and I knew he was taking me there, down into the black, murderous depths, and I knew I would drown once more at the hands of a man I loved.

"Stop it," he said, crushing me against him. "You'll make us fall."

I didn't care. I would rather die in a tangle of broken limbs than drown at his hands. I tried to tell him, but nothing but air came from my throat, and he simply ignored my desperate struggles as he rose vertically over the roiling ocean, and then plunged downward.

I expected bitter cold, but the sea was merely cool and salty. I shut my eyes to keep the stinging water out, closed my mouth on the silent scream and held my breath, fighting him as he pushed me down, down, and my lungs were bursting, my body sinking, as he pulled me to him and covered my mouth with his.

I was too shocked to resist, and he forced my lips open, breathing into me, sweet, pure air for my starved lungs, and my eyes fluttered open. I could see him clearly in the luminous blue water, smell the scent of his skin, and when he lifted his mouth I realized I was breathing.

He stripped the torn and bloody shirt from me, letting it drift away in the ocean, and the salt water washed my wounds, soothing them. I felt my body release its frozen panic, almost on its own, and I lay back, the water wrapped around me, cradling me, caressing me. A moment later we shot upward, his arms tight around me, so that we were floating in the water.

"I should never have left you alone," he whispered against my ear. "But none of us ever imagined that the Truth Breakers would dare to come here. I ran as soon as I heard you call, but I was afraid I wouldn't make it in time."

How could he have heard me call, when I'd had no voice? It made no sense—but then, neither had that strange, momentary shift my body had gone through. He *had* come in time, and that was all that mattered. I let my head sink against his shoulder, my legs wrapped around his waist as he slowly carried me from the sea.

The shore was filled with people, and I was shirtless. He held me against him, shielding me, as Allie rushed forward. I didn't turn my face from the warm presence of his skin, but I recognized her voice, her worried questions.

"She's fine," Azazel said. "I'll tend to her."

I must have imagined it, but I thought I felt the crowd draw back respectfully. He carried me effortlessly into the coolness of the main hall, back into the rooms that had been a haven.

He carried me straight into the huge shower, turned on the hot water, and stripped my sodden pants off me, his hands gentle, impersonal, as he soaped the salt from my body, warming me. The wounds on my shoulders had already begun to heal, and I felt limp, pliant, as he took care of me, wrapping me in a thick white towel when we were done and carrying me into the bedroom.

Someone had removed the smashed doors and cleaned up the broken glass, and a soft breeze came in through the open casement. I could only hope the same people had removed all the body parts. The bed had been remade, but Azazel yanked back the covers and settled me, towel and all, into the welcoming softness.

I didn't want him to leave me, but I didn't know how to ask. I didn't have to. He slid into the bed beside me, his damp, naked body pressed up against mine, and he pulled me against him, wrapping himself around me. Finally, finally, I let out my pent-up breath. I was safe. I was well. I was loved.

No, that was ridiculous. As ridiculous as the thought that I could have shifted form and ripped into one of the creatures who had almost killed me. But there was no other word for it than *love*.

"Yes," he murmured against my temple. He knew my thoughts, I remembered without alarm. What was he saying yes to? It didn't matter. I could believe what I wanted to, what I needed to. At least for now.

Everything was still and quiet. Night had fallen, and moonlight drifted in the open portal. I wanted to stay like this forever. Didn't I?

I could feel him growing harder, thicker, even though we lay perfectly still. Was he asleep? I knew men became aroused in their sleep. As a demon it had been my job to whisper in their ears, to excite them enough to take their wives and plant their reluctant seed. Could I whisper in Azazel's ear and tell him to take me?

His hands slid down to cover my breasts, his fingers plucking my nipples, and the banked fire roared to life again. I pressed my butt against him, rubbing, and his sudden growl was pure animal need. Something that vibrated within me as well. I turned in his arms, and he kissed me, his mouth still tasting of the salt water, and I wanted to drink him in. Wanted to suck at him, as he had sucked at me, and I knew what I was going to do.

"Oh, God," he muttered weakly, and I remembered he could read my thoughts. My body heated with a rush of embarrassment, but he only laughed, low in his throat, and shoved the covers off me.

Chapter Twenty-two

Azazel lay on the bed in a perfect agony of anticipation, yet Rachel had suddenly become nervous. He'd forgotten that, despite her randy thoughts, in terms of pleasure she was practically a novice. She might know what she wanted, but she had no idea how to go about it. He could read her confusion, her shame, and he wanted to hold her in his arms, protecting her from everything, including her own uncertainties. But he could read her longing as well, and he had already proven he was a far cry from a saint.

He took the hand that clung to his shoulder and drew it down his chest, slowly. It was bunched into a nervous fist, and he used his fingers to open it, placing it flat against his stomach. He quivered in anticipation—even her touch would be enough to send him over the edge.

Lie back and think of England, he reminded himself with a streak of amusement. And brought her open hand to his straining erection.

She tried to jerk her hand away, but he wouldn't let her, holding her against his hard flesh, and after a moment she calmed, letting her fingers touch him, learning him, encircling him. He wrapped his own hand around hers, showing her the motion, though it was a dangerous thing in his state of rapid arousal. She tugged and pulled at him with perfect precision, and just when he was about to stop her, she released him. He breathed a sigh of relief, only to feel her fingers drifting over him again, touching the sensitive head, drifting along the ridges and veins, and he could barely stifle his low moan.

She pulled her hand back swiftly. "Did I hurt you?"

His soft laugh was strained. "No," he said. "It felt too good."

"Oh." She seemed to think about that for a moment, and even without seeing her face he knew she smiled in the darkness. He was growing attuned to her every mood, whim, and reaction. "In that case," she murmured, and pulled away from him, rising on her knees over him.

He felt the feather-light touch of her mouth against his throat, and he remembered her bite in the pouring rain, her unconscious mimicry of the sacred bonding ritual. She moved her kisses down his chest, until he felt her small wet tongue against his nipple, and he reached up his hands to hold her there, to guide her, then dropped them again, fighting his own need to control.

She moved down and then halted, and unconsciously his hands fisted the sheet beneath him. Then her hand found him again, and her closed mouth brushed against the sensitive head of him. He moaned, but this time she realized it was from pleasure, and she moved her lips over him, feather-light touches that were an agony of delight. Her mouth left him, and he let out his strangled breath, only to feel it open around him, taking him into her mouth, sucking him in deep, her tongue moving against him, and it was all he could do not to climax immediately. He could do this, he reminded himself. There were far worse things than being tortured by pleasure.

Or maybe there weren't. She was kneeling over him, and it was easy enough to pull her against him. He wanted his mouth on her, tasting her as she sucked at him; but she resisted, clearly not wanting the distraction, so he had to content himself with sliding his fingers between her legs, finding the tangled damp, pushing in as she tightened around him.

She slid her mouth down, trying to take all of him, and he found her clitoris, using his thumb as he thrust his fingers into her. She responded, her mouth moving up and down on him with such hungry urgency that he knew in a moment he'd be lost.

With a strangled roar he reached down and pulled her up, over him, ready to let her straddle him. He placed his cock against her, and she sank down eagerly, a perfect precision of their two needs, and she laughed low in her throat as she took him. And then, to his astonishment, she rolled over onto her back, tugging him with her so that their connection didn't break, and he was covering her, her knees up high around him.

He looked down at her, cupping her face, and kissed her with all the force and power he'd been holding back; and she met him fully, a kiss of rampant desire and demand. He moved then, pulling out and then pushing in again, the eternal rhythm that somehow always felt new, and he could feel the shimmering convulsions tightening around him. He wouldn't last long, couldn't last long, and he sank his head next to hers, concentrating only on their joining, when her soft voice suddenly penetrated his haze of lust, and he froze in an agony of need.

"I want . . ." she whispered in that lost, broken voice that filled him with shame and sorrow, ". . . I want to change positions."

He managed a crooked smile. "Of course," he said, starting to turn and pull her on top; but she resisted, pushing at him.

"No," she said. "There's another way."

He held very still. "There are many other ways," he said finally, his own voice sounding as damaged as hers.

"I . . . I . . ." Embarrassment colored her voice, and he knew she couldn't find the words.

"You want me to guess?" he said with strangled amusement. "We could just try it different ways until we hit the one you had in mind." And then he caught the image from her mind. "Ah, that one. One of my absolute favorites. If you're sure."

"Yes," she said, her voice muffled.

He pulled out, moving back, and she turned over, lying flat on her stomach. He slid his arm under her waist, pulling her up. "No, love," he said. "It won't work that way." He reached between her legs, finding her, and began to push in slowly, the unaccustomed angle slightly tighter.

He didn't mistake her moan for displeasure, and her first shimmer of climax almost pushed him back out again, but he held still; when the convulsion lessened he pushed in farther, a slow, easy invasion that was going to kill him, he was certain of it.

When he finally came up against her he held still, letting her get accustomed to the feel of him, deeper than ever, and she lowered her head onto the sheet. He was too close and he knew it, but he wanted her with him. He thrust, hard, his hips flexing, and she braced herself, welcoming him, and he gave in to it, pumping into her, no longer able to control himself. He felt her begin to climax and put his hand between her legs to touch her, driving her as he spilled into her; and his wings unfurled, wrapping around them both, encasing them in a cocoon of safety and desire.

It felt endless, delicious, closer to heaven than anything he'd known since the beginning of time. He felt her shudder and weaken beneath him, and he held her, cradling her, as the last stray tremors faded away, and his wings folded back in, releasing them.

He rolled over onto his back, taking her with him, letting her collapse on top of him, an exhausted, pleasured little heap of a girl. He didn't need to ask why she'd wanted it that way. Accepting his weight on top of her yesterday had been an act of faith, of letting go of the stubborn need to control that had brought about disaster, just as his own questioning had done for him. By deliberately choosing a highly erotic but symbolically subservient position today, she'd banished the last of her fears. She could take him any way she wanted, as long as it gave her pleasure.

Her lips were at his throat, and she nuzzled him there. "Why didn't you bite me?" she whispered.

He hesitated before giving her the truthful answer. "It doesn't have to be every time. If you don't like it, we don't have to—"

She was stronger than he expected. She rolled over, and he was once more on top of her, cradled in her thighs. She reached up and cupped his face in her hands, brushing a kiss across his mouth, reading his hunger, and he knew that it matched her own. She arched her neck, pushing his face down, and his fangs were already extended for the bite when he touched skin, the taste of her blood incredibly sweet on his tongue.

He had to be careful. She'd lost blood today; and while he'd taken the bare minimum last night, she was still operating on less than usual. He pulled away, licking at the twin wounds, closing them, and sank down beside her, holding her in his arms, totally spent. If Uriel won, if all their efforts came to nothing, he would at least fade from existence knowing that the end of his life had been the very best part of it. And holding her close against him, he slept.

CHAPTER TWENTY-THREE

TWO DAYS LATER, AZAZEL TOOK one last, reluctant glance at the woman lying curled up in bed. The time had come. If he'd been able to, he would have put the Grace of sleep on her, so that she didn't have to experience the next twenty-four hours. Either they would survive or they wouldn't, and he would have spared her if he could. But once mated, he had no power over her, no ability to control her, and no Grace to give her.

Preparations were already being made. They were making ready for battle. Michael, ever the warrior, was all ruthless efficiency as he marshaled his forces. The Fallen and their wives were arming; the house was buttoned up tight. There was no hint as to how the assault would come, but come it would. Today. While Sheol had no sages or oracles, enough of the inhabitants were given a sense of presentiment. Even he had enough of the gift to have sensed their enemies' approach, pulling himself from Rachel's arms to prepare for battle.

"Do we know how it will begin?" he asked Michael as he watched him strap on his leather armor. Azazel was one of the strongest fighters among them, fierce, unblinking, with a power that went far beyond normal limits. But he knew he was the second-best, making up in speed and cunning what he lacked in Michael's finely honed strength.

Raziel was possessed of extraordinary skill with the sword, Tamlel with a spear. Gabriel's wife was an archer of considerable ability, and Azazel had been assured that Allie was lethal with a dagger. Each and every one was gifted in self-defense. They would fight to the death; and rather than let Uriel torment her, Azazel would take Rachel in his arms and kill her himself before taking the death stroke. He would take that pain upon himself to spare her. If it came to that.

"Don't look so gloomy," Michael chided, in his usual high spirits when anticipating a fight. "We will prevail. We have right on our side."

"And just how long have you been on this earth, that you think rightness has anything to do with victory?" Azazel said bitterly, reaching for his own leather armor. A sharp sword could slice through the thickness of the cured hides, but they had used it since the beginning of time. They would use it until the end of time, should it come to that.

But it wouldn't. He wasn't going to let Uriel win.

Michael must have read his thoughts. "That's better. Where's Rachel?"

"I'm trying to let her sleep."

"Through an epic battle? Not likely. She'll be angry that you tried to shield her."

"She has many more reasons to be angry with me—she can add this to the tally," Azazel said, buckling the straps around his torso, then picking up the leg coverings.

"She hasn't forgiven you? She chose you—surely that means she's chosen to absolve you as well."

"Some things are too great to be forgiven," he said, reaching for his sword.

Raziel appeared in the armory door. "They're coming," he said. "We need to assemble on the beach."

Michael clapped a hand on Azazel's shoulder. "We'll prevail, brother. Have faith." He headed out after Raziel, and Azazel slid his second, shorter sword into its sheath, preparing to follow. Only to come up short as Rachel appeared in the doorway, blocking it.

She'd plaited her wild red hair into a warrior's braids and pinned them to her head. She'd managed to find a warrior's uniform in the short period he'd been gone, and the expression on her face was fierce. "Were you just going to let me sleep through this?" she demanded.

"With luck, you never needed to know what was going on," he said, keeping his face blank, his voice neutral.

"Because I don't belong here, is that it? Everyone else is preparing for battle, ready to defend their home and their lives. And I'm supposed to just curl up in bed and wait for the outcome?" Her rough voice vibrated with rage.

"Yes."

She gave him a steely glance. "Give me a weapon."

"Are you thinking of gutting me?" he asked, curious. Curious as to whether he'd let her, as final penance.

"No. To help defend Sheol."

"Go back to our rooms," he said, trying to keep the desperation out of his voice. "You will only hurt our chances of winning."

"Fuck you," she said in her hoarse voice.

The enemy were almost here. He could feel their approach. They'd reached the gates of Sheol, and in moments they would smash them down, breaking the covenant, the laws ordained by the Supreme Being. The Fallen's banishment and eternal damnation were written in stone, but so was their life. Eternal life, eternal damnation, and the unbreachable sanctuary of Sheol. And now Uriel was about to break that law.

"Go back to our rooms."

"Why?"

He took a deep breath. "Because you make me vulnerable. If you're there, I'll be thinking about you, trying to protect you, instead of fighting the battle I need to fight. Rachel, I can't fight Uriel and fight you too. Go back, for the love of God."

"For the love of God," she echoed. "God is the one who cursed us all. Is there any particular reason I should love him?"

He heard the gate come crashing down before the steady march of their enemy. "I can't argue about faith right now," he said in a quiet voice. "They're here."

"Then I'll have your back," she said.

The assaulting host were marching toward the beach, and the army of Sheol, the small, ill-equipped force of the damned, was waiting for them. He looked at Rachel with her fierce braids and fiercer expression, and a slow smile crossed his face. He pulled her into his arms, just ducking the dagger she'd grabbed, and kissed her, not with desperation but with pure joy. Whatever happened, she was his, and it was enough.

"We have to go," he said when he released her. Taking her hand, he headed out to the sandy beach.

Raziel and Michael were in front of the others, a powerful force, and Rachel released his hand, going to stand with Allie. He had no choice, wasting only a moment to accept that he might never touch her again. And then he went to join the other two leaders.

It was an endless army, as far as the eye could see. No leather armor for them: their bright metal glinted in the filtered sunlight. He looked for Uriel in whatever form he'd chosen, but the archangel wasn't leading his army of angels today.

At their head was Metatron, king of the angels, ferocious and unblinking and huge. With a definite grudge to bear.

He stood front and center, towering over his foot soldiers, but his sword wasn't drawn. He wouldn't call his troops into battle until he raised it, and he was making no effort to reach for it.

"So he wants to talk," Michael muttered in disappointment. "Coward."

Raziel glanced at him reprovingly. "You have no wife, Michael. You have nothing to lose."

"I don't lose," Michael said simply.

"Neither does Metatron," Azazel said.

The king of the angels stepped forward, his black eyes meeting Azazel's for a pregnant moment. There was no sign of Enoch—that form had vanished completely. There was only a giant among men, hungry for carnage.

"I would talk," he announced, stopping about twenty feet from the three of them.

"I could kill him now," Michael muttered, his tattooed arms flexing. "His army would scatter without a leader."

"Control him," Raziel snapped, and Azazel put a restraining hand on Michael's shoulder as their leader stepped forward.

It should have been difficult for Azazel to watch Raziel in the place he himself had held for millennia, but he felt nothing but relief. He glanced over at Rachel. Her face was set, but she felt his gaze on her, and she turned, meeting it. And then she smiled at him.

It almost brought him to his knees. She had never smiled at him, not like this, full of love and promise and, yes, the forgiveness that he'd been too great a coward to ask for. He wanted to cross the sand and pull her into his arms, but he couldn't move.

Instead, he smiled back at her.

"What the hell is wrong with you?" Michael

growled. "I don't remember ever seeing you crack a smile in your life, and you decide now is the time to do it?"

He turned to Michael, and his smile shifted to a more ironic grimace. "I'm in love," he said. He looked back at Rachel. *I love you,* he thought, wondering if she could pick up the words.

Her eyes widened, and he knew she'd heard. She might not believe the truth of it, not until he said it out loud, but if he never got the chance at least she'd die knowing it.

Raziel had reached Metatron, and he halted, his hand on his sword, as Metatron began to speak.

"I, Metatron, first guardian of the ephemeral realm, enforcer of the law, protector of the Dark City, king of the warrior angels, demand the surrender of the so-called Fallen of Sheol and their whores to the most proper and right rule of the archangel Uriel, master of the universe."

He heard a snort of laughter from Allie, which should have infuriated him. She quickly composed herself, whispering something to Rachel, who smothered a smile.

Raziel knew the prescribed form. "I am Raziel, leader of the Fallen and the inhabitants of Sheol, a place declared inviolate by the Supreme Being. We deny your right to have dominion over us, and demand that you leave."

Metatron's steely eyes narrowed. "We will not leave until the sand runs red with your blood and that of your mate and the blood of all who dwell here."

Raziel didn't move. "Then what stays your hand? Do you have doubts as to the righteousness of your orders?"

"I have no doubts. Will you surrender?"

"Never."

Azazel waited, his hand poised on his sword, but Metatron made no move. "I will show no mercy."

"Why should we expect mercy from Uriel's minion?" Raziel said loftily.

Metatron ground his teeth. "Uriel has granted me the opportunity to make a bargain with you. Your best warrior against mine. If you win, we retreat. If we win, you give yourselves over to my men. I promise you death will be swift. It's more than you deserve."

Azazel moved forward, joining Raziel. "How can you possibly offer such a thing? Uriel would never countenance it."

Metatron's smile was sour. "I am not the minion you called me. I lead the armies, and it is my right to choose. The archangel Uriel must, on occasion, defer to me."

Raziel cast a swift glance at Azazel, who nodded; then he turned back to the heavily armed soldier. "We agree, though we have little faith that Uriel will accede to your terms."

"It will never come to that. I am the champion of my people, and I will kill your warrior and grind his bones into the sand, and then I will set his wife on fire, so that her screams will fill the air as my men destroy the rest of you. If you resist, you will die by flames as well. If you accept, then the sword will be swift and merciful."

"Our champion is the archangel Michael," Raziel said. "He has no wife."

"He is no archangel. He has fallen," Metatron said in dismissive tones. "And I have not made the terms clear. I am the one to choose your champion. And I choose Azazel."

He heard Michael's roar of frustration, but he didn't turn around, and someone must have restrained him. He was more distracted by Rachel's silent cry of horror. And he knew, to his sorrow, that her anguish was for him, not fear of immolation, the most painful form of death.

He had known it would come to this. He looked at Raziel. "By your leave?" he said formally.

After a moment Raziel nodded, and backed away, joining his waiting army, the pathetically small, ill-equipped family of the Fallen.

Azazel had known most of them for thousands

of years. Michael and Gabriel had fallen later, as well as Nisroc and Jehoel, but most were almost a second self.

But it was for Rachel he felt the most fear. Metatron was a warrior—he lived to fight, just as Michael did. Azazel had managed to defeat him back in the Dark City because of the sheer rage that had suffused him. Here, on an even playing field, Metatron was by far the stronger. The two of them would stage a prodigious battle, and it was hard to guess who would come out the victor.

Though nearly as tall as Metatron, Azazel lacked the bulk of muscles, the sheer physical power. He would have to use his other gifts, cunning and speed, to keep the battle going until the larger man tired, and he could land the killing blow.

"I will fight you," Azazel said, and he thought he could hear Rachel's muffled cry. "And I will kill you," he added pleasantly.

Metatron's grin was savage. "You can try." He spun around, in his element, ready to fight. "I will fight their champion," he called out to his men, "and the outcome of that match determines the outcome of our assault. You are all to adhere to my agreement. No one is to be touched until I give the order. If I am vanquished, they are to be left alone."

And then he turned back, his sword drawn, his smile filled with bloody anticipation. "This is a long time coming, traitor."

Azazel drew his own sword. He was a worker in metals, and he'd crafted it himself, thousands of years ago. Its balance was perfect, its blade razor-sharp, its action smooth and swift. He smiled back at Metatron. "You've lived too long, minion," he purred. "I'm waiting."

Metatron lunged, his full force behind the move, so quickly that another man would have been unable to react in time. But Azazel knew him of old, and he'd shifted before Metatron even raised his sword, drawing his own across his enemy's muscular thigh. He couldn't reach the femoral artery, but he could cause pain, slow him down, and he whipped his sword across the other leg as Metatron spun around, a roar of fury bellowing out.

"Coward!" he shouted, bringing the sword down on Azazel's neck, but finding only air. He spun quickly, the sword at waist level, and it slashed across Azazel's chest, splitting the leather and cutting into his skin. Metatron grinned.

A moment later Azazel's blade sliced his face. It was useless against the steel armor, but the cut was just above Metatron's eye, and the blood poured down, blinding him, as Azazel moved in.

Even blinded, Metatron sensed him, spinning around and slashing, and Azazel felt the blade bite deep into his back. He went down, then rolled away as Metatron hacked at him, the heavy sword barely missing him in the blood-soaked sand. Azazel was up before he could free the sword from the grip of the sand, and his sword sliced deep into Metatron's right arm.

Metatron only laughed, tossing the sword to his other hand. He was breathing deeply as he looked at Azazel. "You think I can only kill with one hand, traitor? I can kill you a thousand ways, and could have done so many times already."

"Then what's taking you so long, minion?" Azazel mocked him.

"Because I want to prolong your suffering. Knowing you are helpless to save the demon Lilith from the fiery death she deserves, you will suffer and slip and fall and die."

"You're wasting your breath," Azazel said in a bored voice. "I am no child to be frightened by your talk. Use your sword instead, and stop posturing. None of our women are impressed."

"Your women will all be dead!" Metatron shouted as he charged him.

It was not unlike bullfighting, Azazel thought, having seen the barbaric practice long ago. The more he maddened Metatron, the more mistakes the king of the angels would make, until he was exhausted, broken, bleeding. It was a dance with a savage partner, and the same joy filled him, the need to kill, to destroy the force that had drawn him in, deceived him, led him to betray not only Rachel but himself; with each slash, each bleeding cut, he was washing away his guilt, his culpability.

He had trained in the sand, was used to the feel and shift of it beneath his feet as he parried and thrust; but blood was caking his feet, and it slowed him just an infinitesimal amount, just enough, as Metatron's blade came slashing down, and he heard Rachel's raw, broken scream.

CHAPTER TWENTY-FOUR

THE SOUND ROARED FROM MY mouth, a shattered remnant of a scream, as I watched the blade slash down on Azazel as he skidded in the wet sand; and the man who had once been Enoch jerked, unaccountably startled, enough so that the blade cleaved Azazel's shoulder, not his neck, the force blunted, and Azazel was able to roll away, leaping back to his feet, graceful as a dancer.

But he was weakening. I could see it, and Metatron was too big, too strong, despite the slashes and cuts Azazel had landed. Azazel's speed and agility had kept him safe, but he was beginning to slow, and if I didn't do something I would see him hacked to death before my eyes. I would watch him die, and I wouldn't even be able to cry.

I could run out, put myself between them, distract them long enough so that Azazel could land a killing blow. But Azazel had already said I made him vulnerable. If I interfered, it might result in his death.

I looked around desperately, but no one was doing anything to help. They seemed to be relying on some utterly stupid code of honor that was going to end up getting us all killed, and a sudden, ancient rage filled me.

Men and their honor. Men and their need for power, for control, for doing stupid things because of stupid pride and an insane belief in some ridiculous notion of what was right. They would kill us all with their pride, and I wouldn't let them.

She was gone. But she was still within me. Lilith, the storm demon. Lilitu, the wind goddess, the raging fury who sent hurricanes and tornadoes and cyclones. I moved my hand, just slightly, and a spit of sand whirled up in a tiny funnel, falling back to the ground.

Azazel slashed at Metatron, slicing him above the other eye, and the blood poured down, blinding him. Metatron dashed it away, smearing it on his face, and struck back, his sword slicing through the leather jerkin Azazel wore, and I could see the blood gushing out, deep and red, and I knew if I didn't move he would die.

I took a deep breath and went there, joined the demon who lived inside me. I spun my hand, and the winds came down, picking up the sand. Azazel tripped and fell, and Metatron loomed over him, sword raised for the killing blow—

When my wind caught him. The sand blinding him, the gust pushing him away as Azazel once more managed to stagger to his feet. I swirled the wind beyond Azazel, buoying him as he gathered the last bit of his strength, advancing on Metatron, who was fighting the funnel of sand that had encircled him.

I moved my hand, and the wind halted, the sand falling to the ground, and Metatron saw Azazel. He grinned, raising his sword, and Azazel sliced beneath his arm, beneath the armor.

Metatron fell to his knees, his face blank with shock. And Azazel brought his sword down on his enemy's neck, hacking into his body.

The warrior fell face-first into the sand, and silence reigned.

There was only the rasp of Azazel's labored breathing, the soft remnants of my angry wind, the shushing of the ocean that terrified me.

I rushed forward, catching Azazel before he fell. He was heavy, but I was strong, and I pulled him toward the sea. A moment later Allie was with us, supporting his other side, and he glanced down at her with a momentary grimace. And then he smiled. A glorious smile that seemed to have appeared from nowhere.

The water lapped at our feet. "I need to go back," Allie said. "You can take him from here."

"Yes," I said. And I carried him into the healing, terrifying water, deeper and deeper, until it closed over our heads and I breathed it in.

I stripped his bloody jerkin off him beneath the salt water, and watched his savage wounds begin to close. I kissed his mouth, breathing him in, and let him wrap my legs around him, holding tight. He pushed up into the air, and his black wings unfurled, carrying us higher, over the sand, and I clung to him, afraid of nothing. Not the deep ocean, not flying through the misty sky, not loving a hard man. Not the demon who still hid inside me, who could help save the man she loved. She would be a secret. I had thought she was gone, hated her; but she was a part of me, a part of the being who loved Azazel, and I welcomed her.

We set down on the sand near the house, and he released me, but I held him against me, protecting him as he protected me. We looked up as Raziel stood before the army of angels, a cold glint in his eye.

"Your champion is defeated," he called out,

"and Uriel has broken the laws of the Supreme Being. You have no place here. Go, and never return."

He got no argument. They began to retreat, when one of them stopped. "May we take the body?"

Allie had managed to turn Metatron's huge body over, and he lay on his back in the sand, covered in blood, his eyes closed. But then I saw he was still breathing, and I joined her, kneeling in the sand and unfastening the heavy metal armor.

"It is Azazel's choice, as champion," Raziel said.

Azazel was staring at his vanquished opponent. "He lives," he said shortly. "Ask him."

To my astonishment, Metatron's eyes opened beneath the heavy mat of blood and sand, and they focused on me for a moment, then past me to Azazel. "I tried," he said in a bare whisper. "I'm dying."

"Yes," Azazel said, glancing at me for an uncomfortable moment before turning back. "Do you wish to be returned to your army?"

Metatron met his gaze, and he slowly shook his head. "Bury me here. I have no wish to return to the darkness."

There was nothing more to say. They began

to retreat, the legion of soldier angels come to wipe us out, and a few minutes later his army was gone.

Allie made a gesture. "We need four strong men to carry him into the water. Carefully, now. His wounds are very bad."

Azazel broke away from me, coming forward with three others. They lifted Metatron's bloody and broken body gently and carried him toward the sea. I followed, because I didn't want Azazel too far away. I had almost lost him, and right now I refused to let him out of my sight.

"You drown your enemies?" I heard Metatron say in the voice of delirium. "As good a way as any. It is a fitting resting place for a soldier."

A moment later he was underwater, and the four men were chanting something beneath their breaths, something strange and musical, as we all waited.

And waited. I was knee-deep in the surf, watching them, and Allie came up beside me. "What a lucky wind that was," she murmured, casting an oblique glance my way.

"Yes, it was," I said, concentrating on the water where Metatron had disappeared. "Is he going to live?"

"I don't know. Sometimes the wounds are too grievous." She smiled at me, a knowing smile. "It's nice to have secret weapons against an oversized enemy."

I looked at her with all the innocence I could muster. "I don't know what you're talking about."

My skills at prevarication were rusty, but even if I'd been an expert she wouldn't have believed me. "Neither do I," she said cheerfully, turning her gaze to the water.

A minute later Metatron shot up. "Bloody fucking hell!" he sputtered. And then he looked around, at the Fallen who surrounded him, at the people waiting on the shoreline, at me, and then at Azazel. He flexed his shoulder, the scar showing the line that had almost cleaved him in half, and then he grinned. "I like your burials at sea," he said.

I LAY SPRAWLED ON TOP of Azazel, sweaty, happy, replete, his hands still stroking my back. My eyes were closed as I took in the taste and the smell of him, the wonder of having him. There was nothing else I needed.

"Yes," he said.

"Did I ever tell you that your one-word sentences annoy me?" I said sleepily, kissing his neck.

"Yes," he said again.

I bit him lightly. "Yes, what?"

"Yes, Rachel."

I laughed. "You know what I meant. You said *yes*. What did you mean?"

"You know what I meant," he said in a grouchy voice. "You need to let me sleep, woman. I've beaten the greatest warrior who has ever lived, with only a little unfair help, and I've pleasured you almost as much as you've pleasured me. I need to rest."

I froze. "What unfair help did you have?" I said uneasily. I probably should have just ignored it.

"The wind," he said calmly. "It was extremely kind of providence to provide it at just that moment, or I would be dead."

"Providence," I said happily.

"We'll call it that for now," he said. "My lovely, delectably wanton demon."

"That's really not a term of affection. You hate demons," I pointed out.

"But you're not a real demon. Just a little tiny bit," he murmured.

I kissed his mouth. "I'm not a demon."

"If you say so," he murmured sleepily.

"You still didn't tell me what you were saying *yes* about," I said, deciding to avoid the subject of demonhood for now.

"Yes," he said again.

I slid down on him, resting my head against

his shoulder. "You're annoying me again. Yes, what?"

"Yes, you need one more thing. Yes, you already have it."

I bit him, harder this time. "You can't say it?"

"Yes, I love you," he said.

And for the first time in my endless existence, I burst into tears.

In the Beginning

I am Raziel, one of the twenty fallen angels spoken of by Enoch in the old books. I live in the hidden world of Sheol, with the other Fallen, where no one knows of our existence, and we have lived that way since the fall, millennia ago. I should have known there would be trouble on the horizon. I could feel it in my blood, and there is nothing more powerful than blood. I had taught myself to ignore those feelings, just as I had taught myself to ignore everything that conspired to betray me. Had I listened, things might have been different.

I rose that day, in the beginning, stretching out my wings to the feeble light of early morning. A storm was coming; I felt it throbbing in my veins, in my bones. For now the healing ocean was calm, the tide coming in, and the mist was thick and warm, an enveloping embrace, but the violence of nature hung heavy in the air.

Nature? Or Uriel?

I had slept outside again. Fallen asleep in one of the wooden chairs, nursing a Jack Daniel's, one of the many pleasures of this last century or so. Too many Jacks, if truth be told. I hadn't wanted this morning to come, but then, I was not a fan of mornings. Just one more day in exile, with no hope of . . . what? Escape? Return? I could never return. I had seen too much, done too much.

I was bound here, as were the others. For years, so many years that they'd ceased to exist, lost in the mists of time, I had lived alone on this earth under a curse that would never be lifted.

Existence had been easier when I'd had a mate. But I'd lost too many over the years, and the pain, the love, were simply part of our curse. As long as I kept aloof, I could deprive Uriel of that one bit of torture. Celibacy was a small price to pay.

I'd discovered that the longer I went without sex, the easier it was to endure, and occasional physical matings had sufficed. Until a few days ago, when the need for a female had suddenly come roaring back, first in my rebellious dreams, then in my waking hours. Nothing I did could dispel the feeling—a hot, blistering need that couldn't be filled.

At least the women around me were all bonded. My hunger wasn't so strong that it crossed those lines—I could look at the wives, both plain and beautiful, and feel nothing. I needed someone who existed in dreams only.

As long as she stayed there, I could concentrate on other things.

I folded my wings back around me and reached for my shirt. I had a job today, much as I hated it. It was my turn, and it was the only reason the détente existed. As long as we followed Uriel's orders, there was an uneasy peace.

I and the other Fallen took turns ferrying souls to their destiny. Death-takers, Uriel called us.

And that's what we were. Death-takers, blood-eaters, fallen angels doomed to eternal life.

I moved toward the great house slowly as the sun rose over the mountains. I put my hand on the cast-iron doorknob, then paused, turning to look back at the ocean, the roiling salt sea that called to me as surely as the mysterious siren female who haunted my dreams.

It was time for someone to die.

I AM URIEL THE MOST high, the archangel who never fell, who never failed, who serves the Lord in his awful majesty, smiting sinners, turning wicked cities to rubble and curious women to pillars of salt. I am his most trusted servant, his emissary, his voice in the wilderness, his hand on the sword. If need be, I will consume this wicked, wicked world with fire and start anew. Fire to scourge everything, then flood to follow and replenish the land.

I am not God. I am merely his appointed one, to assure his judgment is carried out. And I am waiting.

The Highest One is infallible, or I would judge the Fallen to be a most grievous mistake and smite them from existence. They have been damned to eternal torment, and yet they do not suffer. It is the will of the Most Holy that they live out their endless existence, forced to survive by despicable means, and yet they know joy. Somehow, despite the black curses laid upon them, they know joy.

But sooner or later, they will go too far. They will join the First, the Bringer of Light, the Rebel, in the boundless depths of the earth, locked in silence and solitude throughout the end of time.

I am Uriel. Repent and beware.

CHAPTER ONE

I WAS RUNNING LATE, WHICH WAS NO surprise. I always seemed to be in a rush—there was a meeting with my editors halfway across Manhattan, I had a deposit to make before the end of the business day, my shoes were killing me, and I was so hungry I could have eaten the glass and metal desk I'd been allotted at my temp job at the Pitt Foundation.

I could handle most of those things—I was nothing if not adaptable. People were used to my tendency to show up late; the secretary over at MacSimmons Publishers was wise enough to schedule my appointments and then tell me they were half an hour earlier. It was a little game we played—unfortunately, since I now knew the rules, I'd arrive an hour late, ruining her careful arrangements.

Tant pis. They could work around me—I was reliable in all other matters. I'd never been late with a manuscript, and my work seldom needed more than minimal revision. They were lucky to have me, even if biblical murder mysteries weren't a big moneymaker, particularly when written in a smart-ass tone. *Solomon's Poisoner* had done even better than the previous books. Of course, you had to put that in perspective. Agatha Christie I was not. But if they weren't making money they wouldn't be buying me, and I wasn't going to worry about it.

I had just enough time to make it to the bank, and I could even manage a small detour to grab a hot dog from a street vendor, but there wasn't a damned thing I could do about my stupid shoes.

Vanity, my uptight mother would have said—not that she ever left the confines of her born-again Idaho fortress to see me. Hildegarde Watson trusted nothing and no one, and she'd retreated to a compound filled with other fundamentalist loonies where even her own sinful daughter wasn't welcome. *Thank God.* I didn't need my mother to tell me how shallow I was. I embraced it.

The four-inch heels made my legs look fantastic, which I considered worth any amount of pain. On top of that, they raised me to a more imposing height than my measly five foot three, an advantage with obstreperous middle-aged male editors who liked to treat me like a cute little girl.

However, the damned stilettos hurt like crazy, and I hadn't been smart enough to leave a more comfortable pair at my temp job. I'd been hobbling around all day without even a Band-Aid to protect my poor wounded feet.

I'd feel sorry for myself if I hadn't done it on purpose. I'd learned early on that the best way to accomplish anything was to grit your teeth and fight your way through it with the best grace you could muster, and wearing those damned shoes, which had cost me almost a hundred and eighty dollars, discounted, was the only way I'd ever get comfortable in them. Besides, it was Friday—I had every intention of spending the weekend with my feet up, working on my new book, *Ruth's Revenge.* By Monday the blisters would have healed enough, and if I could just tough it out for two more days, I'd be used to them. Beauty was worth the pain, no matter what my mother said.

Maybe sometime I'd be able to support myself with my writing and not have to deal with temp jobs. Snarky mysteries set on debunking the Judeo-Christian Old Testament weren't high on the public's interest meter, the occasional blockbuster Vatican thriller aside. For now, I had no choice but to supplement my meager income, making my weekends even more precious.

"Shouldn't you be heading out, Allie?" Elena, my overworked supervisor, glanced over at me. "You won't have time to get to the bank if you don't leave now."

Crap. Two months and already Elena had pegged me as someone chronically late. "I won't be back," I called out as I hobbled toward the elevator. Elena waved absently good-bye, and moments later I was alone in the elevator, starting the sixty-three-floor descent.

I could risk taking off my shoes, just for a few moments of blessed relief, but with my luck someone would immediately join me and I'd have to shove them back on again. I leaned against the wall, trying to shift my weight from one foot to the other. Great legs, I reminded myself.

Out the sixty-third-floor windows, the sun had been shining brightly. The moment I moved through the lobby's automatic door to the sidewalk, I heard a loud crash of thunder, and I looked up to see dark clouds churning overhead. The storm seemed to have come out of nowhere.

It was a cool October afternoon, with Halloween only a few days off. The sidewalks were busy as usual, and the bank was across the street. I could always walk and eat a hot dog at the same time, I thought, heading over to the luncheon cart. I'd done it often enough.

With my luck there had to be a line. I bounced nervously, shifting my weight, and the man in front of me turned around.

I'd lived in New York long enough to make it a habit not to look at people on the street. Here in midtown, most of the women were taller, thinner, and better dressed than I was, and I didn't like feeling inadequate. I never made eye contact with anyone, not even with Harvey the hot-dog man, who'd served me daily for the last two months.

So why was I looking up, way up, into a pair of eyes that were . . . God, what color were they? A strange shade between black and gray, shot with striations of light so that they almost looked silver. I was probably making a fool of myself, but I couldn't help it. Never in my life had I seen eyes that color, though that shouldn't surprise me since I avoided looking in the first place.

But even more astonishing, those eyes were watching me thoughtfully. Beautiful eyes in a beautiful face, I realized belatedly. I didn't like men who were too attractive, and that term was mild when it came to the man looking down at me, despite my four-inch heels.

He was almost angelically handsome, with his high cheekbones, his aquiline nose, his streaked brown and golden hair. It was precisely the tawny shade I'd tried to get my colorist to replicate, and she'd always fallen woefully short.

"Who does your hair?" I blurted out, trying to startle him out of his abstraction.

"I am as God made me," he said, and his voice was as beautiful as his face. Low-pitched and musical, the kind of voice to seduce a saint. "With a few modifications," he added, with a twist of dark humor I couldn't understand.

His gorgeous hair was too long—I hated long hair on men. On him it looked perfect, as did the dark leather jacket, the black jeans, the dark shirt.

Not proper city wear, I thought, trying to summon up disapproval and failing because he looked so damned good. "Since you don't seem in any kind of hurry and I am, do you suppose you could let me go ahead of you?"

There was another crash of thunder, echoing through the cement and steel canyons around us, and I flinched. Thunderstorms in the city made me nervous—they seemed so *there.* It always seemed like the lightning snaking down between the high buildings would find me an easier target. The man didn't even blink. He glanced across the street, as if calculating something.

"It's almost three o'clock," he said. "If you want your deposit to go in today, you'll need to skip that hot dog."

I froze. "What deposit?" I demanded, completely paranoid. God, what was I doing holding a conversation with a strange man? I should never have paid any attention to him. I could have lived without the hot dog.

"You're holding a bank deposit bag," he said mildly.

Oh. Yeah. I laughed nervously. I should have been ashamed of my paranoia, but for some reason it hadn't even begun to dissipate. I allowed myself another furtive glance up at the stranger.

To hell with the hot dog—my best bet was to get away from this too-attractive stranger, drop off the deposit, and hope to God I could find a taxi to get me across town to my meeting. I was already ten minutes late.

He was still watching me. "You're right," I said. Another crash of thunder, and the clouds opened up.

And I was wearing a red silk suit that I couldn't really afford, even on clearance from Saks. Vanity again. Without a backward glance, I stepped out into the street, which was momentarily free of traffic.

It happened in slow motion, it happened in the blink of an eye. One of my high heels snapped, my ankle twisted, and the sudden rain was turning the garbage on the street into a river of filth. I slipped, going down on one knee, and I could feel my stockings shred, my skirt rip, my carefully arranged hair plastered limp and wet around my ears.

I looked up, and there it was, a crosstown bus ready

to smack into me. Another crack of thunder, the bright white sizzle of lightning, and everything went calm and still. Just for a moment.

And then it was a blur of noise and action. I could hear people screaming, and to my astonishment money was floating through the air like autumn leaves, swirling downward in the heavy rain. The bus had come to a stop, slanted across the street, and horns were honking, people were cursing, and in the distance I could hear the scream of sirens. Pretty damned fast response for New York, I thought absently.

The man was standing beside me, the beautiful one from the hot-dog stand. He was just finishing a chili dog, entirely at ease, and I remembered I was famished. If I was going to get held up by a bus accident, I might as well get a chili dog. But for some reason, I didn't want to turn around.

"What happened?" I asked him. He was tall enough to see over the crowds of people clustered around the front of the bus. "Did someone get hurt?"

"Yes," he said in that rich, luscious voice. "Someone was killed."

I started toward the crowd, curious, but he caught my arm. "You don't want to go there," he said. "There's no need to go through that."

Go through what? I thought, annoyed, staring at the crowd. I glanced back up at the stranger, and I had the odd feeling that he'd gotten taller. I suddenly realized my feet didn't hurt anymore, and I looked down. It was an odd, disorienting sensation. I was barefoot, and if I didn't know it was impossible, I would have said there was thick green grass beneath my feet.

I glanced back up at the rain-drenched accident scene in front of me, and time seemed to have moved in an odd, erratic shift. The ambulance had arrived, as well as the police, and people were being herded out of the way. I thought I caught a glimpse of the victim—just the brief sight of *my* leg, wearing *my* shoe, the heel broken off.

"No," said the man beside me, and he put a hand on my arm before I could move away.

The bright light was blinding, dazzling, and I was in a tunnel, light whizzing past me, the only sound the whoosh of space moving at a dizzying speed. *Space Mountain,* I thought, but this was no Disney ride.

It stopped as abruptly as it had begun, and I felt sick. I was disoriented and out of breath; I looked around me, trying to get my bearings.

The man still held my arm loosely, and I yanked it free, stumbling away from him. We were in the woods, in some sort of clearing at the base of a cliff, and it was already growing dark. The sick feeling in my stomach began to spread to the rest of my body.

I took a deep breath. Everything felt odd, as if this were a movie set. Things looked right, but everything seemed artificial, no smells, no sensation of touch. It was all illusion. It was wrong.

I wiggled my feet, then realized I was still barefoot. My hair hung down past my shoulders, which made no sense since I had short hair. I tugged at a strand, and saw that instead of its carefully streaked and striated color, it was brown again, the plain, ordinary brown I'd spent a fortune trying to disguise, the same plain, ordinary brown as my eyes. My clothes were different as well, and the change wasn't for the better. Baggy, shapeless, colorless, they were as unprepossessing as a shroud.

I fought my way through the mists of confusion—my mind felt as if it were filled with cotton candy. Something was wrong. Something was very wrong.

"Don't struggle," the man beside me said in a remote voice. "It only makes it worse. If you've lived a good life, you have nothing to be afraid of."

I looked at him in horror. Lightning split open the sky, followed by thunder that shook the earth. The solid rock face in front of us began to groan, a deep, rending sound that echoed to the heavens. It started to crack apart, and I remembered something from Christian theology about stones moving and Christ rising from the dead. The only problem was that I was Jewish, as my fundamentalist Christian mother had been for most of her life, and I was nonobservant at that. I didn't think rising from the dead was what was going on here.

"The bus," I said flatly. "I got hit by the bus. I'm dead, aren't I?"

"Yes."

I controlled my instinctive flinch. Clearly he didn't believe in cushioning blows. "And who does that make you? Mr. Jordan?"

He looked blank, and I stared at him. "You're an angel," I clarified. "One who's made a mistake. You know, like in the movie? I shouldn't be dead."

"There is no mistake," he said, and took my arm again.

I sure as hell wasn't going quietly. "Are you an

angel?" I demanded. He didn't feel like one. He felt like a man, a distinctly real man, and why the hell was I suddenly feeling alert, alive, aroused, when according to him I was dead?

His eyes were oblique, half-closed. "Among other things."

Kicking him in the shin and running like hell seemed an excellent plan, but I was barefoot and my body wasn't feeling cooperative. As angry and desperate as I was, I still seemed to want him to touch me, even when I knew he had nothing good in mind. Angels didn't have sex, did they? They didn't even have sexual organs, according to the movie *Dogma.* I found myself glancing at his crotch, then quickly pulled my gaze away. What the hell was I doing checking out an angel's package when I was about to die?

Oh, yeah, I'd forgotten—I was already dead. And all my will seemed to have vanished. He drew me toward the crack in the wall, and I knew with sudden clarity it would close behind me like something out of a cheesy movie, leaving no trace that I'd ever lived. Once I went through, it would all be over.

"This is as far as I go," he said, his rich, warm voice like music. And with a gentle tug on my arm, he propelled me forward, pushing me into the chasm.

Explore the Dark Side of Desire

with bestselling Paranormal Romance from Pocket Books!

www.PocketAfterDark.com

Available wherever books are sold
or at www.simonandschuster.com

26620